"I want to see all of you."

She lolled against the cushions, a golden angel in a den of iniquity, her eyes big and dreamy, her hair a honeyed cloud, her lips plump and dark from his kisses and asking for more. She represented an invitation to sin as sultry as any Persian houri, despite her nightgown, covering her from chin to toe like a nun. True, it was an improvement over the thick flannel shroud. It fell smoothly about her curves, giving him a better impression of her figure than he'd yet been afforded: high breasts, a small waist, and a lovely curve of the hips. Through the superfine cambric he caught a shadowy impression of nipples; dark pink, he fancied. His favorite kind.

With thickened fingers he unlooped the button at her neck, and couldn't resist the indentation of her collarbone, allowing himself a quick taste of the tender skin. She arched into his mouth and the nightgown fell open, revealing round, pert breasts that his palms itched to tou

"You are   t to see all of yo

Romances by Miranda Neville

From Avon Impulse

MIRANDA NEVILLE

Lady Windermere's Lover

AVON
An Imprint of HarperCollinsPublishers

AVON BOOKS
An Imprint of HarperCollins*Publishers*
195 Broadway
New York, New York 10007

Copyright © 2014 by Miranda Neville
ISBN 978-0-06-224332-4
www.avonromance.com

First Avon Books mass market printing: July 2014

Avon Trademark Reg. U.S. Pat. Off. and in Other Countries, Marca Registrada, Hecho en U.S.A.
HarperCollins® is a registered trademark of HarperCollins Publishers.

Printed in the U.S.A.

10 9 8 7 6 5 4 3 2 1

*To Cynthia, who shares a name
with my heroine, if little else*

Lady Windermere's Lover

Chapter 1

London, 1793

It wasn't every day a man turned twenty-one. Come to think of it, this would be the only day of his entire life when Damian, Viscount Kendal, achieved that milestone. His friends had promised him a night to remember, and Robert was paying the bill for the best fare the St. James's Tavern had to offer. They drank several bottles of wine at dinner, and brandy afterward. The occasion merited a celebration as wild, as debauched, as drunken as any they'd ever enjoyed. Robert had marked the occasion of his majority with an elopement to Gretna Green and a new bride, but Damian had quite the opposite in mind.

Freedom. Freedom from the expectations for the heir to an earldom. Freedom from his father.

Liberty. As the citizens of France had tossed off the yoke of the nobility, Damian no longer had to obey the fourth Earl of Windermere. Not that he wanted to string his father up from a lamppost or send him to the guillotine. The French had gone too far. They'd been right about liberty, however. It was heady stuff. He felt nothing was beyond his powers now. Even flight. For a moment he had the sensation that he floated above the table, watching the three of them munch on nuts and sweetmeats and empty glass after glass.

"Let's have another bottle," he said. "This one's mine." He could buy it with his own money, not just his allowance. He was independent, his own man. "I'll pay for the whole damn dinner. After another bottle."

"There'll be plenty of bottles at Cruikshank's," Robert said.

Damian wasn't particularly fond of Robert's favorite Pall Mall gaming hell. He'd rather look for clean, comely girls. He glanced at Julian, who shrugged. The latter had been in an odd mood since he returned from France.

"Cruikshank's it is," Damian said, remembering that the newly wed Robert eschewed muslin company, at least for the present.

The bottles at Cruikshank's contained gin. They were well into a game when nausea nibbled at the edge of Damian's pleasant glow. He muttered something about moving on, finding fresh air and different company. But luck was favoring Robert and there was no way to stop him when he was on a winning streak. Or a losing one, for that matter.

A couple of players dropped out. Julian too. "That's my limit for tonight."

"Coward," Robert said without rancor.

Julian shook his head. "Sensible."

Even drunk and winning, Robert knew better than to argue with Julian Fortescue, who always did exactly what he wanted. "It's you and I, Damian. Let's bet something worth winning. A hundred on this one."

Guineas passed back and forth. As the bets increased, they exchanged scribbled vowels. Damian lost track of whether he was ahead or behind.

"Tame stuff," Robert said. "What about this? Everything in front of us and in our pockets too, on one roll." Suiting actions to words, he pushed the pile of gold and paper forward and tossed in some copper coins, a silk handkerchief, his watch, and the key to his house. Damian followed suit, producing a similar assortment, and a document.

He'd picked up the deed from the family solicitor that afternoon, enjoyed carrying it around, the symbol of his financial independence. And the memory of his dead mother. "Beaulieu," he said, and snatched it back. "I can't wager my estate. I won't."

To Robert the words *can't* and *won't* were like a burr under the saddle. "Do it!" he cried. "I'll bet Longford against it. Devilish fine property. Good income. Just as good as yours. Maybe better."

Damian's hand clutched the heavy parchment.

An angel or devil perched on his shoulder told him this was an important day, one that deserved a grand gesture. He goggled at the dice, then blinked away the smoke of cheap candles. What were the odds? Numbers danced meaninglessly in his brain. Marcus Lithgow would know. But the friend who had taught them all how to calculate the chances was abroad again. In Germany, or maybe Holland. Damian glanced up at Julian, who leaned against the wall with his arms folded, regarding them with a twisted smile.

"Shall I?" he asked. Julian was his best friend, had been for years. He wouldn't steer Damian wrong.

"You're a man of means now. Nothing ventured, nothing gained." All true. Except Damian didn't want to gain, because he had what he wanted. So did he need to venture? "What's the harm? Lose it tonight, you'll get it back tomorrow." That was true. If Damian won, he'd give Robert the chance to win it back. Robert would do the same for him. None of their coterie, boon companions for almost five years, ever lost serious amounts to each other. It was a grand gesture with no real risk.

His grip loosened and he let the deed join the flotsam on the shabby baize of the gaming table. His eyes watered. One hand seized the greasy glass and raised it to his lips, the cheap liquor stinging his throat and burning his gut. With the other hand he picked up the battered leather dice box.

"Done," he said, rattled the dice hard, and let them fly.

The last thing he remembered before he lost consciousness was Robert's cry of triumph.

The following evening Damian boarded the coach for the north of England. He had only enough money for a cheap seat. Traveling outside on the stage in wet, cold weather seemed a just punishment. The rhythm of the horses' gait drummed out the words *stupid stupid stupid*; as the roads grew worse, each jolt of the coach sharpened his misery with the reminder that the painful reckoning grew ever nearer.

He couldn't bring himself to return the servant's surprised greeting with a smile when he stepped in through the massive oak door of Amblethorpe Hall. "Where is His Lordship?" he asked, handing over his sodden greatcoat to the shivering butler. "In the book room?"

"Aye, my lord. Do you wish for any refreshment after your journey?"

"Thank you, no." Facing his father drunk might be easier, but he'd seek no relief from the scourging he faced.

Even in summer, heat never penetrated the granite walls or lofty arched passages of the ancient fortress. The passage to the rear of the house, gloomy in the November afternoon, seemed both endless and all too short. A blazing fire in his father's habitual lair offered physical comfort, but nothing else.

"Kendal! What a surprise." Lord Windermere rose from behind his desk without a smile, but a glint in his eye told Damian that the old man was glad to see him. He took a deep breath and accepted his father's solemn handshake. "I didn't expect to see you for some time. I don't know if you received my letter congratulating you on your majority. Either way, let me repeat my good wishes."

"Thank you, sir."

They'd parted on cool terms at the end of the summer, after the usual row about Damian's friends, habits, and ambitions. God, how he wished he'd heeded his father's request that he remain at Amblethorpe. He wished he'd never left and gone to Eton. He wished he'd never gone to Oxford and met Robert Townsend and Julian Fortescue. He wished his mother was alive.

If wishes were horses, beggars would ride. At the moment he felt lowlier than any beggar. He clenched his fists and tightened his jaw.

"So what brings you here? Have the joys of London palled so soon? How was your journey?"

No point making small talk. "I lost Beaulieu."

"I beg your pardon?"

"On the night of my birthday. I gambled away the estate."

"I see. We had better sit down." Lord Windermere took his accustomed seat behind the desk and indicated the opposite chair. They always sat like that in this room, and usually Damian was the recipient of a lecture. A new prick of regret afflicted him that he'd never conversed with his father as an adult. Just when he had theoretically reached that milestone, he'd proven beyond doubt that he was unworthy of being treated as an equal.

His father's dry tones pierced his despair. "You had better tell me about it."

It would have been easier if he'd ranted and roared, but overt expressions of emotion had never been his father's habit. He listened, his features impassive, to Damian's halting confession.

"I'm sorry, sir," Damian concluded, "although there's not much use saying it. I've let you down. And the memory of Mama."

"She loved Beaulieu. It's all we had left of her."

Damian nodded, his eyes gritty with sorrow. For days he'd avoided thinking of the family's happy times at Beaulieu, lest he break down and weep. Now, above all, he must control himself, as his father always did.

Lord Windermere rearranged the perfectly aligned pens on his desk. He picked up his ivory-handled paper knife, a gift from his late wife, and stared at it for a moment. "We must buy it back," he said.

"It will cost a pretty penny and I don't even know whom Robert Townsend lost it to." As he'd learned the next day, Robert's winning streak hadn't lasted long.

"Once I discover the new owner I will go to the bankers. I shall start putting money aside at once. There are improvements at Amblethorpe that can be postponed and we shall retrench."

Worse and worse. Lord Windermere had a most unaristocratic aversion to debt, as Damian heard each time he overspent his allowance. Neither was he given to extravagance or overindulgence.

"How do things stand here?" Damian asked. "I realize I have no right to ask, but I should know what hardships my folly will cause."

"Our ancient holdings are relatively modest considering the family's rank. As you are aware, your mother was a considerable heiress. With her estate added to mine you would have been very well-to-do. Regaining the ground lost is not impossible, but neither will it come without sacrifice."

"What can I do, sir? It goes without saying that I shall live frugally." His heart sank at a future spent at Amblethorpe without the possibility of escape. "I should look for a profession."

Considering how well he had taken the news, Damian forgave his father's derisive curl of the lip. "Do you intend to recoup our fortunes through your skill with a brush?"

Damian gulped. "No, sir. I shall give up painting. I shall endeavor to do just as you wish from now on."

"As you are my heir, the church is not suitable. There can be no question of the army, I assume. It won't help matters if you are killed."

Damian bit back his instinctive reaction; exclaiming that the family might be better off if he died and let Cousin George have the title was the kind of dramatic flourish his father abhorred. "I have a facility for languages," he said with all the calm he could muster. "You believe I wasted my time traveling abroad the past four years, and I won't deny that you have reason. Maybe I can turn them to good use after all. Does anyone of your acquaintance have influence in the Foreign Office?"

"I'm not sure that is wise," his father said with a frown. "Would you not be better off here, safe from temptation?"

"I can promise, sir, that I shall never touch a card or roll the dice again as long as I live."

"I believe you have learned that particular lesson, but there are other lures. I'm afraid you need to be weaned from the evil companions of your youth."

"I will break with them, sir. All I wish to do is serve my family and my nation as a staunch and virtuous Tory. You'll see what a paragon of good sense I shall be."

Lord Windermere thought for a while. "I don't know him well, but we have mutual friends. I will send you to see Sir Richard Radcliffe at the Foreign Office."

"Thank you, sir. I won't let you down."

"See that you don't."

Chapter 2

Seven years later
London, December 1800

Attending the theater with the Duke of Denford was not the wisest way for Cynthia to spend her first evening back in London. He'd escorted her before, to plays, the opera, and less decorous events like masked balls at the Pantheon. But this was the first time she'd been out with him when she, Denford, and her husband were in the same country.

Receiving word from the Foreign Office of Windermere's imminent arrival from Persia, she'd pressed the horses over winter roads from Wiltshire, thinking she'd find him already at home in Hanover Square.

Her stomach fluttering, she had climbed down from her chaise and up the steps into the marble hall. She found all serene: no excitement at the presence of the master of the house, no evidence of luggage from abroad. The Earl of Windermere wasn't at Windermere House. The servants hadn't seen him or even heard of their master's return. The surge of optimism that she'd maintained for two days on the road dissipated like heat through a leaking roof. There and then, Cynthia determined to deny that foolish hope had ever existed.

There was no reason to be disappointed, she told herself firmly. Disappointment suggested the existence of expectations. Cynthia would be a fool to expect anything from Windermere. He hadn't disappointed her, merely let her down. During just over a year of marriage, most of it spent apart, Damian Lewis, Earl of Windermere, had been consistent in that regard.

Lord Windermere might not have been present to greet his faithful wife, but the devil next door was. Not half an hour after her arrival from the country, the Duke of Denford stepped along the pavement from his house and welcomed her home as Windermere had failed to do. Despite at least two very good reasons why she should refuse, Cynthia was now dressed in her favorite evening gown, sitting in a box at Drury Lane with temptation incarnate.

"I didn't expect to see so many people in town just before Christmas." She leaned over the rail, peering at the sweep of seats opposite, five tiers of them, thronged with increasingly well-dressed patrons, ranging from clerks and servants in the highest gallery under the roof, down to the expensive and fashionable boxes nearest the pit. She and Denford occupied one of the latter, the sidewalls of which offered an illusion of privacy, despite being open to the gaze of the world.

"What an excellent box, Julian. You know I like being near the stage."

"You also like being invisible to most of the gossiping tabbies." He knew as well as she that her flouting of convention was largely bravado. Fewer than half the occupants of the vast horseshoe-shaped theater could see the inhabitants of the front boxes.

"I don't even know why I worry about being discreet. I'm not well-known in town." She waved her hand to indicate the opposite seats. "It's quite possible that not a soul in the place knows who I am."

"They know me."

"That's because you are notorious and therefore interesting to everyone."

"The world is filled with fools."

She turned to look at her companion, whose low voice dropped to an impossibly deep bass when he was particularly amused or especially cynical. His appearance alone was enough to make him stand out. His tall, lean figure was habitually clad in unrelieved black—this evening in satin breeches and an evening coat and waistcoat of velvet embroidered in black silk. Even his neckcloth was black. The gloom of his costume enhanced the satanic effect of dead-straight black hair, which he wore long and tied back in a queue with a silk bow. He sat upright beside her with arms extended, hands resting on the silver-chased knob of the ebony walking stick he rarely left at home. His dependence on the elegant staff was an affectation for a man under thirty in perfect health. Some people, including Cynthia, found it amusing. Others found it just one more reason to detest him. The Duke of Denford had plenty of enemies.

"I believe you enjoy shocking people, Julian."

Denford's mouth curled unpleasantly, then the thin face with the hawkish nose made one of the mercurial transformations that fascinated Cynthia, and had sent her scuttling out of town a few weeks earlier, terrified she would succumb to the heady seduction of the duke's brilliant blue eyes.

"I enjoy shocking *you*," he said. A man shouldn't be allowed such devastating features, especially when he had the ability to change them from ice to fire beneath her gaze.

"I'm not as easy to shock as I was when we first met."

"No," he said. "Thank God for that. You have become a fascinating challenge."

It didn't seem possible for pure sky blue to exude heat, but Denford's eyes made every inch of her skin flush warm. How did he manage it? Without moving a muscle, he examined her face with concentrated intensity for some seconds, then his gaze dropped to the white expanse of her bosom, the bodice cut so low that the blue silk and lace barely concealed her nipples. She felt them hardening, and a curl of fire kindled in her belly. A familiar sick panic gripped her chest at the clash of attraction and repulsion, longing and fear.

She jerked her head toward the stage and stared at the obstinately closed curtain. Surely it was time for the play to begin.

"Why did you leave London?" The question was almost a whisper, close enough to caress her ear.

"Anne wanted to go to Wiltshire," she said with determined nonchalance. "As her temporary chaperone, naturally I had to go with her."

"Was that the only reason?"

"Why else?"

It was true, in as far as it went. Her houseguest Anne Brotherton had a reason to visit Hinton Manor, where she'd remained. But Cynthia had seized on the excuse it offered to escape Denford's dangerous attentions. And Denford knew it.

"You like to accommodate your friends," he said.

"Yes."

"Am I your friend?"

She laughed nervously. "Of course you are."

"I look forward to being accommodated."

Her laugh degenerated to a titter. She grew warmer and more panicked, torn between the competing urges of flight and surrender. Desperate to break out of the sensual net he wove about her, she resorted to frankness. "I'm not like this, Julian," she said, staring with dogged, unfocused eyes at the mass of humanity in the crowded pit. "I am the daughter of a clergyman. I am married. I would never break my marriage vows."

"Would you not?"

"I *will* not."

She sensed him retreat, lean back in his chair. Julian had always been clever that way. He would press her so far, then withdraw before she became alarmed and ran away. Except that one time. The one kiss. Which had resulted in her fleeing London and the temptation to sin.

Because she was, despite everything, a married woman and she would not betray her husband, however much he might deserve it. Besides, she wasn't sure of Denford's motives.

He desired her. She did not believe that his carnal interest was feigned. But he had also once been her husband's best friend.

Earlier that day

A cold afternoon wind off the Thames blew up Craven Street. Damian slouched into the tall collar of his topcoat as he approached his rendezvous, ignoring the Cockney imprecations of a costermonger selling apples. He missed the sound of alien languages and the exotic splendors of the Persian court. After sailing past Gibraltar, he missed the particular Mediterranean blue that warmed the body and enlivened the spirits. His escape from England and his unwanted bride had been brought to a premature conclusion.

It didn't matter. He had to return sooner or later and a year's reflection had made him acknowledge what he'd always known: He had behaved badly to his wife. No one had held a knife to his throat and made him marry her. While she might indeed possess the combination of ignorance, bad taste, and blind ambition that he'd ascribed to her, he'd never given her a chance to prove otherwise. It had been months since he'd received a letter from her, and while it was possible some communication had gone astray, he couldn't really blame her if she'd ceased to write to him.

He knocked on the door of the featureless house, and an equally nondescript servant directed him to the second floor, where Mr. John Ryland awaited him. Ryland was a creature of the British Foreign Office. He might work for Grenville and the Pitt government, but his allegiance went beyond party. There had always been men like him, and always would be: quiet, discreet, ruthless behind a judicious veneer. While Ryland undoubtedly knew where all the skeletons were hidden, Damian had no intention of asking. Neither would Ryland tell him.

Damian accepted a glass of sherry and sat down, knees crossed, waiting to be informed why he had been summoned home to chilly London and an anonymous set of rooms, convenient for Whitehall but obviously not regularly occupied.

"Tell me, Lord Windermere, how did you find Futteh Aly Khan?" Ryland asked, and listened respectfully to a report that was quite irrelevant to his current errand. If the state of negotiations with the Shah of Persia interested Ryland, he would have read the detailed and secret dispatches from the head of the mission. "You enjoyed the place," he remarked.

"I did," Damian said. This was all very well, but only small talk. He wondered when Ryland would get to the point.

"What a pity we had to curtail your exploration. I am sorry for it."

Fighting back a wave of irritation at the prevarications of his chosen profession, Damian waved aside the apology. "I confess to being surprised by the demand. I cannot imagine what diplomatic situation requires my modest skills and experience."

Ryland refilled their glasses. "I assume you are familiar with the Alt-Brandenburg question."

Damian nodded. Alt-Brandenburg was a strategically placed German princedom with a notoriously stubborn ruler. "Familiar, yes, but not *au courant*. Has the prince agreed to the British alliance or does he continue to dally with the French?"

"We had almost brought His Highness around to our way of thinking when he discovered a sticking point. He demands a pledge of our friendship."

"A greater sum than can be found in the secret fund?"

Ryland smiled thinly. "Life and diplomacy would be so easy if it were only a question of money. The prince has got hold of a rumor that the art collection of the late Marquis de Falleron is in English hands and he wants it."

"Good Lord."

"I thought you would be aware of the significance."

"I attended a rout at the Hôtel Falleron when I was a mere youth. It must have been just before the fall of the Bastille." Even among the many splendors of Paris, that evening stood out in Damian's memory as a particularly dazzling one. Julian had been there, of course. Robert and Marcus too. He shied away from the memory of a time and companions he had put behind him long ago.

"You must have enjoyed that, my lord, with your appreciation for the arts."

Better to think of what he had seen rather than whom he'd been with. "The Falleron collection was legendary and, judging even by the small portion I saw, legend did not lie. I seem to recall hearing that the pictures disappeared after the marquis and his family went to the guillotine. If they were to be sold, the event would rival the dispersal of the Duke of Orleans's collection."

Ryland looked at him with an expression so

bland it must presage a blow. Damian was about to find out why he'd been ordered to sail the French-infested waters of the Mediterranean with such haste and lack of concern for his safety.

"It's said that the Duke of Denford possesses the Falleron pictures."

A lump in his throat threatened to choke him at the name. Surely it couldn't be. "I don't know the duke," he said, firmly. "I believe he is quite an old man."

"The fifth duke died almost a year ago, followed quickly to the grave by his nephew and heir, the father of three daughters."

"Unfortunate."

"Male members of the Fortescue family have been haunted by misfortune recently. Illness, accident, and the failure to sire boys. The new duke is a third cousin, Julian Fortescue."

There was no point denying the acquaintance. Ryland obviously knew that he and Julian had roomed together at Oxford, and, having been expelled from that august establishment, explored Europe in the early days of the Revolution, before things got ugly. It wouldn't surprise him if he knew Julian had been at the Marquis de Falleron's soirée. "You are doubtless aware that Julian Fortescue and I have not spoken in years. I have no influence there. If he is in possession of the paintings, approach him. But if he has come into a fortune, he may be hard to persuade. His love of the Masters is genuine and he wouldn't wish to part with them unless he needs the money."

"You know him well. How would he react if he had inherited the Denford title but not the fortune?"

Sometimes the serpentine methods of diplomacy tried Damian's patience. "Has he inherited the fortune?"

"As it happens, the inheritance is in dispute. According to our information the new duke is both short of ready monies and beset by lawyers."

"I don't know whether to feel sorrier for him or the lawyers. In that case, he'll accept an offer, as long as it's generous enough."

"We have made an offer, through discreet channels. He denies that he has the collection."

Damian shrugged. "I find it thoroughly improbable that he owns these paintings. If he bought them during the Revolution he never mentioned it, and we were still intimate then. And why would he not have sold them? He has made his living as a dealer in works of art since he was eighteen years old."

"We have reasons to believe otherwise, and Lord Grenville thinks you are the only one in a position to make Denford admit the truth, and sell the pictures for the sake of the country."

"I am to appeal to his sense of duty?" For the first time Damian found the situation amusing. "Julian has never given a damn about duty, or anyone but himself."

"Will you try?"

Unlike his former best friend, the Earl of Windermere possessed a sense of duty, and a strong one at that. For the sake of his country he would try to revive a friendship that had dissolved in bitterness.

At the same time, he needed to face the reason he'd fled England in a state of panic. For the sake of his family's future, he would try to establish a cordial relationship with his wife.

Later that day, Damian dined at Grosvenor Square with Sir Richard Radcliffe. Though the Radcliffes entertained lavishly, it was an informal meal, with no other guests, spent catching up on London social gossip. Damian didn't like keeping his new mission a secret from Radcliffe, who had been his mentor and confidant since he joined the diplomatic service. But Ryland had made it clear that the business was to be kept under the hatches.

Claiming pressure of work, Radcliffe asked Damian to escort his wife to the theater. Lady Belinda did not believe in arriving at the theater early. "They always start late. Besides, no one worth looking at ever arrives on time," she said, and pressed another glass of brandy on him, giving him an excellent view of her bosom draped in red silk embroidered in gold. As he remembered well, Her Ladyship wasn't bashful, either in private or in public. No one in the theater would miss that scarlet gown.

When they entered the Radcliffes' box at Drury Lane, naturally in the best part of the house, Titania was waking up to find herself in love with an ass. Damian didn't particularly like *A Midsummer Night's Dream*. It disturbed him how the fate of humans was dependent on the whims of fairies, which seemed akin to the turn of the card or the fall of the dice. So he listened with half an ear to Lady Belinda's commentary on the wardrobe choices of the audience and wished her husband had come with them.

Hard to believe that six years earlier, as a very junior diplomat, he'd had a massive tendre for the worldly hostess. She cultivated young followers from the better families, and her much older husband, ever occupied with the affairs of state, encouraged it. Damian sometimes wondered how much his advancement owed to the pleasure of his patron's wife. Pleasure indeed. For a single month, once Lady Belinda had made it blatantly clear that her husband demanded only discretion, Damian had been her satisfied and ultimately exhausted bedmate. He'd been tossed aside for a newer, even younger candidate. A mission to Prussia beckoned, and frankly the Germans had been a bit of a relief after the exigencies of life as Lady Belinda's lover.

A satin-gloved hand touched his knee, and stayed there. "I have heard, Damian," she said, her voice a low purr, "that the Levant is home to many exotic practices."

"I don't know about that," he said. "What seems exotic to us is normal to them. The game of Chowgan, for example, is no more or less thrilling than cricket is to us. It's played on horseback with sticks to hit a ball. It's very fine sport and demands a high degree of skill."

"I'm always interested in sports that demand skill." Her rich gardenia perfume tickled his nose as she leaned in to whisper. "Do the Persians not have seraglios, like the Turks?"

"Certainly. But male visitors, especially foreign ones, are not permitted to enter the zenanas. The women are well-guarded."

"My poor Damian! Does that mean you have been *alone* for a full year?"

As a matter of fact it did. His bollocks roiled at the proximity of a woman who would, if he gave the sign, skip the play and put him through his paces for the rest of the night.

It was tempting. Very tempting.

Then he thought of his wife, who had been stranded in the country a full year. Though she hadn't appealed to him in the past, long deprivation might make her desirable. With some regret he pretended to turn his attention to the stage.

Belinda hadn't given up. "Gentlemen talk. Even if you lacked the opportunity to play exotic sports, I'm sure you learned the rules."

"As a matter of fact I did play Chowgan."

"Damian," she said with an impatient edge. "I

am not talking about games that are played on the back of a horse."

It was stupid to encourage her, but he couldn't resist. "I am astonished you never experienced that particular pleasure."

She enjoyed that. "Will it surprise you to learn that I have tried? I thought to give new meaning to the rising trot but it proved impracticable."

He crossed his legs, trying and failing to dislodge her hand. Instead it moved upward, warm against his satin-clad thigh. "Not even a horse can keep up with you, let alone a travel-weary man," he said, hoping she would take the hint and accept that the delights of the evening would not extend beyond the thespian. As long as her hand didn't travel any farther, she wouldn't know that his cock hadn't got the message about being too tired for action. Thank goodness the box was shadowy.

"Women talk when they are disappointed." There was no question in his mind that the remark was a veiled threat. Not a direct one. Talking about his bedroom prowess, or lack of the same, wouldn't accomplish anything, but Lady Belinda held a good deal of influence in the circles where his future ambitions lay and was ruthless about getting what she wanted. She had the power to make life difficult for him and needed to be placated.

"I have something you will enjoy, once all my luggage arrives. Certain miniature paintings that I cannot display in my wife's drawing room." He kept his eyes on the stage, but a sharp intake of breath told him he'd intrigued the sensual magpie.

"And shall you demonstrate the poses?"

"Alas," he said with what he hoped was a note of finality, "I leave for Oxfordshire in a day or so."

"You should wait for my Christmas dinner party. A week or two won't make much difference."

"My wife may beg to differ. I have not seen Lady Windermere in over a year."

"Is that so?" Now her voice held a note of amusement. "In that case I will importune you no more. I look forward to seeing the paintings."

She removed her hand from his thigh and they sat side by side with perfect decorum, pretending to watch the play. If there was a single member of the audience less interested in *A Midsummer Night's Dream* than he, it was Lady Belinda.

"Isn't that Denford?" she asked, as a chorus of fairies in flimsy costumes cavorted on the stage. "Perhaps you haven't heard, but the infamous Julian Fortescue has turned respectable. Or rather he inherited a dukedom, which had the same effect without him having to go to the trouble of changing his habits."

His stomach clenched. He'd ignored Julian for the best part of seven years and he fervently wished he could continue to do so. But he had a mission. "Where? Has he changed his style of dress since being raised to the purple?"

"Opposite side, third box in from the stage."

It was about as far across the expanse of the theater as was possible, but the tall, lean figure in black leaped instantly to the eye. Once he'd known Julian as well as anyone in the world and he could still pick him out of a crowd without the least difficulty. The years of disappointment and enmity slipped away and he felt the joy of seeing his best friend after a long absence. But only for a moment; then the old bitterness flooded his organs. Though he wished he could continue to pretend that Julian Fortescue didn't exist, he had to reopen relations with the Duke of Denford. Duty demanded it.

"Still in black," he said. "Has he cut his hair?"

"He believes he is Samson."

"You are probably better acquainted with him than I. Now." There was a hint of a question in his statement. If Julian—Denford—was one of Belinda's lovers, wouldn't Grenville have given her the task of persuading him to sell the paintings? She never made a secret of her *affaires*, and Sir Richard's complacency, even complicity, was well-known.

"We are on nodding terms, that is all." The pique in her voice told him that she wouldn't mind playing Delilah, and he concluded that Julian had rejected her advances.

There was one other occupant of the box, a blond woman in blue, too far away to identify. He had the impression of a fashionable beauty, but her general mien struck no chord. It was unlikely that Damian knew her. She raised a lorgnette and looked around and he fancied they came under her scrutiny. Then she turned back to Denford, his black head contrasting with her fair one. Denford appeared engrossed by his companion and Damian couldn't blame him. Even at this distance he could tell that she was exquisite. He wondered if her face matched her air of elegance.

"Perhaps I should go and congratulate him on his elevation," Damian said, pondering the advantage of making initial contact in a public place He had no illusions about the difficulty of the task he'd been set. The last time he and Julian had spoken— ironically about a very different collection of pictures—had seemed to preclude their ever being on cordial terms again.

"I'm sure he won't mind being interrupted."

"Who is the lady?"

"I don't know. I don't keep count of Denford's conquests." The edge of malice in Belinda's voice aroused warning prickles at the back of his neck. She was lying and she was up to no good.

The blond woman was probably married; Julian would hardly be escorting a young and single lady, and the female in question was clearly no Cyprian. Even at this distance she exuded an air of breeding and delicacy, though the latter quality was deceptive if she openly deceived her husband with a man of Julian's ilk. Intruding on them without knowing her identity seemed potentially awkward.

Suppose her husband was a friend of his? Reestablishing relations with Julian was going to be tricky enough without adding an unknown woman into the equation.

"The curtain is falling. You should go now." Lady Belinda nodded to someone in another box and waved him toward the exit. "I can spare you for quarter of an hour."

"I wouldn't dream of leaving you alone." If Lady Belinda pursued her own mischievous agenda, he refused to be manipulated "Also, I might be *de trop* over there. Who knows what Denford may be getting up to in that box."

She smiled sweetly and changed her tack. "Some women have all the luck," she purred, and put her hand back on his knee.

He inched away and calculated how much more of *A Midsummer Night's Dream* he had to endure.

Chapter 3

Through the incompetent machinations of Puck, the four lovers were in a tangle and Titania was in love with an ass. Cynthia shifted in her seat and let her attention wander to the crowd in the pit.

"Not enjoying the play?" Denford asked.

"How did you know?"

"I notice everything about you, Cynthia."

"I had never seen *A Midsummer Night's Dream* acted," she said quickly, "only read it. It's very different on the stage."

Despite making great strides in worldliness, she couldn't help being a little shocked at the skimpy costumes, suggestive posturing, and outright kissing that was featured in the production. Lysander and Hermia had kissed on the lips early in the play and Titania was doing the same to Bottom now, positively devouring him beneath his ass's head. Cynthia kept telling herself that it was only clever acting and they weren't really behaving with such wantonness in public.

She stole a sideways glance and encountered Julian's intense blue gaze. She lowered her eyes to his mouth and recalled the only time that she had been kissed like that, lasciviously, mouth-on-mouth, like the players on the stage.

The momentous occasion had been in a dark corner of her garden on a chill autumn night a few weeks earlier. It should have been her husband—such intimate caresses were the right of spouses—but Windermere had never kissed her thus. This man, the Duke of Denford, had introduced her to the delight. She felt guilty for kissing another man and resented that the man she'd married had not seen to the business himself. Her classmates at the Birmingham Academy for Young Ladies—ignorant girls like herself—had talked about love and marriage and kissing. The three went together, all with the same man.

"In what way do you find the play different?"

"The actors have revealed new aspects of the characters. I had not previously perceived that Lysander and Demetrius are in competition with each other. First they must both love Hermia and then, when one turns to Helena the other must follow."

"You don't give much credit to the intervention of the fairies."

"I believe magic merely reinforces their own inclinations, which is that of former best friends turned rivals."

"My dear Cynthia," Julian said with a deep laugh. "You have grown into a woman of subtlety."

"I hope so," she said, not without pride. "I came to the capital a naïve provincial. I had no idea how to convey my thoughts except in the most straightforward manner. Since I quickly learned that simplicity is not appreciated in London, I could not convey them at all."

"You know you may always speak frankly to me because I am incapable of taking offense. You can tell me what you really mean about the rivals in this play." Julian was far too clever. And while he wasn't always straightforward, he was never afraid to be frank. "Is that what you think?" he continued. "That I want you only because you are married to my former friend?"

"The notion has crossed my mind."

"If you believe that your only value to me is as Damian's bride, then you don't know your own worth and he is a bigger fool than I thought for leaving you alone so long, and letting you think you mean nothing to him."

I know I mean nothing to him. She was too proud to say it aloud. Instead she soothed her vanity by defending her neglectful spouse. "He was called abroad and did his duty, for which I respect him." Her hand convulsed on the gilt handle of her lorgnette.

"And of course he fulfills his duty to you by frequent letters, attentive to your needs."

To that there was no answer.

Long fingers enveloped her clenched fist. "If you will let me," he whispered, "you will find me neglectful in nothing."

He chose his words well. Neglected was precisely how she had felt for so long, long before she met Windermere. Her husband had merely raised hopes that finally she would have someone to call her own, and dashed them. She ignored a shiver of yearning, withdrew from Julian's touch, and raised the glasses to her nose. Her throat was tight. "Not now."

"Why not now? Admit that you are tempted. Why else did you come out with me tonight?"

As his wicked voice stroked her like a sable brush, she determinedly surveyed the faces and figures in the boxes opposite. There were a few she knew, but very few. Despite her rank, she was not of the *ton*. The niece of a Birmingham merchant, abandoned by her brand-new husband, had no entrée to the more rarefied households of Mayfair. If her only recourse had been to the faintly disreputable company of Caro Townsend and her set, including Julian Fortescue, it was Windermere's fault. Through the lorgnette she saw the Countess of Ashfield, a pillar of London society with the eyesight of an eagle, glaring back at her. Another box was filled with drunken bucks; luckily they were on the bottom tier or the occupants of the pit below would be in dire danger of being hit by flying glasses and vomit. The next box was also a trifle crowded: The owner had decided to cram his wife and six young ladies into the narrow space. By contrast, the very elegant lady next door had but a single gentleman in attendance.

She inhaled so hard her chest hurt. She would recognize that gentleman from a mile's distance, with or without the benefit of magnifying lenses.

She didn't know him as well as she knew the man at her side, but on the other hand, unlike Julian, he had shared her bed. He was her lawfully wedded husband. Back in London after more than a year's absence, he had not sought the company of his wife. Instead he was tête-à-tête in a box at Drury Lane with another woman.

Every muscle rigid, she lowered the lorgnette to her lap with exaggerated care.

"What is it?" Julian asked.

"Who is the lady in red in the box closest to the pit door?"

"Lady Belinda Radcliffe, wife of the undersecretary for foreign affairs. Windermere has known her for a long time, through her husband." She heard pity in his voice and felt his hand on her shoulder, like comfort, not seduction.

"Did you know Windermere was back in London?"

"I heard a rumor. But when you agreed to come out with me tonight I thought I must be wrong."

Cynthia blinked hard and didn't trust herself to speak through thickening tears. Instead she tilted her head to press her cheek against Julian's hand.

Across the theater she saw Windermere's gaze linger on them for a few seconds, then he turned back to the beautiful Lady Belinda.

If she were honest with herself, she had hoped he would see her, or at least hear a report that she hadn't been waiting at home like a meek Quaker for her spouse's return. When imagining his reaction to seeing her transformed into a fashionable lady—and escorted by a duke, this particular duke—she hadn't expected indifference. Expectations confounded again, she thought wryly through her distress.

"I heard that rumor too," she managed finally. "But I didn't know Windermere was already in town. I assumed he had been delayed."

If Denford expressed sympathy now, she would leave. She would ask the theater servants to find her a hackney and go home alone. Her sense of humiliation was too great to be borne in sight of another. Gradually her heightened breathing abated. "So he is merely escorting the wife of a senior colleague, then. Very polite of him."

"I'm sure that's the reason," Julian said. She'd almost recovered her equilibrium when he delivered the final blow. "It is common knowledge that Windermere's affair with Lady Belinda was over years ago."

Common knowledge to all except the stupid lowborn wife he'd married for her uncle's money. Foolishly, she couldn't keep her eyes off them. She saw her husband take the satin hand of his former mistress and raise it to his lips. Not so former would be her guess. The letter from the Foreign Office had told her he'd reach London two days ago. Perhaps he had. But those two days—and nights—had not been spent at Windermere House.

Julian's supple fingers massaged the tense muscles of her neck, out of sight of the casual observer. The sensation of flesh on flesh sent tingles of sensation down her back and up between her legs.

Damian, Earl of Windermere, might have come home this night and satisfied the desire that pooled in her most private place, but he preferred a former mistress in red satin. And when, after all, had he ever satisfied her desires?

She wanted satisfaction. Even more, she craved intimacy and human connection.

"I don't want to see the rest of the play, Julian. Take me home."

Even if he changed his mind, Damian had no chance to tackle Denford at the theater. The duke and his blond beauty left before the last act. Damian accompanied Lady Belinda home. Declining offers of refreshment—liquid or carnal—and the use of her carriage, he opted to walk back to his hotel in St. James's. It was a crisp, clear night without the pervasive damp that chilled one to the bone in a London winter. He could almost see the stars, or at least could imagine they were there. London always seemed both domestic and exotic to him. As a child, the occasional visit to the capital with his mother and sister had been exciting. Then, when they weren't gallivanting around continental Europe, Julian, Robert, Marcus, and he would raise hell and shock the straitlaced out of their stays. After he determined to become a responsible citizen and serve the public, he'd chosen diplomacy, and once more spent much of his time abroad.

The pleasant streets of Mayfair held no particular memories, good or bad. He had no intention of going as far south as Pall Mall, site of the great disaster that changed his life. On a whim he prolonged his walk by an eastward diversion to Hanover Square, the site of his family's London abode.

Reaching the square, he detected light through the drawn curtains of the square brick mansion. Intending to leave for the country almost immediately, he hadn't thought it worth opening the house. With his new, and most unwelcome mission, he supposed he'd have to bring his wife back from Beaulieu and occupy Windermere House.

During his absences abroad, the house was let for the season, bringing in a handsome income, but it was odd that there should be tenants in occupation during December. He walked around the square and found the knocker on the door; someone was in residence. Before he could dwell on the possible awkwardness of intruding on strangers late at night, he rapped sharply.

A couple of minutes later his butler admitted him.

"Good evening, my lord," Ellis said, betraying not an iota of shock. "We expected you two days ago. I trust you had a pleasant journey."

"Very good, thank you, Ellis. Who told you I would be in London?"

"Her Ladyship, of course. She only arrived this morning but she wrote and warned us to be ready for you."

"Her Ladyship is here?" The woman was supposed to have stayed in the country and waited for him to return. Looking past Ellis, he noticed changes in the hall. The paint had been freshened, which was an improvement; a large Chinese urn occupied one corner, which was not. Ugly as it was, it paled in comparison to a ghastly Dutch still-life painting featuring a variety of dead birds.

"Has Lady Windermere spent much time in London during my absence?"

"She has been in residence most of the year."

With trepidation he remembered that he'd given her carte blanche to refurbish Beaulieu Manor. If this was an example of her taste, he shuddered to think what she might have done to his mother's house.

"Where is she?"

"When she came in, she retired to the small

parlor. She said she wished to read in peace and would ring when she was ready to go upstairs. She asked not to be disturbed."

"I don't suppose she meant me."

"Certainly not, my lord. Her Ladyship will be very happy to see you at last." A subtle reprimand colored the butler's final words. "Do you need anything? I see that your luggage has been delayed."

"Nothing for now, Ellis. That will be all." He didn't need a witness to a reunion whose course he could no longer predict. He'd anticipated his bride grateful for his arrival in the wilds of Oxfordshire. By moving to London without permission, she demonstrated an unpleasing independence. He passed out of the hall, behind the double staircase to the short passage leading to the rear ground floor rooms.

The small parlor was empty. He tried the library next door and found it dark and unheated. He returned to the parlor, where the fire glowed, though it looked as though no one had tended it for an hour or two. A leather-bound novel lay open on a table next to the chaise longue. The curtains over the French windows were open a crack and the door into the garden was unlocked. Apparently, like him, his wife, had felt the need for fresh air. Detecting no light outside, he stepped out.

"My lady?" No response. The garden was of a fair size for London, but it didn't take long to see that it was empty, unless she was crouching behind the shrubbery. His boots were almost silent on the frosted lawn and he could hear nothing but the occasional rumble of wheels in the street beyond. Back inside he looked out one last time and saw a bobbing light coming from the left side. Acting on instinct, he slipped hastily into the dark library. A pair of shadowy figures, one a woman, appeared against the garden wall. They spoke for a short time, then exchanged a tender embrace. The man faded back into the wall and the woman headed for the house. As she hurried up the path, the lantern illuminated his wife's long-forgotten features. She was prettier than he remembered, and her hairstyle had improved, her blond hair now dressed in a fashionable tangle of curls. Her blue evening gown was modish and in excellent taste. Something about her appearance nagged a memory, and not a distant one. As she neared the house she tossed a look over her shoulder. The other man had disappeared.

Though he hadn't spent much time in the garden in recent years, he remembered an iron gate in the wall, leading to the adjacent garden of . . . Denford House.

Idiot that he was to have forgotten. Julian and he used to joke about their family mansions being next door to each other. But Julian had never set foot in his. From a distant and despised branch of the Fortescue family, he hadn't been welcome at the family headquarters. Now he must own the place.

And Damian's wife had been visiting him. After midnight. It had been she at the theater, of course, sitting brazenly in a box with her lover. He wondered if she had recognized him there. She expected him in London.

Rejecting his first urge to confront her, he collapsed into a chair, listened, and thought.

It was all Julian's doing, of course. His wife was a pawn in their escalating exchange of revenge that started the night Julian had permitted the great disaster to occur. Anger and hurt welled in Damian's chest, as acrid as ever.

Much as it galled him, he would let Julian get away with this latest game, at least for a while. He had to because he'd promised Ryland. But he'd be watching for his chance to get his own back, once he'd obtained the pictures for the Prince of Alt-Brandenburg. Then he'd deal with His Disgrace, the Duke of Denford. As for the Countess of Windermere, he almost felt sorry for her, a naïve young woman caught up in Julian's complex toils.

All was quiet in the next room. Presumably she had returned to her novel, blissfully unaware that her tryst at Denford House had been discovered.

Silently he tiptoed down the passage. Since supernatural hearing was one of the qualifications for senior servants, he wasn't surprised when Ellis appeared.

"Her Ladyship has fallen asleep. Since I didn't expect to find her in town, I am at a hotel. I will move to Hanover Square tomorrow. Better not to tell her I was here. I wouldn't want her to be disappointed."

He would have to decide what to do about his erring bride, but tonight was not the time. His anger at her was tempered with the nagging sense that, however reprehensible her conduct, his own was not above reproach. Even the day of their wedding could not be recalled without an unpleasant twinge of his conscience.

Beaulieu, Oxfordshire, a year earlier, October 1799

Damian had sold himself to Joseph Chorley at a simple ceremony at the village church in the village where his mother had grown up. Only the Chorleys and a few servants were present, perhaps to prevent the church from being embarrassingly empty. He himself had been unaccompanied. He had no desire to summon his cousin or any of his Foreign Office colleagues to share in the joy of an event he knew, in his heart, was a shameful one.

He didn't know whether to be sorry his father wasn't alive to see him regain Beaulieu, or glad that the late Lord Windermere didn't know the sacrifice his son had made. With no sense of triumph, he took possession of his birthright and sat down to dinner in his mother's dining room at Beaulieu, his first meal as husband to a young woman he had accepted sight unseen and met fewer than half a dozen times.

Her big blue eyes stared out at him from a frame of frizzy fair curls, demanding something. Courtship? Love? She knew as well as he that this was an arranged marriage and a damn inconvenient one. Still, he was beginning to think he'd made a terrible mistake.

"Is the fish to your satisfaction?" he asked.

"Thank you, yes."

"May I pour you more wine?"

"My glass is still full, thank you." Of course it was. He'd filled it barely a minute ago. He'd drained his own in the same short period and now helped himself to more claret.

Six years as a diplomat had taught Damian to converse effortlessly with the most challenging of partners in difficult social situations. Neither puffed up princelings nor two-timing courtiers had ever given him as much trouble as his chit of a bride.

"I never saw Beaulieu until yesterday," she said, with an obvious effort to break a silence that was becoming oppressive. "It's a lovely house."

It was the last subject he wanted to discuss. Taking another gulp of wine to moisten his dry mouth, he made a harrumphing sound.

"Do you not think so? This room has a beautiful prospect down to the river and the gardens are very fine."

He stared at her. Was she merely being obtuse or didn't she know?

She cast around the room with an air of desperation. "That landscape over the mantelpiece is pretty," she said of one of Claude Lorrain's better works, "and I like the portrait of the lady in blue. I suppose she must be a member of the family that previously owned Beaulieu."

"She is. My grandmother."

"Are you jesting?"

"My mother grew up in this house."

"What a coincidence." She broke off, her mouth falling open as she took in the significance of his statement. "I see. So that's why. My uncle didn't tell me."

Apparently she wasn't aware of Chorley's extortion, the way he'd turned down ready cash and driven a harder bargain. Desperate to regain the house lost by his own idiocy, Damian had paid in blood and his future life.

Both his father and he had tried in vain to buy it back. Now his father was dead and he had succeeded at last, but the victory felt like ashes. Possession of the place he'd spent his happiest times filled him with nothing but a deep melancholy. Because, he'd realized with a sinking stomach, winning back Beaulieu couldn't bring back those days.

"How did the estate come to pass out of your mother's family?" The question, reasonable enough from his wife, rasped his raw nerves. Oh God, she was his *wife*.

"It's not important. Let us talk about you, instead." Avoidance of the painful topic brought back his powers of speech and there were matters they needed to discuss. Mistake or not, he'd married Cynthia Chorley and had to deal with her. She might not have been privy to the most ruthless aspect of her uncle's negotiation strategy, but she'd still happily accepted a man she barely knew. She at least was getting what she wanted from the match: rank and position. Now to discover if anything could be retrieved from the wreckage. "You speak French and Italian, I believe."

"I was taught them at school."

"Where was this establishment? How long did you spend there?" He spoke in French, not because he cared about the answers but to test her fluency.

The result was not encouraging. She looked blank. "I'm sorry. You spoke too fast."

Once he repeated the question slowly, she answered, in adequate but abominably accented French. "*Je m'excuse*," she said carefully, "*mais . . .*" She switched to English. "Our teachers were English and the language sounds different when you speak it. Did you learn it in France? Surely, with the war . . . ?"

"I was in Paris before revolution turned to

terror. French is the language of diplomacy so I am accustomed to using it in my work. You must too. As my wife you will frequent the society of foreign envoys in London as well as abroad."

"Abroad?" She looked shocked. Good God! How was he to introduce this simple little provincial into his world?

"We shall speak French together. You will soon improve."

The switch of languages did little to make the conversation flow. His wife chose every word with deliberation and kept her observations brief. At least her lack of proficiency spared him any unwelcome personal questions. He could get through this. Except that beyond the endless dinner lay the next stage of marriage, the other part of the devil's bargain he'd made with Joseph Chorley.

Cynthia was pretty enough, he granted, but her appearance was as unsophisticated as her discourse. The evening gown was of a good quality crepe, no doubt a product of one of Chorley's mills, but dowdily cut and trimmed about the neck in a manner that lacked taste and was years out of date. Beneath the excess of frothy lace he guessed at a handsome bosom. Alas, it aroused no sensual curiosity in him. He thought with regret of the skilled courtesan he'd kept in Copenhagen, his most recent post, and hoped he would be up to doing his duty tonight.

He liked European women. The ladies flirted elegantly, while their professional sisters knew how to please a man in bed. Some might call the new Countess of Windermere an English rose. More like a wild flower, in his opinion. Or a weed. An uncultivated bloom in the wrong place. God, he regretted turning down Malcolm's offer of a position in the embassy to Persia. He could be preparing for the exotic East now, eager to discover a new culture and forward the interests of the nation, instead of sitting in a state of depression, contemplating the bedding of a dull virgin.

Perhaps it wasn't too late. The embassy didn't leave for a month, and there might still be a place. He could stand a week or two of marriage, if he knew it would be followed by a long reprieve.

His wife's incoherent French observation on the quality of the syllabub stopped mid-sentence. He'd slammed down his glass and splashed red wine on the tablecloth. "Is anything wrong?" she asked.

"*Je vais bien. Voulez-vous retirer, madame?*"

It was her turn to spill her wine. Apparently she thought him so eager to sample her charms, he would go to bed at the uncivilized hour of eight o'clock. He repressed a sigh. "To the drawing room."

He'd linger over a brandy, spend another excruciating hour with her, then get the job done.

Chapter 4

Hanover Square, London

The return of the Earl of Windermere to Hanover Square was heralded by the arrival of his luggage—a large trunk and three hampers delivered by carrier from the port of Plymouth. Not long afterward his valet appeared in a hackney, bearing a valise, hatbox, and dressing case. The presence of the personal servant warned Cynthia that her lord and master was finally about to dignify his wife with his company.

As the morning drew on without sign of the lord himself, Cynthia wondered if he was lingering in bed with Lady Belinda. He'd certainly never lingered in bed with her, and she hadn't taken the opportunity offered the night before to discover what lingering in bed with a man might involve. Her imagination failed her, and perhaps that was for the best.

Well after the clock struck noon, she heard an

arrival in the hall below. Choosing to receive her husband with a display of formality, she awaited him in the drawing room, rather than the morning room or the cozy back parlor she preferred. She tiptoed over to the mantel to check her hair in the mirror, then settled down in a bergère chair, smoothing the skirts of her most elegant winter morning dress, an expensive ensemble of fine rose kerseymere trimmed in a darker shade of velvet. Windermere would find her very different from the frumpy provincial he had married, in outward appearance at least. Her newfound confidence had dissipated with his imminent return, and her stomach held a swarm of butterflies.

The sound of footsteps on the stairs was accompanied by a rumble of male voices that resolved itself into "I'll announce myself, Ellis" and "Very good, my lord." He wasn't speaking to the butler in French, she thought with an edge of hysteria. Would his first greeting to her be in that language? His farewell, a little over a year ago, had been polite, fluent, and largely incomprehensible. She braced herself for a barrage of Gallic courtesy.

The glimpse across the theater hadn't prepared her for the impact of Lord Windermere in close proximity. When she first set eyes on him, she had thought him the most beautiful man of her acquaintance. Now her acquaintance was much broader but her reaction was the same. A coat of sober gray broadcloth displayed his broad shoulders, tapering to a narrow waist and elegant limbs. Everything about Windermere was elegant. Even his ears, neatly framed by the mahogany hair, rested in symmetry, close to the head. She had forgotten his ears, which she'd noticed for the first time when she walked up the aisle to join him for their wedding ceremony. Her foolish heart echoed the hope of that moment, the incredulous joy that this magnificent man was to be hers; her mind reprimanded that organ for forgetting the lesson that her bridegroom's character didn't match his looks.

As he crossed the spacious room she could see that the year in the Levant had subtly tanned his skin and introduced fair streaks into his hair, adding a hint of disorder that made him even more attractive. She calmed her breathing and concentrated on his face, waiting to discover what would emerge from his mouth, the most perfect part of a face that must surely exemplify masculine beauty. The lips formed a classical bow and turned up a little at the corners. In a less grave man the feature would seem a perpetual smile.

"My lady." Not a hint of emotion infused the words. The fine features were impassive, the eyes a glass wall that concealed all feelings. Some things hadn't changed.

At least he'd spoken in English. So far.

"My lord." She rose and managed to walk a few steps forward without her knees giving way. He took her offered hand and grazed it with his lips, sending a small spark into her knuckles that coursed through her wrist and arm in a rush of heat. She withdrew a fraction of a second before he let her go, despising that his touch still affected her, even though she knew how ultimately unsatisfying it would be.

"I trust I find you well." He stepped back. "You certainly look well." Was that a glint of admiration? If so, it was fast dismissed. "I am surprised to see you in London."

"I find the country does not suit me during the winter months."

He raised his brows. "From your letters I understood you to be satisfied at Beaulieu."

Her fluttering heart grew cold and hard. The less said about his response to her letters the better.

"I enjoy town," she said. "The theaters, the company, and of course the shops. Perhaps you don't recall, my lord, but among your final requests, when you were unexpectedly called abroad, was that I should refurbish Beaulieu. I couldn't be expected to find everything in Oxford, or by correspondence. I needed to see things with my own eyes." Deliberately she looked across the room at the marble-topped French buffet, a monstrous miracle of inlaid woods and gold ornamentation. It was gaudy, expensive, and entirely unsuited to the restrained English surroundings of the room. Guilt about its purchase fought a wicked glee at the immediate reaction of the owner of the house. He blanched, visibly.

"An interesting addition to the room."

"Won't you sit down, my lord?"

She resumed her own chair and Windermere almost tottered backward, collapsing onto the settee with a discernible wince. Quite a handsome piece, upholstered in cerise silk brocade, but horribly uncomfortable. The carved gilt frame dug into the sitter's thighs.

"I assure you, my lord, that I have not neglected your instructions. The redecoration of Beaulieu Manor has been completed."

"I am glad to hear it, ma'am." She wanted to laugh at his appalled expression.

"Shall I ring for refreshment?"

"Thank you, no."

They sat and stared at each other in silence. "How was your journey?" she asked finally, taking a certain pleasure in the fact that she displayed better manners than her smooth diplomat husband. It wasn't what she wanted to ask.

Why did you leave me?

Why did you come home to your mistress?

And, above all, *Why didn't you care that I lost my child? Your child?*

Perhaps he had questions too, though she doubted it. In his eyes she was a convenient source of money and an inconvenient millstone about his neck. He'd be happier if she'd produced the heir and lost her life doing it.

For an excruciating half hour Cynthia listened to

a stilted account of Windermere's passage through the Mediterranean to Gibraltar, whence he'd made the remainder of the journey on a naval ship.

"How fortunate you avoided the French navy," she said.

He nodded. "The weather was good for this time of year. The Bay of Biscay can be very rough."

Though she didn't wish him at the bottom of the sea, she wouldn't have minded if a strong gale had sent him on a detour. To America, perhaps.

It was a relief when Ellis came to announce a visitor, but alarming when he showed in the Duke of Denford. What was Julian up to? No good, that was for sure. And how would Windermere react?

She had never seen Julian disconcerted, and she didn't now. "My dear Cynthia," he said, with his usual aplomb, bowing over her hand with matchless assurance, his eyes meeting hers in a flash of blue mischief. "And Damian!" He pivoted on his cane. "What a delightful surprise! Your servant told me you had returned from the Levant."

"Julian! An unexpected pleasure." Windermere looked undismayed, happy even, to see the man he hadn't spoken to in years. For a moment she thought they were going to share a manly embrace and thump each other on the back. "Or should I call you my lord duke? I understand congratulations are in order."

"I never thought to outrank you," Julian said jovially. "Or to live next door. We used to joke about it."

"I remember it well. Finally we'll be able to make use of the gate in the wall." Cynthia's eyes flew to her husband's face, unable to account for his friendliness. "Perhaps you already have," he added. Did guilt make her imagine a certain hardness in his eyes?

"Having the charming Lady Windermere as my neighbor is the most desirable feature of a very uncomfortable residence. It turns out your family knows better than the Fortescues how to furnish a house. And you, my old friend, have been clever enough to acquire a wife to carry on the tradition."

Cynthia tried to shoot him a surreptitious glare. Windermere was bound to eventually discover the source of the hideous furnishings and paintings she'd brought into the house, but she'd rather postpone the revelation. She wasn't at all sure that her husband would sympathize with the reason. It occurred to her that Windermere's return threatened to put a spoke in the wheel of the cozy arrangement she had with a certain shopkeeper.

"I suppose as neighbors you and Cynthia were bound to meet." Windermere—*Damian*—had never before called her by her Christian name. Not even in bed. Especially not in bed, where conversation had never interfered with the performance of marital duty.

"We were friends long before I gained possession of the barracks. Caro introduced us."

"Caro!" Her husband's posture relaxed infinitesimally. "How did you meet her, my lady?"

"She called on me when I was ill last February."

"She was always the kindest of girls," he replied, showing no reaction to the reference to her indisposition. "Is she still at Conduit Street?"

"She lives in Hampshire, with her new husband, the Duke of Castleton."

"Caro Townsend a duchess!" He laughed. "Hard to imagine. It seems all my old friends have come up in the world."

"Indeed," Julian said. "Marcus is now a viscount with a handsome estate in Wiltshire."

"Not so handsome," Cynthia said with feeling, having just returned from Lord Lithgow's spider-ridden, flood-beset property.

"Clearly I have much news to catch up with since I've been away," Windermere said, for all the world as though he were on the best of terms with the friends of his youth. "Can I persuade you to join us for dinner one evening, Julian? I am engaged with Grenville tonight, but tomorrow perhaps. Unless you have another engagement, my lady."

"If I did, my lord, I would cancel it. It would ill become me to amuse myself elsewhere when my husband has been restored to me after so long."

"Excellent. Shall we say seven o'clock then? Unless you prefer to keep country hours."

"I am no longer the country mouse I was when you left me at Beaulieu, my lord. I would not dream of sitting down to dine a minute earlier."

"I can see that you are not. You have become quite worldly, my lady. Admirably so."

If someone had told Cynthia back at the Birmingham Academy that one day she'd be sitting between an earl and a duke, she'd have called him a fantasist. Keeping up with the byplay between the two men tested her newly developed sophistication. One man had never wanted her, the other said he did. Too bad that the former was the husband to whom she owed loyalty, however undeserved.

She looked at Julian, who had been following the exchange with the wry twist of the mouth that both fascinated and exasperated her, then turned back to her husband. Windermere had a singularly beautiful smile, as she remembered to her cost. In her experience he deployed it seldom and almost never with genuine intent. What he directed at her now sent her heart thudding against her ribs, but it did not reach his eyes. She knew it was a meaningless curve of the lips.

She inclined her head with a graciousness that was wholly feigned. "Why thank you, my lord. Your praise overwhelms me. I live only to please you."

"What do you say, Julian?"

"How could I possibly resist such an invitation." He swept a bow of matchless urbane mockery. "*A demain*, Cynthia," he said, and stalked out like the sleek black cat he resembled.

She didn't miss the flash of emotion that crossed Windermere's face when Julian used her given name, nor the thoughtful look that pursued him out of the room.

"You are very cordial with Denford," she said. "I had heard you disliked him."

"And knowing that, you pursued his acquaintance? Such a loyal wife."

Her behavior did prick at her conscience, though logically Windermere's had been worse. "I pay little attention to gossip. I am glad I did not allow rumor to keep me from a friendship that obviously you don't object to. I am delighted to see you and Julian on such good terms." Her sunny smile felt like a death grimace. "I have lived quietly in your absence without entrée to the *ton*. Caro, Denford, and their friends welcomed me. Now that you are home, I look forward to expanding my circle with your other acquaintances."

"I suppose you are ambitious to be received in more fashionable circles," he said with a sneer. She'd never heard Windermere speak so rudely, and it caused her fierce satisfaction that she'd rippled his glassy calm. She didn't know why he was upset, but that was nothing new. Since the moment he'd slipped the ring on her finger, pleasing her husband had proved impossible.

"Only for your sake," she said with a careless wave, intended to convince him—and herself—that his ill opinion meant nothing to her. "I haven't forgotten you telling me a wife is important to a diplomat's career."

He walked over to her chair and extended one elegant finger to tilt her face upward. Her heart skipped a beat when, for an instant, she thought he was going to kiss her, as a man might be expected to do after a year apart from his wife. But those perfect lips came within a foot of hers and no closer. She made herself meet him eye to eye, wishing she could read his thoughts. They were engaged in an unspoken struggle she didn't entirely understand.

"What?" she whispered finally.

"You have changed," he said.

"Just as you requested. I tried to become the wife you wanted."

"Really? You did this for me?" He made no effort to conceal his skepticism. What had *she* done to make him distrust her?

She couldn't tell the truth, that she'd started out to learn how to be the perfect wife so that her husband would love her when he returned. She was different now. She no longer knew what she wanted of him, except that he should be sorry for the past and—perhaps—do better in the future.

Last night she'd gone to Julian's house intending to assuage her hurt and pay Windermere in kind for his infidelity. But at the last minute she'd found she couldn't commit adultery. Julian had taken her rejection in his usual stride, helped her up from the brocade divan in his library, straightened the bodice that he'd been attempting to untie, and escorted her through his garden back to her own. "Better luck, next time," he'd whispered, and kissed her good night on the lips with surprising sweetness. She'd almost changed her mind because in that moment he offered comfort in addition to sensual satisfaction. She badly needed comfort.

Tears that she *would not* shed pricked her eyes as she stared at her husband's beautiful, inscrutable face. She turned aside and blinked hard. Muttering something about speaking to the cook, she pushed past him and stumbled from the room. The pathetic truth was that she wanted Damian to kiss her sweetly and held out very little hope that he ever would.

And why should she even want it from a man without a heart?

The previous winter

My Lord,

I write from my bed, having been confined there at the orders of Dr. Croft. It grieves me to inform you that I am no longer with child. The doctor thought I was doing well, and approaching the fourth month when one can be more sanguine of a happy conclusion. Three days ago the pains began. I will spare you the details of the event. Unpleasant as it was, the body is healed far sooner than the spirits. I find myself oppressed with grief that I will never know our child. I am sorry, my lord, that there will be no heir awaiting your return. It is perhaps as well that I did not inform my uncle of my condition for his disappointment would be as great as yours. Of course, the child could have been a daughter.

We do not know each other well, my lord, so perhaps I should spare you my grief. Yet we joined in creating the possibility of a child, and for all I know you may feel the loss as strongly as I do.

Cynthia sealed the letter quickly, before she could regret writing to Windermere with such frankness. She had never done so before, her dutiful—and ever less frequent letters—being concerned strictly with practical matters. But her overwhelming emotions in the present case had to be shared and there was no one else. Was her husband not the most proper recipient of her confidence? She could not speak of it to the servants, or to the young woman who came twice a week to the house to speak French. And certainly not to the shopkeepers of London.

The prospect of motherhood had given meaning to a life that was almost entirely devoid of social interactions. Apart from the physical pain of the miscarriage, the infant's loss engulfed her spirits.

She was moping in the drawing room two weeks later when a caller was announced.

She accepted the visiting card that her butler proffered on a tray. The name meant nothing. "Do you know this Mrs. Robert Townsend, Ellis?"

"There was a Mr. Townsend who attended Oxford with His Lordship."

That was good enough for Cynthia. One real acquaintance in London was one more than she currently possessed. For the first time in weeks she felt a glimmer of interest in life and a greater curiosity when a short, slender young woman bounced through the door, bringing an air of energy that brightened the dull February day.

"Lady Windermere?" she said, darting forward. Cynthia had risen to curtsey but her visitor forestalled the formality by seizing both her hands and giving them a comforting squeeze. "I am so very sorry to hear of your illness. I would have come earlier but my housekeeper was in the country visiting her sister, and you know how it is. One hears nothing when the servants are away."

"Indeed," Cynthia said faintly.

"It's a while since I saw Damian, but when I heard that his wife was alone and suffering, I had to come. It is too bad of him to have left you alone."

It took a moment or two for Cynthia to realize that by Damian, the visitor meant her husband. She knew his Christian name, of course. She'd seen it in the settlement documents she'd signed prior to the marriage. It would never have occurred to her to address him by it, and she couldn't imagine anyone else doing so either. What was the relationship between Windermere and this young woman? This very pretty young woman.

Her bewilderment must have shown. "What a goose I am. We haven't even been introduced. I am Caroline Townsend but you must call me Caro. My late husband, Robert, was one of Damian's closest friends."

That seemed harmless enough. "Thank you for calling," Cynthia said, responding to Mrs. Townsend's infectious smile. "Won't you sit down?"

Mrs. Townsend, whose manners continued to display a spontaneity such as Cynthia had never encountered among the middle-class denizens of Birmingham, accepted the invitation after first removing her bonnet and pelisse, revealing a simple white muslin gown of a vaguely classical design and a cluster of bright red curls, cut short and clinging to her head. She perched on the edge of her seat and regarded her hostess like an eager little bird.

"I'm afraid I don't remember Lord Windermere mentioning the name of Townsend," Cynthia said. "But he was called abroad so soon after our marriage that the matter may not have arisen."

"I'm not at all surprised. Robert and Damian

had a falling out years ago. But I used to know Damian quite well, and as far as I know he never had anything against *me*. I don't *think* he would object to our becoming acquainted."

"I don't see why he should," Cynthia said. "And since he is not here to give his permission or otherwise I don't feel the need to guess at his sentiments. I will follow my own inclination and welcome you. I have been in London for several weeks and I don't know a soul."

"Bravo! I am delighted to see that Damian wed a lady of spirit."

Was that what she was? She'd never felt like it before and rather liked the idea. "It is possible that he forbade the acquaintance when speaking French and I didn't understand him."

"Why on earth?"

"He wished me to become fluent, as is becoming to a diplomat's wife."

"There are certain places," Mrs. Townsend said with a straight face, "where it is appropriate to converse in French. In France for one—and in the bedchamber. The French are extremely good at a certain kind of communication. Or so I have always been told."

Cynthia supposed she should be shocked. Mrs. Townsend seemed not to have developed the social restraints that prevented most people from mentioning personal or intimate matters. Or anything else terribly interesting either. While not quite ready to confide that the bedchamber was the one place where Lord Windermere did not address her in French—or English either—she suspected her fascinating guest would be a source of information she had no other way of obtaining.

"Did you say that your own husband had died, Mrs. Townsend? If so, I offer my condolences."

"Caro. Damian always called me Caro and you must too."

"I am Cynthia," she replied to Caro's unspoken question.

"A year ago, and I miss him." For a moment the lively little face settled into grief, fast replaced by a pixyish grin. "Hey ho, life goes on, and Robert wouldn't have wished me to bury myself. Goodness, Cynthia, Damian isn't even dead and it sounds as though you've been living more like a widow than I. You must come to dinner at Conduit Street and meet my friends. Some of them knew Damian too. Julian, of course."

"I don't know who Julian is either. I wish you will tell me about my husband when he was younger, Mrs. Townsend—Caro."

"Robert met Julian, Damian, and Marcus at Oxford but they were expelled quite quickly."

"Expelled!" Cynthia couldn't begin to fathom what her excessively correct spouse could have done to merit such punishment. "I would have guessed Windermere to have been a model scholar."

"I daresay he was," Caro said. "They were all

brilliantly clever young men and no doubt would have done very well if they'd cared to take the trouble, and hadn't been caught breaking into the naughty art collection housed in the Bodleian Library. So they all went to France instead."

"That explains Windermere's fluency."

"Damian was the best at languages, I believe. I met them after they came back because of the Revolution. Damian helped Robert and me to elope, you know."

"No I didn't know. I find it hard to believe."

"Damian wasn't always so stuffy." Caro frowned. "Though he was quiet, more reserved than the others. I think he was shy, rather a gentle soul."

Cynthia stared. "I don't think I've met a man more socially adroit than Windermere." *Or less like a gentle soul*, she tactfully refrained from adding.

"Really? I expect he had to be when he decided to make his way in diplomatic service. But I wouldn't know. I haven't seen him since he abandoned us. We missed him for a long time."

He'd abandoned Cynthia too. "From your account of him, Caro, Windermere has changed a good deal. I suppose all young men do as they grow up."

"Robert didn't. And Julian is just the same as he ever was. I notice you don't call him Damian. Even his name is different. When I knew him, Windermere was his father. My mother wanted me to marry him, you know."

"My husband's father?"

A peal of laughter set Caro's curls a flutter. "Not even my mother was insane enough to expect me to wed an old man, even an earl. No, I take that back. If the late Lord Windermere had shown any interest in me, my mother would have been delighted. Luckily I never met him. Damian, or Kendal as he was then, was the most eligible of the quartet. I never wanted anyone but Robert, but I counted Damian a good friend. He was always kind to everyone."

"Why did their friendship end?"

"Neither Robert not Julian would ever tell me exactly what took place the night of Damian's twenty-first birthday. That was the beginning. Other things happened and Damian stopped speaking to us. Or perhaps it was the other way around. I know they were both angry and ashamed of themselves, especially Julian. Robert didn't care so much, but he had me. And I am sorry to tell you, Cynthia, that he was quite addicted to cards and dice and lost a great deal of money before he died. I hope you are rich for it is quite uncomfortable to be living under reduced circumstances."

"Windermere married me for money," Cynthia said. "My uncle's money, not mine."

"In that case," Caro said, "I think you should spend some of it on clothing." She clapped a hand over her mouth. "I shouldn't have said that. I haven't an iota of tact."

"I'm not offended. My aunt, who has no taste, chose my gowns. I have been meaning to buy some new ones but I haven't felt up to it." Having been cheered and diverted by her visitor, she felt a wave of despondency crush her spirits again.

"Come to dinner tomorrow night," Caro said. "Several of my set will be there. Oliver, of course. He will almost certainly fall in love with you but you needn't be alarmed. And Julian. He used to be Damian's best friend."

"Julian who?"

"Fortescue, except he just became a duke so now he's Denford. Isn't that absurd?"

Cynthia contemplated the ghastly contents of her wardrobe and the fact that she was to dine at the same table as a duke. "I don't have anything to wear."

"Any old rag will do for dinner at Conduit Street. It's a miracle some of the painters ever remember to put on their breeches. If you buy new dresses you shouldn't do it on my account, but to please yourself." Caro gave a throaty chuckle. "An enjoyable party and a new gown may not be worthy replacements for an absent husband, but we must find happiness where we may."

So little was Cynthia accustomed to pleasing herself that the idea frightened her. Then the notion took hold of her mind with a wicked thrill of anticipation. To perdition with her absent husband, she thought, with a defiance she couldn't have conceived of three months earlier. He had left her alone while he traveled halfway around the world, and he was going to have to bear the consequences. If she did something he did not like, then he should have been here to tell her his wishes. She wasn't a mind reader.

"I like the new higher waists," she said, now subjecting the little redhead's ensemble to critical scrutiny. "Your white muslin's simplicity is deceptive. I daresay it was quite costly."

"My dear Cynthia," Caro said. "My dressmaker is going to love you."

Cynthia rose from her sofa with a new determination. "Can we go now?" she asked.

When Windermere returned, he might not find an heir to his earldom, but his wife would be a lady of fashion. With Caro's help she would replace the ill-fitting, overtrimmed gowns her aunt had chosen for her and get rid of the frizzy curls. She would study how to be a worldly London denizen who referred to bedroom matters without blushing. And when she had transformed herself, perhaps this kind, formerly shy man would appreciate her. Perhaps they would have another chance for happiness, even for love.

"Fetch your bonnet," Caro said. "Damian won't

recognize you in a few months. What does he have to say about your poor health?"

"Not a word," Cynthia replied. "He hardly ever writes."

Postal deliveries (by way of the Foreign Office) to and from Persia being intermittent, she heard nothing more from her husband for over two months. When the letter came it was in response to several of her own, though she found little *responsive* in them. Mostly he wrote questions and commands to be conveyed to the stewards of his estates. By way of variation, he charged her with several errands, such as ordering certain garments from his tailor, the Persian climate having turned out to be more variable than he had expected. He asked her if Windermere House had been let for the season, and made some suggestions about the gardens at Beaulieu that she found quite irritating. He obviously knew nothing at all about gardening.

But it was the conclusion to the letter that shriveled her soul. "I am sorry to hear of your indisposition. You must be more careful of your health. Yours etc. Windermere."

Three times she read it, in disbelief. She had poured out her soul and all she got in return were two sentences and a *Yours etc.*

Clutching the neatly written pages until they crumpled in her fist, she sat down at her escritoire.

First she did her duty, writing to the steward and the tailor. Then, before she could change her mind, she dashed off a note to the Duke of Denford.

After meeting her at Caro's dinner party, Denford had paid her marked attention. Flattered and alarmed by his admiration, she'd been shocked to the toes of her respectable slippers by his offering his escort to a masked ball. Attending such an event in the company of a man not her husband wasn't the kind of thing one did in Birmingham.

She wasn't in Birmingham anymore. And since her husband clearly didn't care a rap what she did as long as he received his new clothes, she would please herself.

Chapter 5

Returning home from dinner with the foreign secretary, Damian learned that Her Ladyship had already retired. He followed suit, finding that his valet had set up his gear in the earl's bedchamber. Damian wasn't much acquainted with the room. It had been his father's and was without much character, except for a certain austerity of decoration that fitted the personality of its late occupant: plain walls, dark drapery, and nothing personal at all. His father had never been much of a reader so there were no books. As for pictures, Damian would have been surprised if there was a single one. The late Lord Windermere had use only for family portraits, kept at the ancient family home at Amblethorpe in the Lake District. No, Damian was wrong. A small landscape framed in gold hung over the fireplace. Damian carried a candle over to get a closer look: a gloomy oil rendition of Amblethorpe Hall that matched the dour grayness of the original. As always, he thought of his ancestral estate without affection and Beaulieu without any more pleasure. He supposed Windermere House was as much his home as any other, until duty sent him abroad again. The trouble was, he was no longer unencumbered.

A door connected to the chamber that housed the countess. He'd often visited his mother in that room, once his father had left the house. She liked the company of her children in the morning, after she had risen. How eagerly he and Amelia had awaited the summons that gave them a welcome respite from their studies and plunged them into the enchanted, scented world of Anthea, Lady Windermere. For a moment he was ten years old again, showering his twin with hair powder under their mother's amused gaze. He ached to step through that door and discover that the two females who'd dominated his childhood were still alive and still laughing.

Instead he would find his unwanted wife.

He had to admit that under other circumstances she would no longer be "unwanted." Her looks had improved, greatly, since their marriage. In her personal appearance she showed signs of the good taste so lamentably lacking in her additions to the decoration of the house. He hated to think what she might have done with his mother's chamber.

He'd looked into her eyes that afternoon and had the oddest desire to kiss her lying mouth. If not for Julian, damn him, he'd be quite eager to join her in bed, but his intention of resuming marital congress with his wife had been complicated by the discovery of her infidelity. His immediate reaction was to cast her off, but things weren't as simple as that. Only by siring an heir were the greatest financial advantages of his marriage to be reaped; he needed to maintain relations with Denford, at least for now; and a divorce was unthinkable if he was to have any future success in his career. It was highly unlikely that such a scandal would allow him to achieve the post of foreign secretary.

Clearly he was never going to enjoy the kind of love that his oddly matched parents had enjoyed, but when he wed Chorley's niece to gain back Beaulieu he'd given up that chance. He ought, at least in theory, to be able to live with a faithless bride, as long as discretion could be maintained. Such a marriage was hardly unheard of in the higher levels of society. In one area, however, he'd discovered a sticking point: His children must be his own.

Until he was certain that Cynthia was not with child by her lover, he would not share her bed. In the meantime, he'd pretend to resume his friendship with Julian and get him to sell the pictures to the Prince of Alt-Brandenburg. After that he would decide what to do. Whatever it was, it wouldn't be pleasant for the dastardly duke, and Lady Windermere would need to atone before she was (perhaps) magnanimously forgiven on a promise of future good behavior.

Pacing around the room he was drawn to that door. Placing his ear against it he heard nothing. His wife must have dismissed her maid some time ago, as he had his valet. Then he heard a latch, and soft footsteps in the passage outside their rooms. He sped over to his own exit and discovered her holding a candlestick and headed for the stairs.

"My lady." He bowed ironically.

"My lord." Her free hand clutched at her pale blue satin wrapper, liberally trimmed with lace. With golden hair streaming over her shoulders, she looked more like an angel than an adulteress.

"Is there anything I can do for you?"

"I was going down to fetch my book."

"Why not ring for a servant?"

"They have retired and it's no trouble for me to go. I am not ready to sleep."

She blushed, as well she might if she intended to slip out into the garden and meet her conveniently located lover. Damian made one immediate decision. If he was to be cuckolded again, it would not be by Denford. His wife had enjoyed Julian's attentions for the last time and he would make sure of it, even if he had to personally stand guard.

"Go back to bed, my dear," he said. "If you will tell me the title, I will find your book."

"Thank you," she said. What else could she say?

"It's on the table next to the chaise in the small parlor. It's only a novel."

"I shall bring it to you *tout de suite*."

He had called her "my dear" and he was coming to her room. Expecting him to be eager to start siring an heir, she'd been relieved when he'd failed to appear at the connecting door earlier. Perhaps he was too tired after his night with Lady Belinda. For all she knew, he'd been with his mistress that evening. Although she had little practical knowledge of the sensual habits of men, she'd picked up a good deal of gossip from Caro's circle and knew that some men weren't capable of performing more than once a night. Certainly Windermere had never repeated the act with her: into the room, into the bed, into her. In and out a few times, then out, out, out.

She couldn't help wondering if she was so unappealing that his lack of interest was somehow her fault. She had gathered that both men and women had different levels of skill and attractiveness in these matters. Perhaps she should have taken the opportunity to find out with Julian, who had quite the reputation. If she couldn't take and give pleasure with *him*, it probably was her fault.

On second thought, it might be better not to know. In the absence of any certainty, she could keep up her well-deserved anger against Windermere for his indifference and his betrayal.

She sat at her dressing table and fiddled with her brushes. The events of the past twenty-four hours had left her emotionally wrung out and too agitated to sleep. She hoped reading would calm her and let her sink into blessed forgetfulness for a few hours, before she had to wake up and deal with her erring husband. She now feared that she wouldn't gain that respite.

He didn't bother to knock, merely slipped in and closed the door behind him. He stood and looked at her, without saying a word. Remaining on the padded stool of her dressing table, she stared back defiantly. He'd always seemed the epitome of the English gentleman with his blue-gray eyes and neat brown hair. But a full-length banyan made from richly embroidered silk lent an exoticism to the regularity of his features and figure. She felt a stirring deep inside her that signaled a greater danger to the peace of mind he'd already rocked.

"Miss Burney's *Cecilia, or Memoirs of an Heiress*," he said. "Are you enjoying it?"

"Not as much as *Evelina*. Have you read it?"

"I liked *Evelina* better too. Mortimer Delvile seemed excessively proud, making Cecilia relinquish her fortune rather than marry her and take her name. You cannot accuse me of such behavior."

The marriage settlement included a provision that their children would take on her name. The family name of the Earls of Windermere would henceforth be Chorley-Lewis. Having lost his only son and the chance of establishing a dynasty, her uncle wished to immortalize his name through her. To Cynthia it had made her uncle seem rather pathetic, not a word she would normally apply to the great bully.

"I acquit you of *pride*, my lord," she said. "Mortimer Delvile is a tiresome creature and Cecilia deserves better. Our cases are not comparable, however. Delvile wishes to marry Cecilia for love, not for her great fortune."

Whatever reaction she expected from him wasn't forthcoming. She picked up a powder puff for something to do in the ensuing silence and waited for him to leave. When she dabbed at her neck, a sound came out of his throat, though what it signified she couldn't guess. "Thank you for fetching the book, my lord. You may leave it on the bed." Mentioning the word *bed* made her blush and she powdered furiously to cover it up.

Peering past her reflection in the mirror, she saw him lay the volume on the mattress, but he did not leave. Her eyes widened as he removed a pair of leather slippers with turned-up toes, and placed them neatly next to the bedside table. Next to go, drawing a shocked gasp, was the robe, sliding off and revealing his back and buttocks. Never having seen such a sight in the flesh, she was fascinated and unwillingly impressed. He turned, and before she could see any more, she closed her eyes. Never once during their marriage had he revealed his body to her in the light. Neither would she expect it. The very notion of sleeping—or doing anything else—naked was contrary to the precepts of her upbringing. By the time she dared look he had climbed onto the mattress and settled himself under the covers, half reclining against the pillows, displaying surprisingly broad shoulders and a muscular chest sprinkled with light brown hair. A surge of indignation drove out appreciative curiosity.

What right did the man have to invade her room without so much as a by-your-leave and occupy her bed? He had the right of a husband, of course, to her body. But something about the cool way he'd taken possession of her private apartment, like a storming army, roused her fury. His action wasn't motivated by desire—he wasn't even looking at her. It was pure arrogance.

"What are you doing?" She marched over, almost tripping on her billowing robe, and glared down at him with her arms folded.

"Lying in my wife's bed," he said, quirking his brows as though the question were a foolish one.

"I am not accustomed to sharing this bed."

"I would hope not, since your husband has been absent."

"It's not big enough for two." It was in fact the widest bed she'd ever occupied, even bigger than that at Beaulieu.

"I think we can manage without being crushed."

He generously shifted about an inch nearer to the edge and smiled blandly. He looked ridiculously handsome without his shirt, but she was not in the mood to admire.

She cleared her throat. "My lord."

"Yes?"

"We have lived apart for more than a year."

"True."

"And before that we weren't married for long."

"Also true."

"We don't know each other very well."

"That dearth can be remedied by spending more time together." He settled deeper into the bed-clothes. "Starting now."

She stilled her nervous fingers that were plucking at the lace edging on her favorite wrapper. "What I mean to say is that . . . about marital relations . . . I don't wish." She almost swallowed her tongue in her feeble efforts to articulate this awkward request. "I would ask that until we know each other better that we should . . . not."

"Not?" She wasn't sure if he understood her confused mumbling. Raising his arms behind his neck, which flexed the muscles of his shoulders and chest, he regarded her in a silence that increased her disquiet. Her tongue swept convulsively over her lips and her mouth felt dry. He didn't seem eager to fall on her and demand his rights, but neither did he make any move to depart.

To encourage him to go away and stop disturbing her peace, she offered him the robe that he'd draped neatly over a chair. "No, thank you. I prefer to sleep naked." His lips stretched into that humorless smile she'd got to know so well at Beaulieu.

"And I would prefer you to sleep elsewhere," she said, betraying her frayed nerves.

"I regret, my lady, that I cannot accommodate you. The mattress in my bedchamber is not to my taste. The feathers are too tightly packed and full of lumps."

This seemed highly unlikely in her well-run household, though she hadn't inspected the thing herself. She wavered, torn between arguing and sleeping in the other bed herself, lumpy or not.

"Come," he said, patting the bed beside him. "No need for either of us to suffer. There's plenty of room for both and I promise not to lay a finger on you. There is nothing unusual about a husband and wife sharing a bed, is there?"

"Nothing at all, in the normal course of things," she said cautiously. "We, however, have not been in the habit of excessive intimacy in our living arrangements."

"That will change now that I am home."

Against her better judgment she decided to remain. She didn't see why she should be driven from her own comfortable chamber into the earl's gloomy lair. She'd embellished the already elegant and pleasing room with personal touches: her brushes and dressing set; a shelf of favorite novels;

a delicate inlaid round table on which were arranged the fashion journals and other periodicals she subscribed to; a silver bowl containing potpourri; and the miniature portraits of her father and mother.

"It is my understanding that aristocratic couples occupy separate chambers. Not that I have special knowledge, being from a lower station."

"My mother and father always shared a bed."

"You surprise me." Not least by imparting a private family detail. She couldn't remember another instance of him volunteering such personal information.

She let her wrapper slide to the floor and climbed gingerly into bed, not on the side she usually favored, but she wasn't up to demanding a rearrangement tonight. Unlike him she dressed decently for bed in fine but sturdy linen, buttoned to the neck. "Aren't you cold without a nightgown?"

His shrug sent his muscles rippling. "The room is well heated for winter."

"If you are to sleep in my bed I request that you dress properly."

"Your preference is noted—for the future."

Did that mean he intended to sleep with her all the time? Utterly confounded, she adjusted the position of the candelabrum on the bedside table and opened her book. "I am going to read Miss Burney. I'm sorry if the light troubles you."

She might as well have saved her breath. "I'm

used to sleeping through all manner of disturbances in foreign cities." Then the wretched man had the gall to turn on his side, punch his pillow, pull more than his share of blankets over his broad shoulders, and close his eyes.

Rigid with tension, she stared at the pages, but the English language had ceased to have any meaning for her. She kept stealing sideways glances at him, half expecting him to pounce. Why else was he there, if not to get himself an heir? It made no sense. To her indignation he began to emit a light snore, more of a loud breathing really. She was supposed to sleep through this? Unlike him, she was not accustomed to the disturbances of foreign parts. Though if she were being honest she'd admit that some of the girls at school had been noisier sleepers.

Giving up on *Cecilia* and on trying to understand her husband as well, she blew out her candles and settled down to sleep herself, trying to ignore the way his unclothed flesh radiated heat.

Chapter 6

The servants knew that His Lordship had spent the entire night in her bed. It wouldn't bother Caro, Cynthia told herself firmly, and she had no reason to feel self-conscious about it. Her husband certainly hadn't. When her maid brought in her early morning chocolate, he'd descended from the bed in all his naked glory, shrugged into his robe, and asked the woman to send up his valet, all without a hint of embarrassment. Meanwhile Cynthia clutched the sheet up to her chin and avoided looking at him. She couldn't summon more than a muttered croak in reply to his cheerful "Good morning" and a reminder that they were expecting company for dinner.

The housekeeper was most indignant at the suggestion that any bed under her command should be in anything less than prime condition. Nevertheless, Cynthia ordered her to have His Lordship's mattress restuffed to eliminate the chance that her husband's excuse for his strange visit to her bedchamber was actually the true one. The woman returned a quarter of an hour later considerably chastened. Moth holes had been discovered in the curtains of His Lordship's bed. The room would need to be cleaned and the velvet replaced.

"Never mind," Cynthia said. She always found it hard to be angry with servants who worked so hard. "Perhaps last year's tenants damaged the hangings. Can they not be mended?"

"You're very good, my lady, but I know moth when I see it. If we are lucky we'll be able to re-place sections only, if we can match the cloth."

A lengthy discussion of the problem led to the decision that the proprietress of Bow's Silk Ware-house should be asked to assemble samples of velvet in different shades of red. The interview had barely concluded when the footman announced that Mr. Oliver Bream had come to call.

"Oliver!" Cynthia cried. "Thank goodness you are here. You must come to dinner tonight."

The cherub-faced artist shook his mop of curly hair and grinned. "Glad you asked, Cynthia. Saves me having to angle for an invitation. I came as soon as I heard you were back in town."

"Why else would you be here if not to find a meal?"

Oliver pretended to look offended. "To see you, of course." His eyes roamed around the parlor. "Did you breakfast already?"

Cynthia rolled her eyes. Months ago, when

they first met at Caro Townsend's house, Oliver had fallen madly in love with her, just as Caro had predicted. His feelings had lasted all of a week before moving on to another object, and then another. His passion for his latest paramour always came second to his devotion to free meals, and a distant third to his true obsession, which was his art. In the view of Cynthia and his friends, he had real talent as a painter. Since this opinion was not shared by the rest of the world, he lived rent-free in Caro's carriage house and cadged meals wherever he could.

Having sent the servant for tea and cakes, she patted the sofa beside her. "It's good to see you, Oliver. Tell me your news."

It was soothing to listen to him ramble on about the lamentable lack of skill in a couple of pupils who came to him for lessons in watercolors, the latest iniquity perpetrated by artists more successful than he, and the matchless beauty of Mrs. Langton, wife of a purveyor of canvas in High Holborn.

"Does she return your regard? Will she run away with you?" Cynthia asked, knowing that Oliver chose the most unattainable objects of his pursuit and would be disconcerted if not appalled should he actually catch one.

Oliver swallowed a mouthful of plum cake and shook his head. "Langton is a brute of a man. Very strong. She wouldn't dare leave him. Besides, his canvas is the best in town and I shouldn't like to upset him. He might refuse to extend me credit. I wish she had a different husband."

"You will be able to judge mine this evening."

"Windermere is in London?"

"He arrived at Windermere House yesterday. And he invited Julian to dinner."

"Really?" Oliver said with mild surprise. "I thought they disliked each other." As a longtime intimate of Caro and her set, he was well acquainted with the history. But Oliver was never overly concerned with matters that weren't of personal or artistic interest. It made him a safe confidant. Anything she said would likely be forgotten by tomorrow.

"Windermere and Denford haven't spoken in years."

"Oh right. I remember now." He frowned. "What was the row about?"

"Caro said she could never get the truth out of Robert, and Julian shuts up like an oyster whenever I ask him. I've always guessed his attentions to me have been largely an effort to annoy my husband."

"I thought you liked Julian?"

"Of course I do, but that doesn't mean I entirely trust him."

"That's very cynical, Cynthia. Not like you."

"Am I not cynical? Perhaps you are right. But neither am I naïve. I used to be, but not any longer.

Why would a woman of my very modest attractions have inspired instant admiration in a man as worldly and jaded as Denford? Yet the very first time we met, he treated me as though I were a fascinating beauty."

She noticed with amusement that Oliver didn't contradict her assessment of her charms. He'd long ago forgotten his brief infatuation. Instead he spared her a glance away from the alluring array of pastries. "You're very pretty, Cynthia."

"Better than I was, now that I have acquired some town polish. When Julian first met me I was a provincial dowd. I knew he was using me and I used him back. He's a very amusing escort and I was in need of company. Though I believe we have become genuinely fond of each other."

He had awoken desires that she had thought put to rest when Windermere disappointed her. But now she was almost certain that those dangerous urges had been aroused mainly by a wish to irritate—or attract—her neglectful husband. "As friends," she added firmly.

"I like Julian too," Oliver said. "Even if he doesn't understand painting."

"Indeed," Cynthia said. "He has abysmal taste. The Holbein portrait he bought a couple of months ago is a horrid thing."

Oliver grinned sheepishly at her teasing. "I'll admit he has an eye for the older painters, but he has no notion of where the future of the art lies."

Cynthia had listened to Oliver's views of the noble future of painting—with specific reference to his own oeuvre—a dozen times and was disinclined to indulge his obsession now. "I am glad you will be here this evening because I don't fancy sitting between those two at dinner without help."

"Do you think they will fight?"

She laughed at Oliver's expression of terror and fascination. "If it comes to that I shan't expect you to intervene, or get in the way of any flying fists. We'll leave them to it."

"What's for dinner?"

"My cook is planning something special for the return of the master of the house."

"Good! In that case I shall brave it"—as though there were any chance of Oliver missing a meal—"no matter the danger. And no matter what either of them does."

"I have a very good idea what Julian is up to, but I haven't a clue what Windermere has in mind."

Sitting down to dinner between his wife and her lover was a situation awkward enough to daunt even an experienced diplomat. First thing that morning, Damian had summoned reinforcements in the form of his cousin and his cousin's wife. It turned out Lady Windermere had done the same. As the party assembled he wondered how this mismatched group was going to converse. He couldn't see George Lewis, the stolid Tory MP for Kendal, having much to say to Oliver Bream, who was some kind of artist, evidenced by a wild shock of hair and traces of paint on his hands. Denford would doubtless regard the ensuing debacle with sardonic enjoyment. How the hostess anticipated the disparate gathering he had no idea. He'd avoided Cynthia all day, alarmed by his desire on waking to remain under the covers and make love to her. Letting nature take its course when husband and wife found themselves in bed together was not currently an urge he could entertain.

With all the leaves removed from the dining room table, the party of six was seated so that conversation could be heard by all. Damian was dutifully listening to Louisa Lewis's account of her three sons, when Bream, seated on his other side, interrupted the devoted mother's peaceful flow.

"That is an exceptionally ugly picture," he said loudly.

The artist was staring at the space over the mantelpiece where, Damian noticed for the first time, a chinoiserie mirror had been replaced by a huge portrait of a lady in the fashion of King Charles II's reign.

Cousin Louisa looked startled and peered nervously over her shoulder. "She is quite plump," she said, "and her eyes stick out, but her blue velvet gown is handsome."

Bream waved aside the observation. "My point

is that it is very badly painted. Where did you find such a beastly thing, Cynthia?" He addressed his hostess across a horrified George Lewis, who wasn't used to such loose manners.

Damian looked down the table at his wife and raised his brows. He'd like to know the answer himself.

She seemed to be avoiding his eye. "I bought this one because the gown matches the curtains in here. Sir Peter Lely painted it, did he not, Denford?"

"Lely, or one of his assistants. An inferior work by an inferior artist. Mrs. Lewis is quite correct about the eyes. All Lely's subjects look like pugs."

Poor Cousin Louisa, who'd spent the whole of dinner stealing appalled glances at Denford, appeared about to faint at being addressed directly by the disreputable duke. Unwillingly, Damian felt the urge to laugh. George's wife was a good woman but very dull. They were a well-suited pair.

"Matching a picture to the drapery is an unusual notion," she murmured. "Very soothing to the digestion."

Oliver Bream bristled with indignation. "Art is supposed to elevate the mind, not calm the stomach."

Since the topic of art was very much on Damian's agenda for the evening, he asked Bream about his own work and the table talk became general. He described what he'd seen in Tehran, and spoke of the antique paintings of Persia. He could almost imagine himself back at Oxford, or in Paris, having the same kind of heated discussions he'd once enjoyed with Julian, Robert, and Marcus.

Except that everything had changed. George and Louisa Lewis he could ignore; his wife's presence, while not intrusive, could not be forgotten. He was aware of every move and gesture, whether directing the servants or deftly seeing to the comfort of her guests. His ears strained to hear her every word.

"I had no idea you knew so much about art, my lord," she said at one point. Of course she didn't. When he had known her he'd been too bilious with rage and disappointment to reveal anything of himself, or afford her more than the most basic courtesy. In the year since, he'd admitted to himself that he'd treated her unfairly.

"If you are interested, I'll take you to the Royal Academy," he said on impulse. "But perhaps you have already been."

"As it happens I have not. I would enjoy that."

"I hope you enjoy yourself," Denford said. "But I doubt it. You know I despise modern painting." He turned to Damian. "I haven't changed."

"Are you still of the same mind about ancient sculpture too?" he asked.

"The Italian and Dutch are the only true masters, and a few of the French. I never could keep your taste from erring."

"You were too narrow in your view," he retorted. "I broadened your horizons."

For a moment he felt happy, then came down to earth with a thud when he remembered that he was no longer the wide-eyed Viscount Kendal sharing a youthful enthusiasm for paintings with the equally ardent Mr. Fortescue. Julian was his enemy, and the avid interest of the lovely woman opposite him was likely inspired by her lover, not her husband. Silence fell over the company with his sudden shift in mood.

"An angel must have passed over us," his wife said, before the moment became awkward. She smiled through the flickering candles at him, her skin glowing in the soft light. Then she turned to Denford, seated to her right. "You never told me how you met Windermere," she said. "Only that you were at Oxford."

"I found him in a dark cellar at the Bodleian Library, peering at Greek statues."

"I was studying the classics, and the university collection was not in a cellar, though I grant that the visibility was less than ideal."

"I brought him into the light and introduced him to the glories of Raphael, Michelangelo, and Van Dyck."

"He took me upstairs to show me Oxford's gallery of Old Masters," Damian said. "My father was not an admirer of the arts and I was grateful for the revelation." A yearning for the innocent mischief of those days seized him. Why must everything have gone so wrong?

"I would like to see them too," his wife said. "There is nothing so fine on display in London."

Julian shook his head in disgust. "It is a disgrace that a capital as great as London does not possess a first-rate public art gallery. The king is a man of taste and I am surprised he has not seen to the matter."

"Perhaps His Majesty's poor health stands in his way," she said. She pursed her lips with a sympathy that appeared unfeigned and he noticed that her mouth was small and pink and shaped for kissing.

"In that case his ministers should see to it, but they are a crowd of uncivilized louts."

He had to stop thinking about Cynthia and pay attention. Denford had said something interesting. Was he hoping to sell the Falleron collection to King George? If so, he'd catch cold at that plan. Grenville would stop any public funds being released for the purpose, as long as the Alt-Brandenburg question persisted.

While Denford performed a witty—and not wholly undeserved—dissection of the members of the Tory government, Damian leaned back, sipped his wine, and observed the interaction between his wife and her lover. They seemed to know each other well. Almost too well, like an old married couple rather than a pair engaged in an adulterous affair. It must have been going on some time for them to be so comfortable together. He wondered if the liaison was well known in London. Lady Belinda knew, he realized. She had laughed slyly at his failure to recognize his own wife.

Yet how could he have known her? Close up, the features were the same, but in every other way she had changed. She might have appalling taste in art and furniture, but she had made the best of her own appearance. Gone were the stiff curls and overfussy gowns, to be replaced by a coiffure and wardrobe that wouldn't disgrace the beauties of any court in Europe. The careless cluster of curls suited her heart-shaped face, and she had learned to clothe her short, curvaceous figure in a way that made any man worth his salt wish to take her to bed. The fact that another man had done so became a matter for regret as well as anger.

He wanted her. Much more than the superficial attraction he'd felt for Lady Belinda that night at the theater, which had been based purely on the strain of celibacy. He wanted his wife. He wanted to rumple the golden locks, explore the texture of her skin, and taste those perfect lips. He wanted to take her upstairs and discover if she looked even better unclothed.

The impulse needed to be controlled. There were too many reasons it could not happen.

At the other end of the table, Denford murmured a private aside to her and she responded with a co-quettish nod, a suggestive pout of her kissable red mouth, to the former's amusement.

He also needed to control his temper. A new irritation had entered the ocean of bad blood that lay between himself and Denford: jealousy.

Now Denford was telling a story, gossip about people he didn't know, making him feel an outsider in his own house. She threw back her head and laughed at the denouement, displaying a throat whose purity and elegance twisted Damian's heart.

He summoned the serene surface he'd developed during years of public service and smiled.

Cynthia was enjoying herself. She wasn't accustomed to entertaining much, except in the most casual way. This odd little gathering was the closest she'd come to a formal dinner party. Having a husband to act as host and assist in managing awkward moments was a comfort to her. She wondered if he approved of her own contributions. In the old days at Beaulieu he made no secret of his doubts that she was capable of presiding over his household as a worthy hostess. But tonight she thought she was doing quite well. He hadn't gone so far as to smile at her, but he had offered to take her to the Royal Academy. When, as happened quite often, she sensed his steady gaze on her, she felt tight in her own skin, an alarming but not disagreeable sensation. She also worried that she had something caught in her teeth.

Julian was going on about something, probably being his usual witty self, but she scarcely listened.

Through the forest of candles glowing over the linen, silver, and crystal of her carefully chosen table setting, her attention was drawn to Windermere. *Damian*. How absurd that Julian called him by his Christian name and she did not. She remembered the first time she saw him and how handsome he had seemed. If anything, he was more beautiful now. His Persian tan made his gray eyes bluer. She imagined tracing the straight, firm eyebrows that added character to his face, and exploring the dimple in his chin.

With her tongue.

Good God, where had that come from?

Then he smiled at something Julian said, and she realized for the first time that he also had dimples in his cheeks, barely perceptible, when he was amused.

She'd like to amuse him, she realized. She'd like to say or do something that would reveal those delicious indentations of flesh, which she'd then taste . . .

She should not be sitting at her dinner table thinking such things. It wasn't decent. And even if it was, he didn't deserve such attentions. Nothing had changed, even though she wished it had.

Perhaps it would. Perhaps she could forgive the past and forge a new relationship with Damian that would involve dimples. They were married, after all, and there wasn't anything either could do about it.

A gasp of horror interrupted her thoughts. It

came from her left, from George Lewis. No doubt Julian had said something outrageous and shocked her husband's cousin. What had they been talking about? Oh yes, the iniquities of Mr. Pitt's ministry. Not that Julian cared a bit. It amused him to pick an argument, and poor Mr. Lewis was a Tory member of Parliament.

"Don't take any notice of Denford, cousin," she said. "He likes to shock."

Cousin George recovered his poise and his natural pomposity. "I confess, Your Grace, to some surprise that you continue in your trade of buying and selling pictures since you inherited high rank. Like my revered cousin the late earl, I see a nobleman's interest in art as suitably restricted to the glorification of his house and family."

"What would you expect me to do?" Julian replied. "What would you do if you suddenly became Earl of Windermere?"

"I certainly don't expect it. I have no doubt my new cousin will soon present her lord with a pledge of her affection. I have never thought to inherit Cousin Damian's estate."

"But if you did. If Windermere fell under a hackney carriage tomorrow, what would you do?"

"I would continue to do my duty to my family and the nation in the House of Lords instead of the Commons."

"And I continue to do what I have always done, which is to buy and sell pictures."

"Will you not take your seat in the Lords?"

"I don't think you would like what I would get up to there," Julian said with a bark of a laugh.

"Tell me what you hope to accomplish next year, cousin," Cynthia said hastily.

"I wouldn't wish to bore you, my lady, with the details, but one of the first bills likely to come up is a renewal of the Spitalfields Act."

"What is that?"

"It sets the wages of silk weavers in Spitalfields, east of London."

"I know where Spitalfields is," Cynthia replied. *Only too well.*

"The factory owners oppose it. It lays them open to competition from mills in other parts of the country that are able to pay lower wages."

"And you, Mr. Lewis? How do you intend to vote?"

"There are arguments on both sides." He looked over at Windermere. "Do you have an opinion, cousin? I must be guided by the head of the family, in whose gift my parliamentary seat lies."

"I promised your uncle I would use my influence against the renewal of the act." Damian nodded to her, as though she would be pleased. "He sees the law as likely to raise the price of silk. Now that we are at war with France, the competition from imported materials is unimportant. We need to strengthen the industry in London."

George nodded approvingly. "Very wise, Windermere. Do you know that certain factions of the Whigs are trying to get the wage protections extended to women workers? Can you imagine anything so absurd?"

"Why absurd?" Cynthia asked.

"Surely it is obvious? Women do not have to support wives and families. They don't need to make as much money. Not, of course, that the law would set the wages for women weavers as high as that of the men. No one is suggesting it should go that far."

"Women sometimes have to look after their families too."

"If so they are no better than they should be. A decent woman has a husband."

Although Cynthia could have named half a dozen women whose circumstances contradicted George's claim, she didn't like to argue with a guest—or her husband—at the dinner table. "If this law is not a good thing, how did it come to be passed?" she asked instead.

"Fear, Lady Windermere. Fear and intimidation. The various Spitalfields Acts were passed under threat of riots, and the silk weavers were rewarded for disorderly conduct."

Cynthia thought of the squalid streets around her uncle's factory; the dirty, crowded houses; the poverty and desperation of the people. The need for work in which even a small improvement in wages made the difference between starvation and a life that anyone at this table—or any servant in her house—would find insupportably mean. "I cannot find it in my heart to blame men or women for trying to better themselves."

Windermere broke into the conversation. "When they do so at the expense of good order, the result is the kind of horror I saw in France during the worst of the Revolution. I would hate to see blood running in the streets of London."

Julian threw back his head and laughed. "Bravo, Damian! Ten years ago I would never have thought to hear such a speech from an admirer of liberty, equality, and fraternity. Your father would be proud."

Damian's features twisted into an expression Cynthia had never seen and could not read. Disgust, perhaps, or cynicism, or some blend of the two overlaid by a veil of sorrow. She wished she knew what it meant.

Chapter 7

"**A**re Mr. and Mrs. Lewis good whist players?" Denford jerked his head at the table where Damian's cousins had settled down to play a rubber against Cynthia and Bream.

"Fair enough," Damian replied.

"It doesn't matter. They'll win. Oliver always trumps his partner's aces. Since you arranged the game, you should be ready to pay your wife's debts."

He bit back a query about his wife's skill. He had no clue how well she played cards, while Julian, no doubt, was well aware. The thought infuriated him, and he had only himself to blame for his ignorance. If he had stayed in England, he would know about Cynthia's whist skills and a lot of other things too. And Julian would never have had the chance to seduce her. Yet she had been so different then . . . or perhaps not. He hadn't taken the trouble to find out.

He took a deep breath and tucked his feelings away. He had a job to do.

"Will you join me?" he asked. "Brandy?"

They settled in a pair of chairs next to a malachite table as far from the cardplayers as the length of the drawing room allowed. Once Damian had known Julian's expressions as well as his own, could distinguish the true emotions that sometimes cut through the wall of cynical worldliness. He hoped he still could and would be able to tell whether Julian lied about the Falleron collection.

Julian accepted a glass, breathed deep, and tasted. "A fine cognac," he said. He didn't need to mention that they had discovered the joys of French wines together in the cafes of Paris. Damian felt sure that they were sharing the same memory. But when his former friend raised his eyes from contemplation of the golden brown spirits, his expression was cold and mocking.

"Why am I here, Windermere?" he asked. No more false bonhomie and Christian names. "What do you want? If I remember correctly, the last time we spoke at any length was some six years ago when you took a great deal of pleasure in informing me that Lord Maddox wasn't going to sell his pictures to me as previously agreed."

"Maddox wasn't the first collector to change his mind."

"Thanks to your father."

"It was thanks to my father that you even met Maddox. The fact that your sale didn't go through had nothing to do with us."

Denford dignified this excuse with no more than a curl of his lip. This final episode in the decline and fall of their friendship was the major sticking point in Damian's current mission. The irony that he was supposed to persuade Julian to sell a collection of pictures had laid heavily on his mind and—a little—on his conscience. He knew what a setback the failure of the Maddox purchase had dealt Julian's fledgling career.

"I'd raised the money and you knew how hard that was for me," Denford said. "Control of such a prime group of Masters would have established my reputation and let me open my own gallery to rival Bridges. Instead I had years more of begging and contriving."

"And now you are a duke. Being in trade is bad enough but at least buying and selling pictures is an acceptable occupation for a gentleman. Good God! You should be grateful now you never opened a shop."

"The title is empty since I have come into precious little of the fortune as yet. A lot of nonsense about what gentlemen should or should not do troubles me not a whit. I've never given a damn what anyone thinks of me or of what I do."

Damian nursed his brandy and eyed his opponent with an air of calm that he hoped equaled Julian's. The anger and bitterness into which their friendship had dissolved lingered under the surface, but neither let it show. He had this sudden urge to grab the Duke of Denford by the throat and strangle him with his affected black neckcloth until those blue eyes betrayed . . . something.

So he didn't give a damn? Well, he should. Julian *should* care about what he'd done to Damian seven years ago. He *should* care about what he was doing to him now. He had no business seducing another man's wife in retaliation for what was the merest pinprick compared to the blow Damian had suffered. He was going to pay Julian back, once he'd concluded his current, infuriating mission.

"I shouldn't have gloated over the Maddox business," he said, managing not to choke. "I'm sorry for it now. But there was a lot of bad blood between us."

"Blood that you were the first to spill."

Although he disputed that assessment, Damian let it pass. "Water under the bridge."

"By all means let it flow away. Then perhaps you can tell me what you want."

"The Falleron collection. Do you know where it is? I don't expect you to consider the importance of the Alt-Brandenburg alliance, but there's a fortune in this for you. The Foreign Office is prepared to sweeten the prince's offer with monies from the secret funds."

Julian's scorn would have cut through glass. "Prince Heinrich is a tasteless oaf. I wouldn't sell masterpieces to such a boor."

"I didn't know you were acquainted with him."

"I attended a reception at his palace in '97. He was surrounded by blowsy mistresses and smelly dogs to whom he spared what scraps of food from the table he did not consume himself. The very idea of his laying fat, lustful fingers on the exquisite flesh of a Raphael Madonna is enough to turn my stomach."

"Do you expect me to believe you care whom you sell to, as long as the price is right?"

"You disappoint me, Damian. You used not to be so coarse."

That rankled. He had been in the habit for so long of thinking of Julian as a heartless, mercenary creature who acted only in his own interest. And while he still believed it, he also remembered Julian's genuine passion for great works of art. Somehow he felt his actions now—his attempt to manipulate Denford to his will—had a grubbiness about them.

But it wasn't just his own future in the government that was at stake. It was the good of the nation.

"So you admit that you have the collection?"

"I admit nothing."

And yet he had referred to a Raphael Madonna, and the Marquis de Falleron had possessed a famous one. It didn't prove that Denford owned the collection, but Damian was beginning to be convinced that he did. He felt the pricking under the skin that told him he was on the right scent.

He settled back in his chair, sipped his brandy, and smiled faintly. "I remember your excitement that evening at the Hôtel Falleron. You're the expert, but I believe it is unusual for a collection of that size and importance to vanish. Did you ever hear rumors of what became of them?"

"Rumors are cheap."

He surveyed Julian through narrowed eyes. The duke was preternaturally still, his face set in stone like a medieval saint. "You were in Paris when the Terror began. I believe the marquis and his family were early victims of Madame Guillotine."

Had Damian not been looking he wouldn't have spotted the infinitesimal twitch at the side of the twisted mouth, the momentary cloud in the clear blue eyes. "I left soon afterward and never knew what happened."

Soon after what? His wording seemed odd. Before Damian could press, Julian struck back. "I left France and returned to 'perfidious Albion.' You went into the right profession, Windermere."

Damian didn't make the mistake of not taking the insult personally. French diplomats had long accused their British counterparts of being "perfidious" in their promises. Julian was referring to what he'd always claimed was Damian's betrayal.

"What some call perfidy, others regard as looking after the interests of the country."

Denford smiled unpleasantly. "Patriotism? On that topic I agree with Dr. Johnson. When you rejected art for the grubby contrivances of government, you fell among scoundrels."

"Really? I thought I was doing the opposite. Let's not talk about old rivalries, however." He'd gathered useful information and would like to probe for more.

"Not old ones, no." Julian glanced over at Cynthia, who was laughing at some idiocy of Bream's and looked carefree and lovely. "Cynthia looks ravishing tonight."

The demands of diplomacy, perfidious or otherwise, were tossed aside. Sometimes plain speaking was called for. "Leave my wife out of this. Leave her alone." His jaw clenched.

"As you have?" Julian jeered.

"I am home now."

"For how long? Will you take her with you next time you are called away on an urgent diplomatic mission?" He managed to make service to the nation sound self-serving and seedy, rather like a visit to a brothel.

"That's none of your affair. You should not have involved an innocent like Cynthia in our old quarrel."

"You believe I am using her for my own ends?"

"Why else would you be chasing after her?" He carefully kept from letting out that he knew the pursuit had been successful.

"You have a poor opinion of your own bride."

Again Damian felt shabby. And stupid. For it

was rapidly bearing in on him that his lady was no longer the dull little provincial he'd married, if she ever had been. Could Julian actually be in love with her?

A well-bred but distinct commotion arose at the card table.

"Upon my soul," Cousin George said. "I do believe you revoked, sir." Apparently, Bream, not content with trumping his partner's winners, had done the same to his opponent's when he had no right. "You trumped my king of hearts when you still had a small heart in your hand."

"Really," Bream said vaguely. "I thought hearts were trumps."

"Even if they were, you still have to follow suit."

"I always forget."

Cynthia put down her cards and stood up. "Let me ring for the tea tray. Will you tally the score, Cousin George? Setting aside the last hand when Oliver made the mistake, I believe you are a handy winner. We were quite outplayed. Dear Cousin Louisa, you must be parched."

The contretemps cleaned up and brushed aside, she walked over to the bellpull, a few feet from Damian's chair.

"Has my lord been entertaining you, Julian?" She gave Denford a sideways glance that Damian interpreted as coy.

"Windermere and I have discovered a surprising amount to talk about after all these years."

"It's odd that I am better acquainted with you than with my husband. And you know *him* better than I do."

"How piquant that I should be what you two have in common. I shall have to bring you together."

"We can share you."

Damian was unable to believe what he was hearing. He had of course heard of such "sharing" arrangements, but he'd never fancied the idea himself. Even when he and Julian had been close, they'd never pursued that particular vice. As far as he knew, a certain Venetian courtesan was the only woman they had both bedded, but certainly not at the same time.

Except she wasn't the only one. There was Cynthia too, his faithless wife. Disguising his shock, he stared at her through narrowed eyes. She smiled at him, apparently without guile, then turned to Denford. He couldn't be sure, but he thought her mouth widened a little when she regarded her lover. And yet he could swear there was nothing lascivious in either look. He was having a hard time imagining this angelic, golden woman in sweaty congress with even one man, let alone two at once.

Julian on the other hand looked amused. "I don't think I would like you to share me with anyone," he said. "I'd rather have you to myself."

Cynthia blushed, the color making her appear prettier than ever. "That was a goosish thing for

me to say. I only meant that I am glad . . ." She
trailed off, flustered. "I am glad to see you mending your past differences." She turned to Damian.
"You must know, my lord, that without Denford
and other friends I would have been uncommonly
lonely during your absence."

He flinched at the reproach in her clear blue
eyes. "I am sorry for that, my lady. I heeded the
call of duty. My work will always be important to
me, but I see that it is time for me to tend to my
domestic affairs as well as foreign ones."

He had the urge to toss Denford out of the house
forever, and turn his efforts to mending fences with
his wife. He had no hesitation now about where to
apportion blame for her straying. She was an innocent lamb in the jaws of a wolf.

Cynthia enjoyed the bedtime ritual of brushing
her hair because she remembered her mama doing
it for her. Even after she married and acquired the
services of a personal maid, she continued to do it
herself. Not in a melancholy way; her childhood
had been a happy one. She preferred to dwell on
past happiness rather than its premature loss.

Tonight the probable arrival of her husband
drove away memories of life in the curate's cottage.
She prepared for the event by twisting her hair into
a severe plait and donning her sturdiest winter
nightgown, a voluminous flannel garment suitable

for unheated bedchambers. She climbed into her side of the bed feeling overly warm.

Windermere, displaying further evidence of a flamboyant taste in nightwear that didn't match his sober daytime attire, was resplendent in crimson velvet with gold frogging. She forbore from comment, even when he discarded the robe to reveal—thank heavens—a shirt reaching almost to his knees. Undistracted by more interesting parts of his anatomy, she allowed herself to note that he had shapely calves and ankles and long, elegant feet lightly dusted with dark hair. The room suddenly seemed stifling.

"I'm sorry about your mattress, my lord," she said, pushing aside a couple of blankets. "The man was unable to come in and restuff it today. The housekeeper tells me that she needs more notice. She apologizes for not being aware of your stuffing preferences. The mattress on the master bed was, she says, stuffed according to the common taste."

"I have uncommon tastes, I fear. I prefer a looser stuffing. No matter. When the—er—mattress stuffer can get here is time enough. I am quite comfortable in your bed."

"Are you sure my stuffing isn't too tight for you?"

"Thank you, but I found it quite comfortable, at least on the right side of the bed. If I find the other side isn't loose enough I shall ask you to switch places with me again." He climbed into bed.

Not sure why the whole conversation seemed vaguely indecent, Cynthia glanced sideways to find him looking disgustingly at ease and shockingly handsome. If the marriage had turned out the way she'd naïvely hoped, what would they be doing now? *That*, she supposed, but was that all? Would not a husband and wife on good terms, who had just entertained guests, discuss the evening? *That* with Windermere had been disappointing, but a conversation appealed.

"I enjoyed meeting your cousins," she said.

"Did you? I always thought them a dull pair."

"I understand he is your second cousin."

"My father had only sisters, which is why George is next in line for the earldom."

She felt on treacherous ground here. Having a discussion that touched on begetting an heir in the very place that heirs were commonly begotten seemed fraught with peril. "He seems a very worthy man."

"There's not an ounce of harm in George." She waited nervously for him to say something about the topic that hung over her like a thundercloud. When once again he said nothing, she wondered if her uncle had been wrong when he said Windermere was desperate for a son. He didn't behave like a man intent on procreation.

"You had no brothers, and I never knew you had a sister either until the steward at Beaulieu told me. I don't know if she was older or younger."

"Amelia? Did I never mention her?"

"You told me very little at Beaulieu, and most of that in French."

"We were twins."

Her heart caught. "As an only child I have no experience of such a relationship, but it seems to me that twins must be especially close." She touched his arm timidly. "Will you tell me about her?"

"What do you want to know?"

Everything! she wanted to cry, but his expression and voice were distant and bleak, and she had to draw him in gently, not drive him away.

"Did you look alike?"

"People said so. Our coloring was the same but I couldn't see the resemblance myself. She was just Amelia to me."

"Do you have a portrait of her? I should like to see it."

She held her breath, waiting for him to deny her request, or retreat into his shell of reserve. Without saying a word he rose and went through to the earl's chamber. Her heart almost burst with relief when he returned, bearing an oval miniature in a pearl-encrusted frame.

"Here."

She looked at her husband, who was returning to bed, and back at the portrait, comparing points of similarity, including the turned-up edges of the mouth. There could be no question of their relationship. Amelia was a feminine version of her twin, and even as a young girl gave promise of ravishing beauty. "Those who said you looked alike were right. I like her smile. She looks humorous."

"She was always laughing, like my mother."

"And your father?"

"He was more serious."

"Like you."

"When I was with Mama and Amelia I laughed."

Cynthia's attention was drawn to the technique of the portrait. "It's painted on ivory, isn't it? The creamy surface lends a lovely glow to the colors. Who was the artist?"

"My mother."

"Truly?" She looked closer, running a fingertip around the pearl border. "She had a real talent!"

"Painting was her passion. She took lessons from excellent masters."

"I believe there are some of her watercolors at Beaulieu. A series of studies of country folk: farm laborers, a dairymaid, and so forth. I recognize her style."

"You have a good eye."

"I'm surprised they remained in the house after your family sold it." She held her breath. Beaulieu meant so much to her husband that he'd married her for it. But part of the story—how it came into Joseph Chorley's meaty hands—was missing.

He did not bite. "I'm glad to have them back" was all he said.

"Did your sister paint too?"

"She had no facility with pencil or brush, but she played the pianoforte and sang like an angel."

As they relapsed into silence Cynthia could sense the strength of his emotion. Last year Windermere had possessed her body, briefly, every night for almost two weeks, yet she'd felt progressively more estranged. Now, reclining side by side in bed, not touching, she felt an intimacy growing between them, delicate tendrils of mutual knowledge that had the potential to meet, entwine, and form a stronger bond. If only she didn't say the wrong thing and destroy the tenuous connection.

"Do you play?" she asked.

"Not a single note." The words were humorous, the tone grim.

"Will you tell me what happened to Amelia? Unless it's too painful."

"There's nothing much to tell. She died in the same outbreak of measles as my mother. Half the village of Amblethorpe was affected and more than a dozen succumbed."

"You were spared."

"I was safe at school. I left for Eton at the end of the summer without the slightest notion that I'd never see them again. Three months later I received the letter from my father telling me that Mama and Amelia were both dead."

"How old were you?"

"Fifteen."

"I'm sorry." She hesitated to talk about herself.

Yet there was no chance their marriage could improve if they did not speak of important matters, her own as well as his. "We have that in common. My father and mother also perished of an epidemic disease when I was ten." Speaking of her loss always made her feel lonely.

"What happened to you?"

"When the influenza came to our village, my parents sent me to Birmingham to Uncle Chorley while they nursed the sick of my father's parish. They caught the illness themselves. I never saw them again. At least you and your father had each other. You must have been a great comfort to him."

"Perhaps."

He looked as bleak as she felt. Cynthia had the urge to embrace him and tell him that he was not alone, he had her. And she had him. Ridiculous, since he'd never given any indication that he cared.

"I am sorry. It is sad to have neither family nor friends, as I know. Thank goodness for Caro. I've never had a better friend than her. From what she has told me, you were a regular member of Robert's set in the old days."

He'd been relaxed against the pillows as they conversed. Now he stiffened, very much the reserved diplomat despite being clad only in a nightshirt. Still she pressed on, wanting to know about this aspect of his past. "Whatever the reason your friendship ended, it must have been a wrench."

"It was all for the best," he said briskly. "Taking

up with Julian and Robert at Oxford was a mistake, and my only excuse is that I was a little maddened by grief for Mama and Amelia. The time I spent with them was the folly of youth, sowing my wild oats. I have other friends now, men of substance and ambition who, like me, lead a useful life." He sounded as pompous as his cousin George Lewis. He clearly wasn't going to fulfill her curiosity about his quarrel with Julian. "Although much of the last seven years has been spend abroad, I have many acquaintances in London, especially in government circles. You will remember that we spoke of how you would aid me in my diplomatic duties."

"*Bien sûr, monsieur,*" she said, wishing she could drop a curtsey. The chilly, arrogant man she'd married had returned.

"I had expected to join you at Beaulieu for Christmas, but since you are in town we may as well stay here. Sir Richard and Lady Belinda Radcliffe are giving a dinner on Christmas Day. Sir Richard has been my patron in the service and they are particular friends."

"I see," she said, trying not to show her disappointment that their first appearance together as a married couple should be at the house of his mistress. "Are you sure you can trust me not to disgrace you?"

"Do you possess a suitable gown for a formal occasion attended by members of the highest government circles?"

"I believe so, but not having soared to such rarefied levels, I cannot be sure. You are welcome to inspect my wardrobe."

"I trust you, my lady. Your style of adornment is in perfect taste."

"You do me too much honor. I hope Denford will be invited to this event. I'd feel more comfortable with a familiar face."

She'd flirted with Julian this evening, hoping to awaken jealousy in her husband. Since that had clearly failed, she would go back to using Denford to annoy him. Windermere was too well-bred to grind his teeth but she could tell he wanted to. She welcomed his display of emotion and her own ability to detect it.

Chapter 8

A visit to Bow's Silk Warehouse, repository of glorious bolts of brocades, twills, calicos, and chintzes, was the perfect antidote to the turmoil of life with her husband. The careful examination of velvet samples for my lord's bed hangings was so much easier than puzzling out the meaning of his continued presence in her bed. Then, since Cynthia hadn't expected to be in London before Christmas, she indulged herself in a little seasonal shopping.

Usually thrifty with her pin money, the only income over which she had absolute discretion, she loosened her purse strings when tempted by the Oxford Street merchants, especially the sellers of toys. Her servants and other dependents needed practical gifts, she kept reminding herself. Then she'd find the very thing to bring a smile to the face of a particular child and she couldn't resist. She might have no children of her own to spoil, but she had a little household of families who depended on her, and she hadn't seen them in weeks. Tom would love this cup and ball, and Nancy this doll. A set of toy bricks were perfect for little Pudding.

Before she headed east to distribute her largesse, a twinge of guilt reminded her of the man who, unknowingly, provided the means to look after her band of waifs. Ordering her carriage to Bond Street, she wandered into the more elegant emporia there, looking for something for her husband, in vain.

She couldn't locate the perfect gift for a man she barely knew, but she did buy a lace cap for baby Hannah. It was utterly impractical and completely adorable and she couldn't wait to see her in it. She had an especially soft spot for Hannah and her mother, Aggie, the first girl Cynthia rescued.

Postponing the decision about a Christmas present for Damian, she made the journey through the City of London to Spitalfields in the East End and a house in Flowers Street. Cynthia feared the return of Windermere meant she would no longer be able to maintain the house. Judging by his comments about the Spitalfields Acts and the factory workers at dinner the previous night, she didn't expect him to be sympathetic. She was quite sure he'd be even less so if he ever discovered the ruse she'd concocted to raise money.

Her coachman, who had first taken this route under protest, now knew the way. Most of the inhabitants would be at work, but the children would be there. She knocked at the door, expecting the usual excited youthful chatter, punctuated by infant wails. Instead the widow who presided over the household greeted her with a grave face.

"My lady," Mrs. Finsbury said. "I'm glad to see you. We have another. Meggie turned up here last night. Her father threw her out of the house."

Behind her stood a girl, thin, pale, and obviously with child. Dark rings around reddened eyes testified to her distress. "It's all right, Meggie," Mrs. Finsbury said. "Her Ladyship is here now and she won't let you starve.

Another mouth—and eventually two—to feed.

Several months earlier

Cynthia had been looking at materials to replace the faded drawing room curtains at Beaulieu when a young woman was shown in staggering under the weight of a hamper. As she shoved it up onto Mrs. Bow's counter, her meager cloak fell open.

"Are you quite well?" Cynthia asked. "Should you be lifting things in your condition?" She looked enviously at the girl's noticeable belly. She'd never even reached that stage.

The woman—or girl rather—flashed a look of alarm between Cynthia and Mrs. Bow and hastily rearranged her garment to cover the evidence. "I ain't in no condition," she said. "I'm strong enough to work. The master said to bring over these swatches and be sure to bring them all back. I'll wait outside."

"Go and sit down in the back room," Mrs. Bow said. "No need to be out in the cold."

As she examined the gorgeous products of the Finch Street Silk Weavers, Cynthia found herself haunted by the sunken eyes and pale, moist skin of the mother-to-be, who couldn't be more than fifteen. Later, stepping out to her carriage, Cynthia caught sight of her, once more awkwardly burdened by the basketwork hamper, and saw her stumble. Samples poured out into the gutter and the girl scrambled to rescue them, emitting soft wails of distress.

"Help her," Cynthia ordered her footman. Most of the delicate silks were unharmed, but a couple of the swatches were soiled. The girl started to cry in earnest.

"Load the basket into the carriage, John," Cynthia told her servant. "We will deliver the girl and her merchandise home. She isn't strong enough to walk all the way herself."

The girl, who introduced herself as Aggie Smith, seemed quite overwhelmed by the luxurious carriage. Cynthia, who wasn't so far removed from a much simpler life, understood her awe.

"Would you like a bonbon?" She let Aggie suck on the lemon sweet for the length of a street or two before raising the delicate topic. "You shouldn't be working so hard when you are with child. You'll hurt yourself and the baby. Why does your husband allow it?"

Not that the great Earl of Windermere had done anything to see to *his* pregnant wife's needs. Women had to help each other, even if she was a countess and Aggie a messenger for a factory. The least she could do was save this overburdened urchin from a long walk in the rain.

Aggie shrank into her corner of the seat, wrapping her thin arms about her. "I'm not wed, m'lady," she muttered.

"I see." A blow, though not entirely unexpected. "There must be a father. Will he not take responsibility?" The terror and despair on Aggie's features were answer enough. The wretch must have abandoned her. "Alone or not, you must look after yourself and you should not be carrying that heavy basket. I shall speak to your master and tell him it is his fault you dropped it."

"Please, my lady. Don't do that. If he finds out I'm expecting I'll lose my job."

"That's unfair." Even as she said it, she knew the statement was a foolish one. A female always took the greater blame for loss of virtue. One of the maids at her school had been dismissed, even though everyone knew that the school porter was responsible. The porter was too valuable a servant to lose and he was wise enough to confine his seductions to those of the laboring classes. "What about your own family, Aggie?"

"I'm an orphan. The babe'll have to go to the Foundling Hospital but if I keep it a secret I can maybe keep the job after. The silk places pay good wages." Aggie spoke with a bleak resolution that broke Cynthia's heart.

"Do you want to give up your child?" she said softly.

"Want ain't got nothing to do with it."

Cynthia had desperately wanted her child, and lost it. She was determined that Aggie would not so suffer. She had an idea how to persuade the owner of the Finch Street factory to keep Aggie on, and to provide her with easier work until after her child was born. She herself was a prospective customer worth a handsome sum. If Mrs. Bow, whom she knew to be a decent woman who treated her employees kindly, would join her in threatening to withhold her custom, the man might relent.

"I shall help you, I promise. I shall make your master change his mind."

"He never will, not that one. Ask any of the girls."

"What do you mean? He has dismissed others in the same state as yourself?" Cynthia felt a prickling of apprehension at the back of her neck. "Tell me the truth, Aggie."

"He's the one that did it. We try to avoid him but it's hard."

"Why do you all stay then?" She didn't need Aggie's look of incredulous impatience to know the answer. "Good wages."

"And times are hard. There ain't too many places to go."

Confronting this violator of innocents was the boldest thing Cynthia had ever attempted. On arrival at the premises of Finch Street Silk Weavers, a surprisingly wide and expansive edifice stretching several hundred feet on the narrow thoroughfare, she sent in her bewigged and liveried footman to announce to the owner that the Countess of Windermere wished for an audience. That should impress the man. A respectable-looking clerk showed her the way. The premises were neat and clean and exuded an air of purposeful industry, belying the immoral cruelty of its overseer.

Heart racing, she went through the door that the clerk opened with a slight bow. She stopped on the threshold, her hand covering her mouth at the sight of a man she knew well. Aggie's attacker was her uncle's London partner. That meant that Finch Street Silk Weavers was part of the Chorley fortune, producer of the wealth that had bought her an earl for a husband and was paying Mrs. Bow's extortionate bills.

"My dear Cynthia. Or Lady Windermere, I suppose I should call you. Such condescension for you to call at my humble offices." Wilfred Maxwell's grating tones sent a frisson of disgust over her skin. He arose from behind the desk, a man of overweening self-confidence whom many would call handsome. No more than thirty-five years old, he had dark hair untinged by gray. His powerful body would have no difficulty overcoming the resistance of any woman.

Cynthia had always found him utterly repulsive. Maxwell had made it clear he wanted to wed his senior partner's niece, and she had been terrified that her uncle would approve the match. Whatever her complaints against Windermere, however impossible her marriage sometimes seemed, at least she wasn't wed to this disgusting creature.

"Mr. Maxwell," she said faintly. "I was not expecting to see you here."

The horrid man had the nerve to take her hand. She withdrew it quickly, thanking the Lord for gloves. A sneer twisted Maxwell's fleshy lips. "Too good for me now, Your Ladyship?" he said.

"Pleased as I am, of course, to see an associate of my uncle's," she said, "my present errand is not a happy one. I come from Mrs. Bow's warehouse."

"Do you have some complaint about the samples I sent over? Even had I known that the good Mrs. Bow's customer was the illustrious Countess of Windermere, I could not have provided better."

"My contention does not concern the product but the messenger."

"Aggie Smith!" he roared, brown eyes bulging as though he might have an apoplexy. "The girl can't be trusted with the simplest task." He pushed past Cynthia to the door. Grateful again for the protection of fine kid gloves, she grabbed his meaty arm with both hands.

"Don't you dare," she said, wondering how she dared herself. "I know what you did to her. And to others too. I shall write to my uncle and tell him what kind of a man he calls partner."

Maxwell stopped, his muscles tense beneath her fingers. Then he relaxed and let out a deep belly laugh. "You go ahead and write to Uncle Joseph. You are sadly mistaken if you think Joseph Chorley and his partners in business give a damn what kind of a man runs his factories, as long as the money flows in the right direction, and plenty of it. This and every other mill under my rule turns a handsome profit. As long as that keeps up, Uncle Joseph isn't going to concern himself if I take my pleasure with human dross. I can always find plenty more like Aggie Smith. Better-looking girls, and better workers."

A moment's consideration told Cynthia the truth behind Maxwell's bluster. Sad to say, Joseph Chorley was a man without principles or morals.

Maxwell hadn't finished. "Go, my fine lady. You may think yourself too fine for the likes of me, but remember this. I intended to wed you and become the heir to the old Chorley's fortune but he sold you instead to Windermere. Windermere gets money while Chorley gets your fancy earl's support in Parliament. Don't think you're worth more to them than Aggie Smith. You are just dressed finer, that's all."

Cynthia stalked out, her face burning with impotent rage. Then a new determination kindled. She might be a meaningless pawn in the games played by men. Such was the fate of women. But she would find a way to save Aggie Smith and others like her.

Chapter 9

While waiting to be sure Cynthia was not with child, Damian had to prevent her from sneaking out to meet Denford. Judicious questioning of his coachman revealed that her daytime excursions tended to be innocent enough, mostly a vast amount of time spent at modistes, silk and furniture warehouses. Occasionally she ventured through the City of London to the Spitalfields area where Mr. Chorley had several factories. He must remember to ask what drew her to such an unfashionable quarter. He'd never had the impression that she was involved with her uncle's business. Indeed, it would be most irregular for a lady, especially one who had wed an earl to improve the social standing of her family.

With her lover conveniently in the next house, there was no need for them to venture far afield in search of a trysting place. To foil her access to Fortescue House through the garden gate, Damian locked the doors into the garden from the parlor and library and pocketed the keys. If she tried to go out, she would have to ask the servants. Unable to find the keys, the butler would inform him of the problem. He wasn't sure what he'd say, but he'd think of something. He was a diplomat, accustomed to excusing the inexplicable and talking out of both sides of his mouth.

The whole business left a sour taste in his mouth. As he spent more time with Cynthia, he fought the urge to trust a woman who was manifestly untrustworthy. Soon, he fervently hoped, he would know if she wasn't with child. Then he would reassess the state of their marriage and decide how to go forward. Of one thing he would make damn certain: Any child she carried in the future would be fathered by him. It would have to be. Sharing a bed with a woman he wanted and couldn't touch was straining his nerves. For two nights he got into bed and went straight to sleep. Conversation was too dangerous.

He returned from a meeting at the Foreign Office, intending to spend the rest of the day in the library, looking over some reports sent by his man of business. A scent of hothouse flowers wafted through the opposite door, drawing him to the open door of the parlor. His wife sat on an upright chair looking at the French window. A folio-sized sketchbook was balanced on her knee while she plied her pencil.

As he crossed the threshold, the pencil fell to the

ground and her head jerked around. "My lord! I did not expect you this morning."

"I don't think I said anything about my movements."

"No," she said. "You did not." She spoke without a hint of reproach, but it did occur to him that a husband should, out of courtesy if nothing else, inform a wife of his plans. He wasn't used to being married, and perhaps it wasn't so terrible after all. Coming home to a warm, sweet-smelling welcome from a pretty wife seemed very appealing. It would be even better if he were bedding the pretty wife and if she hadn't bedded another man.

"I didn't know you drew," he said. Of course he didn't. He'd never asked her.

She laid the sketchbook flat on her lap and nodded serenely. "I always enjoyed it at school. I took it up again while I was staying in Wiltshire with Anne Brotherton. I helped her by recording objects excavated from a Roman villa. This morning I decided to try my hand at the garden. The windowpanes break up the view and make it easier to tackle."

"I see. Natural squaring off."

"Did your mother teach you about that?"

He shrugged. "I've visited artists' ateliers in France and Italy. I am familiar with the basic techniques."

"Shall I ring for tea?"

"Not for me, thank you. I have work to do."

He walked to the door, stopped, and turned. "Do you mind if I fetch my reading and keep you company?"

"Not at all," she said with a hint of surprise.

"Tell me if I am disturbing you," he said when he came back with a bundle of papers and found her staring at the window, a delicate crease between her brows.

"You won't. I'm not very good. Not like your mother."

"A lady is not expected to show a high level of skill at what should be merely an enjoyable pastime."

"I strive for excellence, nonetheless. I doubt I will ever be as good as Oliver, for example, but I don't aspire to sell my work."

He wanted to look at her sketch, curious to see whether she was being modest. But he remembered how much he'd disliked showing his own work until he thought it ready for exposure to the critical eye. Settling at her small escritoire, he tried to concentrate on the reports from Amblethorpe and found them dull. He knew it was his duty as the owner to attend to the management of the northern estates. He'd listened to numerous lectures from his father about how an inattentive landlord was an unsuccessful one. As his father's bluff accents, tinged with a hint of northern dialect, assaulted his brain, he felt his fingers itch as they had done so often during his father's harangues. The scritch-scratch of his wife's pencil on thick rag paper was a siren call. He forced himself to read a list of leases.

So passed a silent hour that wasn't uncomfortable, though he couldn't say he felt at ease. He was too aware of his companion, and kept stealing glances at the golden head bent over the paper, the gentle frown of concentration. Every now and then she would catch him looking at her. She'd blush and hastily turn back to her sketch. He wondered what she was thinking. Probably lost in her work with the absolute absorption that art demanded. He suppressed a pang of envy and thought about sheep and drainage.

"The light is fading," she said finally, standing up and setting aside her drawing.

"Are you finished for the day?"

"I think so." She closed the sketchbook and walked over to the window. All he could see was the blue paper wrapper of the manufacturer. He wished she'd offer to show him what she'd done that afternoon. "I suppose I had better draw the curtains," she said, "but I never want to. When the days are short I hate to waste even a few minutes of daylight." She rested her nose against the window, staring out into the garden.

Was she thinking of Julian and how she hadn't been able to meet him at night?

"What's that?" she said.

He heard it at the same time, a soft squeak or cry. She reached for the door handle.

"You'll catch cold," he warned. "It's drizzling."

"There's something out there." She rattled the glass doors. "This door is locked and the key is missing. There is some poor creature out there. What was Ellis thinking, removing the key? I shall speak to him about it."

"I'll ask him," Damian said quickly.

"Hurry! It's starting to rain in earnest."

Having retrieved the key from a desk drawer in the library, he unlocked the door. "It was on the table in the next room," he said. "One of the footmen must have moved it by accident. No harm done."

She slipped outside and down the terrace steps to where a kitten stood on the path, indignantly mewing. She scooped it up and brought it inside.

The small gray cat knew a cozy berth when it found one. It ceased crying and curled up against his wife's bosom. "Oh look!" she cried. "It's purring."

He'd be purring too.

"It probably has fleas," he said sourly.

"I wonder how it got into our garden. I'll have to send inquiries to all the houses on this side of the square."

"London is full of stray cats."

She crooned, stroking its little head and muttering endearments. "If it doesn't belong to anyone, I shall keep it. I always wanted a pet. I wonder if it's a male or a female."

Damian fought off an idiotic pang of jealousy. It was a cat, for heaven's sake. He carefully plucked the creature from her breast and held it up. Its little stomach panted under his palm. "Female," he said, and happily relinquished her to her benefactress.

"Do you mind if I keep her, Damian?" she said. She looked at him eagerly and he wondered if she was aware she'd addressed him by his Christian name for the first time. "Do you object to cats?"

"I've never had one in the house. My father preferred dogs." Big, raucous beasts that accompanied him shooting. He never permitted an animal in the house that wasn't of sporting use. "I have no objection."

"Oh thank you!" she said with a smile that made his heart jump. For a moment he thought she was going to kiss him. "Are you hungry, my sweet?" The kitten mewed again. "I'll take you down to the kitchen and find you some milk and a bed. I'm sure the cook will be delighted to see you."

All further remarks were addressed to the feline and Damian was left alone, forgotten. He drew the curtains against the twilight and threw a couple of pieces of coal onto the fire. About to return to his work, his eye was drawn to the abandoned sketchbook. It was hard to resist taking a look, but he restrained his curiosity. Instead he picked up the pencil, riffled through his papers until he found a blank sheet, and started to draw. In his mind's eye he saw the pure line of Cynthia's profile: the smooth forehead, slight upturned nose, the perfect bow of her upper lip, the small but determined chin. With a few strokes the face took form as his pencil moved faster, adding shading as he'd been taught so long ago in Paris. He'd always had a knack for producing a likeness, but when he stopped and held the paper at arm's length, he was dissatisfied. They were Cynthia's features, close enough, but there was no life to the portrait. It communicated nothing of her character. Perhaps it was because he didn't really know her character. Or perhaps he hadn't the skill. He heard his father's voice again, this time telling him not to waste his time on an art that was suitable only for females and certainly not for any gentleman. He ripped the paper into four neat pieces and threw them onto the fire.

Without letting himself think about it, he flipped open the sketchbook. Drawings of battered Roman artifacts covered several pages. There was a portrait of a dark-haired young woman with an intelligent face. His heart beat faster when he turned the page to find a man's face, but it wasn't Julian, as he had feared. He knew those handsome, smiling features: Marcus Lithgow, another of his former friends. More pieces of broken pottery, and then the view from the parlor window. She hadn't got far with it, barely sketched a tree seen through one pane. Neither was it the last drawing in the book. He turned the page and discovered why he'd caught her looking at him that afternoon. It was he, all right—she drew a fair likeness. But that wasn't his expression.

The face she'd caught in three-quarter profile lacked any kind of feeling. It was sleek, cold, impenetrable—even a little ruthless.

Chapter 10

Damian paused at the door. The strain of celibacy was becoming acute, and he assessed the risk of letting his wife sleep alone. Even if he didn't hear her leave in the middle of the night, the garden door key was hidden again. But she would think it odd if he suddenly absented himself. As far as he knew, there had been no change to the mattress and apparently there was something wrong with his bed curtains. He'd better put himself through the discomfort of her all-too-desirable proximity because, after all, she might try and sneak out. It had nothing to do with a sudden reluctance to sleep alone. Nor was it because he had enjoyed their afternoon together.

He found her already in bed. "We have company, I see." To avoid looking at her, he concentrated on the new pet, running a finger along the curving spine of the kitten, curled up on her lap. "She purrs a lot."

"She's well fed and comfortable."

"Does the new member of our family have a name?"

She gave him a quick, surprised glance. It was an odd thing for him to say. He'd never thought of them as a family.

"I was thinking something Shakespearean. Viola, or Miranda, or Perdita, perhaps, since she was found in a storm."

"Rather a dramatic way to describe a little rain, don't you think?"

"Perhaps," she said with a smile. "And maybe those names are too grand for such a tiny, funny creature."

The kitten rolled onto her back, and stretched out her paws. "That tummy looks *very* well fed. Careful or she'll grow pudgy."

"Pudge! I like it. Hey, sweeting, what do you think of your new name?"

Pudge signaled her approval by closing her eyes and purring even louder.

"Is that noise normal?" he asked. "Will it keep us awake?"

"If it bothers you, the mattress in your room has been restuffed."

"Or Pudge might prefer a new mattress."

"She has already tried every other bed in the house, including yours, and none was to her taste. If you are going to sleep in here, you will have to put up with Pudge's presence."

"Even though they say that two is company and three a crowd?"

"It's up to you, my lord, but the cat remains." She looked up at him with a little pouty smile, illustrating why overwrought poets compared their mistresses' lips to rosebuds. Even in an all-enveloping nightgown, she was as enticing as an Eastern dancer wearing nothing but diaphanous veils. Perhaps he'd better have his valet order such a flannel garment for him. It would be an extra barrier between him and his increasingly attractive wife. On the other hand, he had every intention of resuming marital relations as soon as he knew she wasn't with child, and he didn't want her to find him undesirable. She had, after all, told him she didn't wish to lie with him. She thought it was her decision alone that they shared a chaste bed. Since he very much hoped that their bed would not be chaste for long, it was time to start wooing her.

He climbed in beside her. He gave her credit for not wishing to give herself to both lover and husband at the same time, but little did she know that her affair with Denford was over. Seducing her himself was one way of making sure.

"You called me Damian this afternoon," he said. "You address both Bream and Denford by their Christian names."

"They are Caro's intimates. Everyone in her set is on easy terms, as you no doubt recall."

"Yet you persist in addressing me as 'my lord.'"

"And you call me 'my lady.' I assume such formality is what you prefer. It doesn't seem strange to me. My uncle and aunt always address each other as Mr. and Mrs. Chorley."

"My own mother and father were formal too, but I don't know how they spoke to each other in private."

"We're not in private. Pudge is here."

"At the risk of shocking Pudge, do you think we might use each other's given names, Cynthia?"

"Yes, Damian," she said, her voice husky with surprise. "It would be . . . proper, I think."

He seized her hand and gave her knuckles a lingering kiss. Her cheeks grew pink; she said nothing, but she left her hand in his.

"I hope we can get on better than we have in the past, Cynthia."

"I hope so too, but, as I said before, I'd like time to know you better."

"I confess that *I* wish to know my wife better too."

Stroking her palm with his thumb did not have the intended effect. She snatched away her hand and regarded him with narrowed eyes. "You had a chance when we were first married and seemed to have very little interest. If you recall, all our conversations were in French, which had a most inhibiting effect on the exchange of information."

Oh God! Those terrible, awkward evenings, when he'd used the excuse of improving her languages to keep her at a distance. "I owe you an apology for that. I meant it for the best, but I was wrong." He smiled winningly. "I don't make you speak French anymore."

"That's an improvement. But if you want to know me you must hear what I have to say and it may not always be pleasant."

"Complain away," he said magnanimously. She must want to berate him for leaving her two weeks after the wedding and leaving the country within a month. He was willing to admit she was justified.

"During our honeymoon you left me alone most of the days."

"I was busy about the estate."

"You made me speak French, which I couldn't do. And then at night," she went on, stumbling over her words, "you came to me as though I were, I don't know, nothing. Of no more importance than a piece of meat."

"What do you mean?"

"You never even kissed me!"

It came as a nasty shock that the lack of care he'd afforded her in bed had not gone unnoticed. She was right. She had meant nothing to him at the time, and their coitus was merely a duty he'd had to get through.

He didn't feel that way now. When he was ready to take her again, he'd do the job properly and make sure she attained her own pleasure. Julian had no doubt seen to it. A lump formed in his chest and threatened to choke him. He was angry with himself and furious with Julian. Oddly enough, he didn't feel nearly as angry at Cynthia. She had been neglected by him and led astray by Julian. The poor girl, unfamiliar with the wicked ways of the world, didn't know any better.

"I'd like to kiss you now. Will you let me?"

And because he was afraid of getting the wrong answer, he took her head in his hands and lowered his mouth to hers. He started out slowly, just a brush of his lips over hers, moving gently and resisting the urge to taste the sweetness within. He kissed her as though undertaking a diplomatic overture: make contact, assess the reception, soothe any resistance.

His restrained approach was rewarded by a noticeable reciprocation. He pressed a little harder. She placed her hands on his shoulders, her fingers firebrands through his linen shirt.

He parted his lips, sipping at her mouth. To his joy he felt her warm breath mingle with his as she opened to him, but a hesitation when he ventured to trace the opening with his tongue. "You're beautiful," he whispered, and retreated a step, massaging the soft skin of her temples with his thumbs. He waited, senses alert to her reactions, wanting to make their first kiss as perfect as their beddings had been mediocre. A new start for them, he thought hazily, but his attention was fixed on the physical. When her breath deepened and all tension ebbed away so she was all melting and pliant against him, he advanced the kiss, tasting her for the first time and finding her as sweet as he had anticipated.

He didn't allow himself to take her passionately. They couldn't come to the natural conclusion this evening. So he kept things warm, not heated, a slow, almost lazy enjoyment of each other. But he leaned back against the pillows and drew her down to him, kept one hand threaded into her silky hair while the other circled her waist, finding the womanly curves beneath thick flannel as exciting as the finest linen or satin. They kissed for what seemed a long time until his desire flared too hot to be ignored.

With reluctance he broke the kiss. Not ready to end the connection, he rested her head against his neck. Her breath, as elevated as his, warmed his skin. With an unsteady hand he stroked her disordered hair and ran two fingers up and down the nape of her neck. She nuzzled his collarbone in approval and he made a mental note that she enjoyed being touched there, a tiny addition to the sum of his knowledge about his wife. Her movement disturbed him all the way to his distended cock. Gently he disengaged from the embrace and laid her on her side next to him. She gazed at him with eyes wide and dreamy.

"Was that a good first kiss?" he asked lightly, recovering his voice and his wits.

"Our first," she murmured. "Very good."

Of course it wasn't *her* first. At the very least Julian had seen to that. Yet she did not kiss like a woman of great experience. He'd sensed a certain innocent wonder in her lips. He began to wonder how long, how often, she and Julian had been lovers and rejected an insidious hope that he was wrong and she had not, after all, betrayed him. That was stupid and belied the evidence of his eyes.

She settled down on her side of the bed, stroking the kitten, who slept on undismayed. "Damian," she began, and stopped.

"Never mind," she said.

He awoke early, aroused by a faint moan in the bed next to him.

"Are you well, Cynthia?"

"No I am not. I must ask you to leave and send for my maid."

Alarmed, he opened the curtains to let in the gray dawn light. She was curled up into a ball, clasping her stomach. A sheen of sweat coated her forehead. "What is it?" he asked urgently. "Shall I send for a physician?"

She managed a wan smile. "It's only my monthly pains. They often take me quite badly. My maid knows what to do."

He was sorry for her discomfort, of course, but happy for the cause. She was not with child.

Chapter 11

Damian leafed through a dozen miniatures, each about a foot tall, depicting soaring Eastern palaces, marble arches, and exotic gardens. The graphic nature of the central action of the paintings contrasted with the elegance of their settings. Amid divans and cushions painted in vibrant colors enriched with gold leaf, dark-skinned, almond-eyed beauties disported, pleasured by the personal weapons of bearded warriors. Portrayed with the greatest artistry, the focus of each scene was the same: penis in vagina. Or in one case, mouth. The positions varied, as did the backgrounds, but the point was the same: to illustrate the act of love and incite the viewer to participate.

Damian was feeling quite excited, an inconvenience since he was due at a meeting with Radcliffe in half an hour. Not that he'd had the chance to forward the wooing of his wife, who was still indisposed. For two days she'd barely left her room and was very ill indeed, according to the reports from her maid when he punctiliously inquired after her. The monthly condition took some women that way, he had heard somewhere.

He'd unpacked the portfolio to give to Lady Belinda, as promised. An adventurous lady, she had initiated him into some of the delights portrayed therein and would doubtless be happy to try any that had somehow eluded her experience. Damian looked back over their affair and felt a measure of disgust, both with her and with himself. As a lustful youth he'd accepted what she had to offer; his mature self recognized that he didn't much like the lady.

Then a Radcliffe footman had delivered a note changing the location of his rendezvous. Since he was summoned to the Foreign Office instead of the Radcliffe's Grosvenor Square house, there was no point taking the drawings with him after all. He set out for Whitehall at a brisk walk, enjoying the nip of frost that cut through the smoke and odors of London.

He reached his destination in a suitably sober frame of mind and was shown into an elegantly furnished sitting room. The holders of high government places knew how to make themselves comfortable. Sir Richard, short and impeccably dressed in a manner appropriate to his sixty-odd years, arose from a desk that was almost certainly the work of a famous French *ébéniste*.

"Come in, my dear boy, and tell me how you are enjoying being back in London."

"Very well, thank you."

They settled in front of the fire, beneath a beaming portrait of a young King George III.

"Not missing the warmer climes of Persia?" Radcliffe asked with a faint whiff of distaste. When Damian first turned down the Persian mission it had been on Sir Richard's advice. The latter claimed the posting outside Europe would do nothing to advance Damian's career and had urged him to find a wife and establish himself in London, while waiting for a less distant ambassadorship to come available. He had been distinctly annoyed when Damian changed his mind at the last minute.

"As it happens, it often snows in Tehran."

"I leave the details of conditions on the ground to the envoys." Having dispensed with the weather, the topic that no conversation in England could proceed without, Radcliffe got down to business. "How are you getting on with Denford?"

"I wasn't aware that you knew about that business."

"Grenville has no secrets from me." Radcliffe no doubt hoped that was so. Damian guessed that the foreign secretary played his cards close to his chest when dealing with a man who aspired to replace him in the near future. Damian's own ambitions were, of course, for the longer term.

Whatever the relations between Grenville and Radcliffe, since the latter was cognizant of the negotiations with Denford over the Alt-Brandenburg matter, Damian was glad for the opportunity to consult his mentor. "What do you think of the business, sir? Will the sale of the art collection really seal the alliance with the prince? It seems tenuous to me."

"Your instincts are always excellent, Windermere." Damian's chest swelled at the nod of approval. "Prince Heinrich's demands are capricious and who can say what will finally persuade him to place his seal on the treaty. But we must try everything and it never hurts to have an extra string to one's bow."

"We can't even be certain that Denford has the Falleron collection."

"Our intelligence indicates otherwise."

"I'd like to know about that."

Radcliffe waved a sere but well-tended finger at him. "We don't reveal our sources to every member of the diplomatic corps."

Considering the sacrifice to his feelings that the pursuit of Denford demanded, Damian thought he deserved some leeway. But he knew from experience that Sir Richard was a wily old dog who would say and reveal exactly what he wanted and no more.

"Tell me," Radcliffe continued. "Have you spoken to Denford?"

"I invited him to dinner. He denies possession of the pictures."

"Do you believe him?"

"Probably not."

Radcliffe's thin smile graced a face sleek with satisfaction. "Aha! I knew you were the right man for the job and I told Grenville so. You were wasted in the uncivilized Levant."

"I'm obliged to you, sir."

"You know Denford well enough to see through his lies."

"I knew Julian Fortescue, as he was then, when we were mere youths. I haven't been on terms of friendship with him for years."

Radcliffe stood up. "I haven't offered you refreshment. I like a glass of hock in the morning." Damian accepted the offer, sipping the fruity German wine as he waited for Radcliffe to get to the point.

"How old are you now, Windermere? Twenty-eight? And Denford about the same. Old enough to get over a youthful quarrel. That, for the sake of your country, is what I expect you to do."

Even to his mentor, a man who had been like a father to him when relations with his own sire had been strained beyond mending, Damian hesitated to confide the present conflict with Denford, one that couldn't be attributed to youthful folly. He didn't wish to confess himself a cuckold, and he wanted to protect his wife. There was no need for Sir Richard to know what she had done.

And yet he remembered Lady Belinda's amusement when he failed to recognize Cynthia at Drury

Lane. She knew. If she knew, Radcliffe knew. And if Radcliffe had proposed Damian for the task of persuading Denford, Damian had been manipulated in a way that left a nasty taste in his mouth.

"Very handy that Denford is living next door to you. Couldn't be more convenient. And then there's his friendship with your wife."

"I beg your pardon? What can you mean?"

"Why nothing." Radcliffe responded to Damian's sharp tone with a bland smile. "It is common knowledge that Lady Windermere is a member of the Townsend set, that disreputable and no doubt highly amusing group that you yourself once belonged to. She and Denford have been seen together all over town. Not surprising that a beautiful young woman left alone by her husband should seek entertainment. Another unfortunate result of your Persian adventure. You should ask her to exert her influence over her *friend*." It was impossible to miss the stress on the last word.

"My wife is not aware of my diplomatic work."

"Make her so, my dear boy. Lady Belinda and I are as one when it comes to affairs and I find her of inestimable use."

He imagined encouraging Cynthia to discover Julian's secrets over pillow talk, and the idea made him absolutely furious.

"I can manage Denford on my own," he said firmly.

"Make sure you do, dear boy. It isn't the first

time I've placed my reputation behind your competence and you haven't yet failed me yet. Drink up and let's proceed to business."

"Has the last quarter of an hour been small talk, then?"

"No need for sarcasm. I wish to speak to you about the Spitalfields Act."

"I told Mr. Joseph Chorley, my wife's uncle, that I would oppose it. I don't see what it has to do with the Foreign Office."

"I have other interests, as do many members of the government, even to the highest levels."

"Are you in favor of the act? I'm afraid I don't know as much as I should, but I am, of course, eager to hear your views."

"I'm with your uncle-in-law—Chorley, is it?—in this matter. Renewal of wage protection for the silk workers is nothing but injurious to the wealth of the nation."

"Then we have no difference."

"I had feared Lady Windermere might have convinced you of the opposite view. In this case I shall be glad to see her excluded from your affairs."

The topic had come up at dinner and Cynthia hadn't said anything, beyond a question about women's wages. He thought it proper for her to care about the welfare of the gentler sex, and even more proper that she had deferred to George Lewis's explanation.

"Why on earth should Lady Windermere have

an opinion?" he said. "If she did, she would surely listen to her uncle."

"So I would hope. But the Townsend set was always notorious for its radical views. I fear Lady Windermere may have fallen under the influence of those artists who used to frequent Mrs. Townsend's salon."

Damian thought of Oliver Bream's single-minded pursuit of solid refreshment. "I'm not too worried."

"And what of such firebrands as Denford? He spoke well of the French Revolution long after it was either fashionable or wise. If Lady Windermere should speak to you of supporting the act, you may be sure it comes from him. Your goal, my dear boy, is to persuade Denford to produce those paintings and counter any influence he may exert in other areas."

In the seven years since Radcliffe had taken him under his wing and guided his career, Damian had never been so out of sympathy with the man. The whole business made him feel grubby. Being polite to Julian had seemed possible, barely, when Ryland had first handed him the task. Ignoring the fact that Denford was involved with his wife had seemed bearable, just, when he'd regarded Cynthia with indifference.

Whatever his feeling for his wife now, they were far from indifferent. His stomach roiled at the very notion of her intimacy with Denford. If he'd ever thought himself a sophisticated man of the world in a fashionable marriage where fidelity came second to statecraft, he wasn't any longer.

"I don't want to deal with Denford."

Radcliffe frowned at this rash statement, blurted out without forethought. "I'm disappointed to see you lose control of yourself. I thought I had trained you better. How often have I told you that revealing your feelings is to give the other party an advantage."

Damian swallowed and tried to present his case rationally. "The whole business with the pictures seems a long shot. Surely there must be another way of getting at the Prince of Alt-Brandenburg. Or of persuading Denford, for that matter."

"You forget yourself," Sir Richard said in tones of deep displeasure. "It is not for you to question the judgment of your superiors as to the value of your mission. Can you so easily dismiss your duty to your country and your own future usefulness as an agent of the Foreign Office? On a personal level, let me remind you that seven years ago you came begging for my help to establish yourself and recover from the consequences of your youthful folly. Walk away now, and you let me down. You also show that you have learned nothing. Think what your father would say if he was still alive."

Radcliffe had found the one argument he couldn't ignore.

Chapter 12

Recovered from her indisposition, Cynthia spent the day in her parlor with Oliver and their sketchbooks. He was planning a series of giant canvases depicting the women of Troy, to be executed in oils just as soon as he found a wealthy patron with large walls. She couldn't remember precisely what philosophical point Helen, Hecuba, and Andromache were supposed to illustrate. She had, however, told him quite firmly that Beaulieu Manor was far too small for such a grand production.

"Are you quite sure?" he coaxed. "Look at this composition. I've managed to combine the sacrifice of Hector's and Andromache's daughter and the murder of their son in one painting."

"For God's sake, Oliver," she said with unwonted acerbity. "Could you possibly come up with a more gruesome subject?" She was in no state to find any kind of nobility in the death of children. "Why don't you paint something cheerful for a change, then perhaps you'd actually sell a picture."

"Doesn't Windermere have another estate, in the north somewhere? I shall speak to him about commissioning my Trojan women for that house."

"I don't know much about Amblethorpe," she replied, "but I doubt Windermere would be interested."

"I don't see why not. He used to be a painter himself."

"Who told you that?"

"I don't know. Just an impression I had. If he had to give up his own art, it stands to reason he'd be interested in other people's."

Setting aside the illogic of Oliver's hopeful conclusion, Cynthia was intrigued by another possible insight into her husband's character. "I don't think you can be right, Oliver," she said shaking her head. "Someone would have mentioned it to me." She returned to her drawing of the new kitten. "Stay still, Pudge. Why can't you go to sleep?"

Oliver looked with disfavor on the little creature, who was chasing a pencil around the floor. "Just as bad as dogs. I hate painting animals, and for some reason old ladies always want to be pictured with their lapdogs."

"Poor Oliver." Cynthia smiled at what was an old complaint. "It's a hard life being a working artist."

"I'm hungry," he said, to no one's surprise.

"Give me five minutes to finish this and I'll ring for tea."

Oliver restlessly examined the ornaments on the mantelpiece, then, thankfully, wandered out of the room. She could hear him rummaging in the library across the passage, a room she rarely entered. Whoever had purchased the books did not share her taste and she preferred to borrow novels from the subscription library. He came back into the parlor carrying a small portfolio of the kind used to carry collections of drawings and prints.

"What do you have there?" she asked.

"A most interesting collection. They are Indian or Persian, I think. I've occasionally seen such things but never had the opportunity to examine them up close. I wonder how they mixed the colors. It looks like some kind of distemper. The gold is very finely applied." He squinted and pointed at the richly gilt details of a Moorish arch, apparently oblivious to the fact that, beneath the arch, an almost naked woman appeared to be about to swallow a man's private member.

Cynthia shrieked, blushed, and closed her eyes. "Do you think you should be showing pictures like this to a lady, Oliver? Really?"

His boyish features creased in concern. "I'm sorry, Cynthia. I suppose they are a little warm."

"A little warm" was one way of putting it, "totally indecent" another. "Put them away at once," she ordered.

Oliver obeyed, but while he finished off a plate of cakes, her thoughts kept drifting away. Having driven him out of the house more abruptly than usual, she stole into the library. Dreading interruption, whether from a servant or, heaven forbid, her husband, who had been absent all day, she leafed through the richly painted parchments, eyes ready to pop out of her head. Page after page depicted men and women in amorous congress in the most blatantly graphic fashion—and in ways utterly unlike her own experience of intimate relations.

Her aunt Lavinia Chorley had described the marital act as horrifying and painful and recommended she close her eyes and try to think of something else until the dreadful business was over. Though Cynthia had been hopeful things would go better for her with the young and handsome Windermere, she was nonetheless terrified as she waited in bed the night of her wedding.

He'd entered the room, blown out the candle, and got into bed with her. No kissing, of course, but he had, she supposed, made some effort to show affection. He'd gathered her in his arms and she had enjoyed that, though she was far too bashful to relax or return his embrace. When he stroked her breasts she'd been utterly embarrassed, having no notion that those feminine appurtenances would actually be touched by gentlemen. But that insult to her privacy was nothing to what followed, when he raised her nightgown to her waist. She'd felt she would surely die of mortification. Wishing only to be done with it, she'd counted the slow, agonizing, endless seconds when he'd settled between her legs and taken her, quickly and painfully. At last, after he made a curious noise between a cry and a grunt and she felt an alien rush of warmth deep inside her, he rolled off her. Another cursory embrace, a quick kiss on the temple, a muttered "Thank you," and he was gone.

What he'd thanked her for she didn't know, because he showed no more evidence of pleasure than she had. In the light of the next morning she'd found it quite impossible to meet his eye. She was actually grateful that they spoke only in French. She understood scarcely a word he said and spoke only in monosyllables herself.

So the scene was set for the short period in which they had shared a house, their daytime discourse as awkward as their brief nightly couplings. Cynthia had blamed herself when Windermere left. Only later did she learn that it didn't have to be like that. In the liberal circle surrounding Caro Townsend, she'd heard that both men and women took great delight in the business.

The dusky-skinned ladies in her husband's wicked pictures—they must surely have come into the house with him as a souvenir of Persia—accepted the attentions of their men with wide-eyed serenity. Some of them even appeared to be taking the more active role in couplings. Was that woman really about to put that thing in her mouth? The very idea seemed utterly outlandish. All the activities varied considerably from the one she and Windermere had shared under the blankets in bed at Beaulieu. Perhaps they didn't have beds in Persia, or if they did they were only for sleeping. These startling acts were performed in gardens, on verandas, on cushions, or just on the floor.

The shocking pictures stirred a longing that must be lust. She pressed a hand against the mound between her legs and rotated her hips to set up a friction, feeling both relief and a heightened ache. Beneath her gown and petticoats she was growing wet.

A noise outside the room broke into her trance. Horrified, she snatched away her hand. How dreadful to be discovered touching herself so indecently! Ellis might appear at any moment with a letter, or to light the lamps. She slammed shut the portfolio and tied the laces with trembling fingers. As she retreated to her parlor the passage was empty except for Pudge, chasing a little ball of woolen yarn Cynthia had given her.

Amid the delicate paneling and gilt furnishings of her favorite room she felt alien, savage, no longer the perfect domestic lady with her cat. She wanted to burst out of her skin, or at least out of her clothes, and rub herself against something in the most indecorous fashion. She was a wild thing with a yawning appetite, but not for food or drink. Hard as it was for her to admit, she wanted a man.

Well, she thought. She had one. She had a husband. While he hadn't been much good in the past, his kiss the other night promised improvement. Perhaps he had acquired these pictures for educational purposes. If he wanted to learn how to please a woman, better that she should be the beneficiary of his studies than another woman. Lady Belinda Radcliffe came to mind.

With a forefinger she traced the rim of her lips, reliving that all too brief union of breath and heat. She'd enjoyed Julian's kisses but she could no longer remember them. Yet every moment of Damian's was imprinted on her skin.

She hadn't forgiven him for the past, but he was her husband, the only one she was ever likely to have. While she might not trust him with her heart, there was no reason she couldn't enjoy his body. It was time to let him back into her bed in the full meaning of the word.

Cynthia dined alone, her husband having an engagement at his club. Now she was alone in bed, listening to unidentifiable sounds filtered through the connecting door, muffled thuds whose cause she couldn't guess. Wearing her prettiest, thinnest nightgown made her feel a fool. Since it seemed she would not have the company of a large, warm body for the night, she might as well wear flannel. Having been ejected from her room three nights ago, Damian apparently needed to be told the exile wasn't permanent. To the indignation of Pudge, whose small, warm body was curled up in the crook of her neck, she pushed aside the covers just as the door, finally, opened.

Her husband stood in the doorway dressed in his Persian banyan and slippers, looking softer and less sure of himself than usual. Or perhaps the sleek mask appeared to have slipped because his dark hair was slightly damp and all awry. Illusion or not, the slight air of disorder suited him. Her heart danced a jig.

"Good evening, my lord," she said breathily. "Is there anything I can do for you?" She essayed an alluring smile and felt even more foolish.

Whatever the result of her own effort, his smile allured her all right. "I came to extend an invitation. I thought you might like to try my new mattress."

Now her heart raced in earnest. "Mine is very comfortable," she managed to murmur.

"I have no complaint about the quality of bedding in either room, only the company."

"Is it me or Pudge you object to?" She sent him an arch look and her confidence grew. Flirtatious nonsense she could manage.

"The question barely merits a response. I should have said the lack of company is what irks me." His voice dropped. "I have missed you."

"Oh?"

"I have something to show you in my chamber,"

he said, crossing the room and extending a hand. "Will you honor me with your presence?"

The intensity of his gaze robbed her of her voice again. It dropped from her face to rake the length of her semi-recumbent body. Considering this attention was exactly what she wanted from the evening, her shyness was absurd. Instead of the unruffled confidence of those well-pleasured Persian ladies, she felt stiff and gauche, as though she were the old Cynthia waiting in terror for a disagreeable marital duty. With a jerk she withdrew her exposed knees into the shelter of her nightgown, alarming Pudge, who jumped off the bed and scampered into the adjoining chamber.

"If you want your cat back you'll have to come and get her." His grin turned gleeful, almost boyish. She'd never seen Damian so little the polished diplomat.

"Since you put it that way," she said with dignity, "I accept your invitation, my lord." She slid off the bed, straightened her skirt, and placed her hand on his arm with mock formality.

"I must remember, my lady, that extortion and kidnapping work with you where a polite request fails."

The earl's dour bedchamber was transformed. The dark red velvet counterpane had been torn from the bed and laid on the floor, covering the rather ugly Wilton carpet. Cushions, taken from all parts of the house, were arranged in careless heaps in a semi-circle, creating a sort of nest. Soft lamplight flickered over the scene, and an exotic and totally unfamiliar scent pervaded the room.

"I thought I'd offer you a little taste of Persia," he said.

Her body thrummed with nerves and excitement. Damian had brought those wicked pictures home with him. Did he intend to imitate them with her? Some of them? All? Her cheeks heated violently as she remembered certain activities. He didn't know she had seen them. Of course it was possible he intended merely to entertain her with traveler's tales of the East, but she didn't think so. She might still be relatively innocent, but she recognized a setting for seduction when she saw it.

"Take a cushion," he said.

She sat primly, tucking her legs beside her, her back scarcely touching the wall of pillows. Through the fine cambric of her nightgown she could feel velvet under her bottom and thigh. In those pictures the couples had been naked. She lowered her eyelids and imagined the caress of velvet on bare skin, the heat of his eyes on her utterly exposed body. Her wanton thoughts shamed and thrilled her as a wet heat flooded her privates. She took a deep, calming breath and felt a strange herbal smoke fill her nostrils.

Pudge's little head butted her knee. As she lowered her hand to respond to the demand for attention, Damian swooped in and removed the kitten.

He carried her gently but firmly out of the room, placed her on Cynthia's bed, and returned, shutting the door behind him. "What we are about to do is not suitable for the sight of children," he said.

"And what would that be?" she asked with delicious anticipation.

"Eating and drinking and talking, and so forth."

"That sounds innocent enough."

" 'So forth' covers a multitude of sins."

Damian would have liked to use the erotic miniatures as an aid in the seduction of his wife, but he feared such explicit portrayals of amorous behavior would drive her into a fit of the vapors. She might have entered into an adulterous affair with Julian Fortescue, but he was certain that she was neither brazen nor highly experienced, nothing like Lady Belinda Radcliffe.

He made himself remember what he'd tried to forget: the joyless nature of their previous couplings. As the man of experience he should have done better, made greater efforts to soothe the frigidity of her frightened virgin body. Now he would spare no trouble to dispel their own past, as well as any desire to return to her lover. But to make her entirely his, she would need to be softened up, gentled into his bed like a shy mare. Luckily, indecent pictures were not all he'd brought back from Persia.

Among the hideous things that Cynthia had inexplicably brought into Windermere House was a pair of censers, the sort of overelaborate French object Damian most disliked. Intended for incense, there was nothing holy about them. On the contrary, they were perfect for the burning of hemp resin. The popular Eastern intoxicant was most powerful smoked in a hookah, but Damian didn't want to render his wife stupefied, merely relaxed.

He found her enchanting: prim and shy one minute, then a siren would peep out from the proper interior, sending blood rushing to his groin and his desire shooting into the heavens.

"What do you think of the bhang?"

"What a funny word," she said with a giggle. "What does it mean?"

He took up one of the censers and knelt on the velvet lawn, letting the fragrant smoke fill the space between them. "Breathe in," he said. "This is resin of the hemp plant, known to the Turks as hashish. The traveler Samuel Purchas claimed that eating it causes mirth and dalliance and makes one appear to be drunk."

She sniffed cautiously. "And what will smelling it do?"

"Not so much. Merely make us relaxed and happy. Careful," he said when a fat, fair curl almost landed in the fragrant cinders. "We don't want to set you on fire." He tucked the errant lock behind her ear.

"Are you relaxed and happy?" She gazed at him

gravely, while taking another deep breath. "It's hard to tell with you."

"Becoming more so every minute."

"That's a very peculiar object."

"You bought it, my lady."

"Did I? How very odd of me." She blinked. "I never really looked at it before. Those black figures holding up the bowl are women with hooves."

"What the French describe as *faunesses*."

"You don't think my French is very good, do you?"

"Never mind that now." The last thing he wanted to remind her of was his behavior at Beaulieu. He set the ebony and gilt censer carefully on the floor, close enough to waft its magic in their direction but out of kicking range. He intended it get them recumbent and kicking as soon as possible.

"Say something to me in French and see if I understand it."

Remembering her painful incomprehension of his honeymoon small talk, he spoke rapidly and said exactly what he meant. "*Je veux te foutre.*" As expected, she looked baffled by the vulgarism. Talking dirty was a form of stimulation Damian happened to enjoy and he could take advantage of her limited knowledge of French to indulge himself without shocking her. Blood roared to his cock, which pressed against the silk of his banyan. Apparently unaware of his arousal, Cynthia watched his face with a silly smile on her sweet pink mouth, which gave him ideas and made him even harder. She looked so innocent and pure in white linen, buttoned to the neck. "*Je veux te foutre*," he repeated.

He wanted to fuck her, very badly, and much else besides.

"*Je veux te baiser dans ta cave et te fair jouir pendant que tu suce ma queue. Je veux que nous jouissons, tous les deux.*"

"That all sounds very, very lovely. It's a beautiful language."

"Very, very lovely. As are you."

"The language of love. I know a French song," she confided with a grave air.

"Sing it." Against all reason he hoped it was a naughty one.

"*Sur le pont d'Avignon*
"*L'on y danse, l'on y danse.*"

No such luck.

She sang the French nursery rhyme in a light, tuneful soprano, like the world's most desirable governess. He joined in through four verses and the chorus, their harmony spoiled by laughter on her part, and distraction on his. He couldn't be expected to remember what beautiful ladies were doing on a French bridge when he had an even lovelier one in his English chamber.

"*L'on y danse tous en rond,*" she concluded with a gasp. Giggling like a schoolgirl, she collapsed against him, giving him the chance to sweep her backward into the nest of cushions.

"You see," she said. "My French is excellent."

"*Im-pec-ca-ble*." He hovered over her, supported by his arms. "So good that you deserve a reward."

"What?" She giggled again.

The bhang was doing its job. Mirth had been achieved, now on to dalliance. His mouth hovered, inches from the rosy lips.

"If you stop laughing, I'll give you a sweetmeat."

Her eyed grew huge. "And if I don't?"

He knew what he wanted to do and he rather thought she wanted the same. "You'll have to wait and find out," he fenced, "but I don't advise it."

His reward was not another giggle but a rich laugh from deep in her belly that invited him to nameless delights. Having expected to direct the night's encounter, he felt his control slipping away. His wife, deliberately or not, was exerting her own influence on the progress of events. With a groan he forgot about the dish of Persian delicacies that had been the planned next step in his seduction. Resting back on his side, he placed his hands on her hips and tugged her against his aching erection at the same time that she cast her arms about his neck.

He couldn't have said who kissed whom first but declared it a tie because when it came down to it, who cared? All that mattered was she was intoxicating and finally he was going to put an end to far too long a celibacy. Somehow his exhilarated brain kept a grasp on his good intentions. His physical condition was approaching desperation and he doubted he'd last long enough to please anyone in his current state. He needed to slow down.

She lolled against the cushions, a golden angel in a den of iniquity, her eyes big and dreamy, her hair a honeyed cloud, her lips plump and dark from his kisses and asking for more. She represented an invitation to sin as sultry as any Persian houri, despite her nightgown, covering her from chin to toe like a nun. True, it was an improvement over the thick flannel shroud. It fell smoothly about her curves, giving him a better impression of her figure than he'd yet been afforded: high breasts, a small waist, and a lovely curve of the hips. Through the superfine cambric he caught a shadowy impression of nipples; dark pink, he fancied. His favorite kind. With thickened fingers he unlooped the button at her neck, and couldn't resist the indentation of her collarbone, allowing himself a quick taste of the tender skin. She arched into his mouth and the nightgown fell open, revealing round, pert breasts that his palms itched to touch. "You are lovely," he whispered. "I want to see all of you."

He could have bit his tongue, thinking he was going too fast, but he needn't have worried. The fragrant smoke or some other cause had shredded her inhibitions. With two shrugs and a wriggle she got out of her nightdress, tossing it aside, and arranged herself on the claret-colored velvet like a goddess in an Italian painting. She took his breath away. How could he have ever made the mistake of thinking her short and dumpy? She was a pocket Venus, perfectly proportioned, with ravishing curves to her arms and thighs, and narrow waist above a gently swelling belly.

"You are absolutely made to be naked," he said with a voice full of awe. "It's a crime that such beauty should be hidden."

"A hanging offense or transportation?"

Her smile would entice a monastery of abbots to mass fornication. She stretched like a sensual cat, undulating her hips to draw attention to the blond thatch of her pubis. The anticipation of possession tortured him. It was impossible to believe that he'd had her before, unaware what a treasure he had captured. But now he had to make sure that she was so incredibly satisfied that she would never again give Julian Fortescue as much as a passing thought.

And so, with the utmost concentration, he pleasured her with all the skill he could muster, using hands and mouth to adore the sweet breast, the soft belly, and finally the wet, spicy gateway to her sex.

"Oh Lord, Damian," she moaned beneath the ministrations of his tongue, urging him to greater efforts.

"No you don't," he muttered as she twisted from side to side. Grasping her curvy little bottom, he held her still, gaining a little extra glee for himself in reining in her movements. He made her take her pleasure from him, despite her fluttering attempts at escape from the intensity of sensation.

"Stop!" she cried. "Don't stop!" No way would he stop. Following the rhythm of her ascent to bliss, he increased his pace until she gave a shriek and shot into fulfillment. Her taste, her earthy woman's scent, her cries of joy, flooded his senses. He felt the quivers of her climax in his mouth and gave her a few more strokes, sending her over the top again.

Letting her trembling subside, he scrambled up and caught her in his arms, relishing the astonished delight on her face. "I had no idea," she said, shaking her head and rubbing her nose in his chest in a clumsy, endearing way.

Take that, Julian Fortescue, he thought smugly. *Some of us know how to please a woman.*

"Damian," she whispered.

"Yes, my sweet?"

"That's no way to make a child."

"No," he said between a laugh and a grunt. "That bit comes next." Pray God she'd be ready soon. He was ready to explode.

"You do want a son, don't you?"

"I can't say it's the topic uppermost in my mind now."

"I am sorry there was no child," she whispered, "but I suppose you really didn't care."

He had no idea what she was talking about. It was Chorley who was obsessed with an heir, not him. He had no interest in a squalling infant, only in a bout of fast, sweaty, mind-destroying copulation as soon as possible. He was so hard he thought he was going to die.

"Don't think about that now," he whispered, running a trail of kisses down her neck to her bosom. "Let's just enjoy ourselves." He took one pink nipple between his lips and felt it stiffen as he sucked. Her breath slowed as he caressed her midriff.

"Damian," she said dreamily. "What's that smoky stuff called?"

"Bhang. Or hashish."

"It causes mirth and dalliance?"

"That's right. And drunkenness, just the appearance of it."

"What's the difference?"

"You don't feel so bad the next morning."

"Tha's good." She slurred her words and her breathing changed again, coming slow and deep. "Tha's very good. I feel very good now. Do you feel good, Damian? I hope so."

"Very good, and I fully expect to feel even better in the near future."

Soon. Very soon indeed.

He made himself pay a minute's more attention to her glorious breasts—no hardship, and eliciting sweet murmurs of pleasure—until he could take no more. Now, at long last, it was his turn. Anticipation of burying his aching cock in her tight, wet heat sent his brain awhirl. He positioned himself over her but held off a few more seconds. Her smug smile, promising that she would enjoy the coming union as much as he, surely merited a kiss.

His lips descended to be met by a huff of warm breath and a funny little snort.

"Cynthia?" Her eyes had closed. "Hell and damnation."

She had nodded off to sleep.

No more bhang for Lady Windermere, he resolved.

Chapter 13

Cynthia awoke feeling extraordinarily well. She'd sometimes drunk too much wine at Caro's parties and the mornings had not been enjoyable. This bhang stuff was marvelous: all the benefits of wine without the headache. Also, just possibly, her husband had contributed to her state of physical content.

She couldn't recall how the evening ended or how she'd returned to her own bed. Other memories were so dreamlike that she questioned their realty. Had she lain before Damian, naked as a Persian lady, letting him look at her and reveling in his admiration? Her belly turned hot and heavy. She peeked under the sheet and realized that she was naked, still. In that case, the next thing must have happened too. The thing he'd done to her with his mouth. Since she could never have conceived of such a thing in a thousand years, it hadn't been a product of her imagination. Her powers of invention were beyond anything so extraordinarily delicious. The very recollection made her blush from head to foot with shame and clench inside with longing for a repetition.

Had Damian . . . had they . . . coupled? She wished she could remember. She didn't want to have missed it since she was fairly certain it would have been much, much better than the last time.

Not a sound could be detected in his bedchamber. Either he was up and about or still abed. She had no idea of the time, except that a crack of light through the curtains told her it was past dawn. On most occasions since his return when he had shared her bed, Damian had left before she awoke. A few days ago she had found a daylight encounter across the pillows excruciatingly awkward; today she would have been intrigued . . .

The difference between their earlier marital relations and last night could not have been greater. She wondered if he'd gained the knowledge to give pleasure from exotic naked creatures among the marble palaces of Persia and wasn't sure how she felt about that. He was her husband and owed her fidelity, just as she owed it to him. *She* had kept faith with the marriage.

Barely.

She had come very close to betraying her vows with Denford. Could she really blame Damian if he had succumbed to temptation? She should forgive him, even if the thought of him cavorting with another woman made her feel a little queasy. Correction. Damian cavorting in a distant land with an unknown woman he'd never see again. That made her queasy. The thought of him doing deliciously indecent things with Lady Belinda Radcliffe in London made her want to howl.

But she was feeling optimistic this morning, rather as she had the morning of her wedding. When she had walked into church on her uncle's arm, sunshine poured in through the clear windows in the nave, bathing the lovely golden stone in light. A single rose window of stained glass cast its kaleidoscope of color onto the path before her, the well-trodden stone floor that carried her inexorably toward the vicar, waiting to conduct the ceremony that would make her Countess of Windermere, and the man who would bestow the title on his wife.

Cynthia had willed him to turn, to look, to smile at his bride. To show some sign that he welcomed this marriage to an ordinary girl of undistinguished birth and little beauty. Would he ever love her? Aunt Lavinia had assured her that if she obeyed him and gave him a son, he would love her as a husband always loved a dutiful wife. As for Cynthia's own feelings, all he needed to do was treat her with ordinary kindness and she would honor him; it wouldn't take much more to make her fall all the way in love.

He'd disappointed her dreadfully, but she didn't want to cling to her grudge. Perhaps he hadn't bedded another woman since their marriage, neither Persian temptress nor London siren. In that case, since evidence suggested he knew better, the dismal nature of his previous lovemaking must be attributed to carelessness and indifference. Optimism urged her to hope the change for the better would be permanent.

She rang for her maid and learned that His Lordship had gone out riding. She dressed to look her best, and as she descended the stairs, a scent of spices sweetened the air. Her cook was preparing Christmas delicacies. Since her parents' deaths, Christmas had never been a happy season for her. Last Yuletide had been spent at Beaulieu Manor with no one but the servants for company.

This year she'd looked forward to spending the holiday in Hampshire with the Duke and Duchess of Castleton. When Windermere's return drew her back to London, she'd made preparations, ensuring that the servants had a suitable feast as well as extra wages on St. Stephen's Day. Perhaps it was the aroma of cinnamon and cloves and nutmeg in the hall that filled her heart with the joy that legend, literature, and faded memories ascribed to the birth of Christ. She wanted wassail and carols, holly and mistletoe. And gifts. The arrival of the new girl at Flowers Street had postponed her gift giving there. And she had nothing for her husband. Christmas Eve wasn't too late to find the perfect token to celebrate their better, even ecstatic future, together.

She contemplated the possibility of a marriage she'd once dreamed of. A marriage like that of her parents. They might have died when she was only ten, but she could still remember the warmth and affection that infused their curate's cottage and lingered through all the years at school and the chilly air of her uncle's house. The warmth that had given her hope that she too would one day come together with a man in mutual respect and even love. The worst thing Windermere's desertion had done to her was to destroy that aspiration. With every act of negligence and betrayal it had drained away until she was left without prospect of the love she craved.

Now, perhaps foolishly, hope had been reborn, a fluttering dove demanding release from the cage of her disillusioned heart. Before she allowed it freedom she had to face the unkindest cut dealt her by her husband. Remembering the cruel letter, the few careless words engraved on her mind, her blood didn't boil as it used to, but her happy glow dulled a little.

Returning from his morning exercise, Damian was sorry to be informed that Her Ladyship was up, breakfasted, and in her parlor. He would have enjoyed finding her still in bed and in need of arousal. Instead he had no reason to postpone one or two disagreeable matters that needed to be addressed. Once he had cleared the air with Cynthia, laid down the law, kindly but firmly, about her future behavior, then they could move on to pure pleasure. Please God, before he went mad.

He found her on the floor in her parlor surrounded by paper and cloth and ribbon and two large hampers.

She looked up, eyes sparkling and cheeks delicately tinged with pink. He picked his way through the clutter and offered his hand. "You are busy this morning, Cynthia."

"Getting ready for tomorrow." She let him help her to her feet, looking delightfully rumpled. On impulse he seized her waist, pulled her close, and gave her a quick kiss.

"I haven't hung the mistletoe yet," she said, flustered.

"I don't need any ancient custom to kiss my wife," he said, and kissed her again, more thoroughly.

The dazed look in her eyes reminded him of last night. A good sign that he'd achieved the effect without benefit of foreign stimulants. He pulled her closer, against the evidence of his burgeoning interest. She, alas, retreated, pulling out of his arms. "It's not even ten o'clock, my lord. I have much to prepare and I still have shopping to do."

"Shall I come with you?"

"That would be delightful," she said, though obviously not pleased by the suggestion, "but not this time. You would find my errands very dull. You wouldn't wish to wait through a fitting with my dressmaker."

"Just as well. I expect Bingham in an hour. Don't forget that we dine with the Radcliffes tomorrow."

That pleased her even less. "I thought we might enjoy our Christmas dinner together."

"I'd prefer it too, but I promised. It's impolite to cancel an invitation that we have accepted."

"That *you* have accepted."

She was being unreasonable, he thought, but he wished to be conciliatory. "I am not used to consulting anyone else about my engagements. I promise to do better in the future." She nodded with a mere twitch of a smile. For some reason she wasn't looking forward to the Radcliffes' feast. "If you are nervous about such a distinguished gathering, you need not worry. I am sure you can manage well, and I promise to stay at your side and assist you in any awkwardness. You will quickly learn how to comport yourself."

"Thank you, my lord. I cannot tell you how relieved I am." He might almost have thought her sarcastic but her face was quite innocent of edge.

"Come, sit with me. I have something I wish to say to you."

She nodded. "We do need to talk."

Settling her on a sofa, he perched beside her and took her hands. "First of all, let me say that I enjoyed last night and look forward to more such occasions." She blushed scarlet and he swooped in to whisper, "Though they may end in different ways," and kissed her again.

She drew back and coughed. "My lord . . . Damian. You said you had something to say to me."

"I do. I want to clear up a few things that lie between us. After that I believe we shall be able to do extremely well together."

"I feel the same way."

He opened magnanimously. "Our marriage started badly, I know, and largely through my own fault. I won't offer an excuse but perhaps an explanation. I felt I had been dragooned into the match by Mr. Chorley."

Her eyes widened but she said nothing, merely tilted her head.

"I had finally set aside enough money to purchase Beaulieu. I thought I had come to terms with the owner when I learned he'd sold it to Chorley instead. Your uncle made it very clear that if I ever wished to repossess my mother's estate, it would be through a marital alliance with his family."

She freed her hands and raised them to burning cheeks. "I am sorry. I didn't know."

"I suspected you might not. Yet you agreed to the marriage. You spoke your vows."

"I was not forced to accept you," she said softly, and looked away.

"There is no shame in a woman agreeing to an advantageous match. We both wed with perfectly rational ambitions and I was wrong to blame you when all the duress was on the part of your uncle." She nodded with a little more vigor. He had the impression she was holding something back. If it saved her pride not to have to admit she liked the idea of wedding an earl, he would allow her that indulgence. "I'm glad we've cleared that up," he said.

"Have we?"

"Certainly! We have admitted that neither of us came into the marriage with the most praise-worthy of motives. Let us put them behind us and move forward."

"Since we are married, Damian," she said, "mutual harmony is a desirable state."

He leaned in and whispered, "After last night I am especially anxious to establish that harmony."

She blushed deeply and looked down at her lap, deliciously confused. He could imagine finally coming to a place where he had nothing to regret about his bride. First he needed to deal with great-est obstacle that lay between them. After that . . . Was it likely that a proper wife would like to take a trip to the bedchamber in the middle of the day? No, forget a hypothetical wife. Would *his* wife, would Cynthia, be ready to be made love to in broad daylight? Tempted to try his luck right away, he made himself attend to the less pleasant order of business. First the medicine, then the sweetener. For both of them.

"There's one more thing. I refer to what happened in my absence. It is not a subject I wish to discuss in detail, but we need to put it behind us." Her head jerked up to meet his gaze. He would have expected guilt; instead she looked eager. "I must insist," he said firmly, "that you cut off your connection with the Duke of Denford."

He was being generous and reasonable. Like many civilized men before him, he was ready to put aside her unfortunate transgression in the interests of his family's future. Unfortunately, he wasn't feeling civilized. Instead his chest felt ready to explode and he wanted to berate her in a way no diplomat worth his salt would do. And then he wanted to hunt down Julian Fortescue and administer a long overdue beating.

He summoned his control and spoke calmly, with an air of undeniable command. "There is no need for you ever to see or speak to him again, except when unavoidable in the course of normal social events." There. The law had been laid down.

She seemed puzzled. "I thought you and he had made up your differences. You invited him to dinner."

"As it happens I have business with Denford. What's between him and me, past and present, is none of your affair."

"He is also our neighbor. Am I supposed to cut him on the street? I have been alone this past year, my lord, and Julian has been my friend."

He couldn't believe his ears. Instead of penitence she was arguing with him. He realized she only now addressed him as "my lord" when she was annoyed. Yet she was the one who was at fault. Did she intend to carry on a relationship with her cicisbeo under the very eyes of her husband?

He wouldn't have it. The Earls of Windermere were no decadent Venetians. Even if he were to agree to the kind of complacent marriage that was common enough even in England—like that of the Radcliffes, for example—she should at least expect to wait until there was an heir or two. Did she have no idea how to behave?

"Friend! Is that what you call it? That will do very well in public, my lady, but let us remove our gloves." He rose to stand in front of the fire, hands behind his back. She perched on the settee, cool as a cucumber in demure ivory muslin, seemingly unaware that he knew the truth. He'd see how cool and demure she'd look now. "I will not tolerate scandal, nor a cuckoo in my nest," he said flatly. "I am prepared to forgive and forget what happened in my absence, but your affair with Denford is over. He is no longer your lover."

She twisted her hands together and turned aside. "Whatever you may have heard is untrue. He has never *been* my lover."

"You face refutes your claim. Look at me and deny that you have betrayed me."

Instead of holding contrition, her eyes clashed

with his. "I do deny it. I have kept faith with you though you certainly haven't deserved it, you—you—" She sputtered, apparently unable to find a word to describe him. Or maybe what she had in mind wasn't repeatable.

"You lie, madam, and I can prove it. I saw you with Denford at Drury Lane." He wasn't about to admit he hadn't recognized her.

"What of it?" she said, taken aback. For the first time she looked self-conscious, but this sign of guilt didn't last long. She rallied her forces. "And I saw you with Lady Belinda Radcliffe. What's sauce for the gander should be sauce for the goose, my lord!"

"Lady Belinda is the wife of a close colleague."

"Hah! Very close."

"Any flirtation there may have been between us was over long before our marriage. Do you honestly believe that I would take my wife to spend Christmas Day in the house of my mistress? You have a very strange notion of propriety."

She rose from the sofa and retreated toward the French window, where she stood with her hands on her hips, glaring at him. "What do I know of your notions of propriety, being a mere provincial nobody? What do I know of your manners and morals? If you cared so much for your vows you would have taken me, your wife, to the theater and I would not have needed a different escort."

This piece of specious reasoning made him want

to tear his hair out. "How was I supposed to know you were in London? I left you at Beaulieu and expected you to stay there."

"For how many years?"

"That has nothing to do with it," he said, avoiding shaky ground. "The point is, I didn't know you were in London or that the house was open. That is why I stayed at a hotel." He moved closer to give himself the advantage of height. "And we're not talking about my imagined sins but your very real ones."

"Don't wag your finger at me," she almost shrieked, stamping her foot. "You have no proof of my supposed affair with Denford because there is none." She folded her arms and stuck her nose in the air.

"I have only the evidence of my own eyes. I know what happened after the theater."

"Yes," she snapped. "The duke escorted me home." But a trace of uneasiness leached through the mask of bravado. How could it not?

He raised his eyebrows. "To the house next door to his."

"It's not my fault that his ancestors and yours bought adjacent houses back in the Dark Ages."

"It has proven most convenient for you, however. That gate between our gardens shall be walled up."

She folded her arms and raised her little pointed chin. "What's that to me?"

A huge depression settled over him. "I saw you, Cynthia," he said softly. "I came home that night and stood in the dark library, watching you return from Fortescue House. I saw you kiss him." He wished desperately that he had not.

Her indignation evaporated and her shoulders slumped. "Oh." She pinched her lips together and fell into deep thought, looking for an excuse, an explanation. He wished there was one.

"Damian," she said on a deep breath, sincerity painted over her beautiful, lying features. "It's true that I went to Julian's house that night. I went because I was angry with you. I confess that for a short time I contemplated breaking my vows. But I changed my mind. I swear that Julian and I have never been lovers, only friends. The kiss you saw meant nothing."

If any man other than Julian were involved, he might have accepted her story. He had too much respect for Julian's appeal, his cunning, and his desire for revenge to believe he would have failed. He paced over to the fireplace, staring sightlessly at the array of ornaments on either side of the big gilt clock. There was a gap in the arrangement where he had removed the censer the night before. Blinking, he tried to regain the spirit of optimism and forgiveness with which he had begun the day and this conversation. He wanted confession, pardon, and absolution to dissolve his black melancholy.

Of two things he was sure. Julian Fortescue

would not have her. And the day after an arrangement was reached over the damnable Falleron collection and that idiot Prince Heinrich of Alt-Brandenburg, he and Julian would settle their differences once and for all.

Diplomacy would not be involved.

She stood with the light behind her, a little gold and white angel. Only the convulsive fisting of her hands betrayed anxiety. She met his eye shamelessly, defiantly.

"For God's sake, Cynthia," he cried. "Won't you admit what you have done and promise not to see him again? After last night I know we can be happy together. Let us make a fresh start starting today. I'll forgive you and I swear we will never speak of the past."

"You may forgive and forget, Damian," she said with a terrible bitterness, "but I don't think I can. Not yet. Now, if you will excuse me, I have things to do."

She swept out of the room like a queen, leaving him wondering how the morning had ended with him feeling obscurely in the wrong.

Chapter 14

Behind the crumbling brick façade of Hamble & Stoke's Warehouse of General Goods in Long Acre lay a treasure house worthy of a gothic romance, if a slightly dusty one. Cynthia always forgave the soiling of her skirts as she explored the crowded aisles of the three-story building, poking through the holland-covered furnishings and stacks of oil paintings. She owed the knowledge of this out-of-the-way emporium to Caro and Julian, both of whom did business with Mr. Hamble from time to time. At first she'd merely found it an entertaining alternative to the more fashionable warehouses farther west. Then Mr. Hamble—she had a feeling Mr. Stoke was no longer in the picture—had accommodated her in a matter of business that required discretion. A business that would be hard or even impossible to continue now that Windermere was back.

"What do you think of my latest buy, then, m'lady?" The elderly proprietor found her staring at an ornate secretary desk of exaggerated proportions. "From the estate of a military gentleman. His widow didn't like it."

"She had better taste than he, then," Cynthia replied. "It's deliciously hideous."

"Not fine enough for the nobs with big houses and too big for them that would appreciate it."

"In other words, perfect for me."

Hamble used his apron to polish the folding front, revealing intricate but crude marquetry. "I bought it for a song and I can give you a good price."

She envisioned the monstrous piece fitting between the windows in the drawing room, where it would clash vilely with a boule buffet she'd bought in June. After the morning's confrontation with Damian, any compunction about her purchases had dissipated along with her plan to buy him a Christmas present. Regretfully she shook her head. "I'm sorry but today I think I need something a little less noticeable. Something small but expensive."

"Like that pair of incense burners with the naked lady satyrs. 'Orrible they were." He noticed her blush and put it down to embarrassment of the wrong sort. "Very fashionable, they are. Nothing to upset a lady's husband. I heard His Lordship was in London," he continued, not to her surprise. The secondhand trade in luxurious goods required an intimate knowledge of the activities and movements of the capital's notables. "You needn't worry, my lady. There's nothing fishy looking about the bills and invoices."

"I am afraid His Lordship will wish me to curtail my expenditures. At the very least he may wish to impose his own tastes on my household purchases." She'd noticed him look askance at some of the more outrageous items of furniture at Windermere House. "I hope you didn't buy this piece with me in mind."

"Morris over in Soho has a lot of new rich customers. He'll take it off my hands."

Hamble's dismissive sniff made her smile. Julian always said the old Cockney was as hoity-toity as a dowager duchess. She had often wondered why he didn't move his shop to a better address. He certainly had the knowledge to cater to a more exclusive clientele.

"I am glad, Mr. Hamble. I am grateful for all your help."

"I hope I can continue to assist you," he said, nodding his grizzled head. "I don't often see your class of lady in my warehouse."

Engrossed in their conversation, neither had noticed the front door open. "And that, my dear Hamble," said a deep voice, "is entirely your fault. You could open up in Bond Street but I daresay you lack the requisite level of obsequiousness."

Cynthia jumped and spun around. "Julian!"

"Your Grace."

"Fancy seeing you here, Cynthia."

"Did you expect me?" she said warily. He was the last person she wished to meet today, especially under circumstances that could be interpreted as clandestine.

"I came to see if Hamble would like to take some bad paintings off my hands. Your presence is a delightful bonus. Come to think of it, one or two of the pictures would suit you very well. How convenient that we should all meet like this."

"I'm not buying pictures today."

"What a shame."

"My lady has expressed an interest in smaller objects."

"I know where you keep them. Let me take Lady Windermere up to the first floor while you have a look at the pictures my servant is bringing in." He offered his arm in a manner that brooked no denial. "My dear Cynthia," he said, as they climbed the bare wooden stairs. "Why do I have the impression that you aren't pleased to see me? I am crushed."

"We shouldn't be meeting like this. I am not comfortable."

"And after I accepted my dismissal with such grace too, just so that we could avoid awkwardness."

It was the first time they'd been alone since they'd parted in the garden the night of the theater, but that wasn't what she meant. She could have

changed the subject, or changed her plans and
gone downstairs again. Wiser still, climbed into
her carriage and driven away. But she was tired of
secrets and discretion. She felt free to say anything
she wanted to Julian precisely because he wasn't
her husband and she didn't ultimately care what he
thought or believed. She stopped on the landing,
dropped her arm, and stepped back. She always
had to tilt her head to meet the duke's eyes, which
reflected their usual cynical amusement.

"We shouldn't meet like this. Damian accused
me of having an affair with you."

"If only it were true."

"Stop it."

He rested both hands on the silver knob of his
cane and stared down his large nose at her. "I don't
see why you are upset, my dear Cynthia. Isn't that
what you wanted him to think?"

"No. Yes. I suppose so. When he was away I
wanted him to hear rumors and be sorry."

It had started as an amusing game, shocking the
members of the *ton*, the people of Damian's world
who had ignored her. She wanted her husband to
see she didn't give a damn about him and his neglect, and to show him that another man desired
her, even if he did not. She clenched her fists. "I feel
tawdry."

And worse. A knot had been forming in her
stomach since she'd swept out of her husband's
presence that morning in a state of high indig-

nation. By choosing Julian for her instrument of "showing" Damian, she might have ruined her chances of repairing her marriage.

"You used me," he said, with a one-sided grin. "You trifled with my affections."

Through her distress, a smile tugged the corner of her mouth. "And you used me in the same way."

"Of course."

"So we are even."

"Certainly not! I am a big bad duke and you are a poor little girl from the country, not used to the wicked ways of town."

"True. Caro always warned me you were up to no good and I was too trusting to see it."

"It's really quite remarkable that you resisted my best seduction and confounded my expectations. But it is not too late to change that lamentable state of affairs. I know a place we can go to be alone and no one will know. Unless, of course, you decide to tell Damian all about it afterward. I do wish you would. You could break the news in the garden while I watched through the gate."

Julian always amused her and today she needed it. "Thank you for the kind offer, Your Grace, but I believe I must once again decline. Instead you can advise me on the purchase of some small objects for which Hamble can overcharge me."

Julian opened the dusty glass doors of a baroque cabinet and removed a malachite vase with gilt handles and a black marble plinth. "It would make a splendid Christmas gift for dear Damian. It's a poor substitute for having you in my bed, but I'd like to inflict this brute on Windermere. I wonder how much Hamble would have the gall to bill him for it."

"You are a wicked man, Julian, though you make me laugh, against my better judgment. I must ask you to stop speaking to me about my husband, unless you do it with respect."

Julian raised a hand to fend off her fierce demand. "Where's the fun in that?"

"The only thing I want to hear from you about Windermere is what happened between you."

She'd asked about the cause of their quarrel a dozen times before and expected to be turned off with another meaningless evasion.

"Come," he said, and guided her across the room. He removed the dust sheet from a low settee, not unlike the one in her morning room, but covered in a gloomy tapestry.

She sat down gingerly, finding it surprisingly comfortable. Julian sank down beside her. Though he leaned back and stretched out his long, black-clad legs, she felt his tension. "Don't say you are finally going to tell me?"

"I think it's time." She had rarely heard him speak so gravely. "It started on his twenty-first birthday. Robert and I took him to dinner to celebrate. We all drank too much and went on to Cruikshank's."

"What is that?"

"A gaming hell."

"Oh dear." Cynthia knew all about Townsend's addiction to play that had ended by leaving Caro almost penniless.

"We drank, we played, we drank some more."

"*Damian* did? I know he wasn't always as sober as he is now, but still."

"He drank. We all drank. We played hazard and drank some more. Damian lost."

"How much? Was it a lot?"

"Not how much, but what. He'd come into possession of his mother's estate that day."

Cynthia gasped and covered her mouth. "Beaulieu! He lost Beaulieu. Did he lose it to you?"

"I dropped out of the game because I couldn't afford the stakes. He lost it to Robert."

"Robert was his friend. Couldn't he get it back?"

Julian's voice dropped to a croak. "Damian passed out dead drunk after the losing hand. Robert joined another table. By the next morning he'd lost everything he had on him."

"Beaulieu," she whispered.

"His inheritance from his mother gone in one mad night. He was never the same again."

"I understand why he changed after that, and why he broke with Robert. But why you?"

"He blamed me." His voice was soft and emotionless. "When he passed out I dragged him into a hackney and took him home. He said if I'd been there I could have stopped Robert."

"Could you?"

"Yes."

She laid her hand over his. "I don't see how it was your fault. It sounds like you only did what you thought was right."

"Damian lost Beaulieu and I lost Damian. Bloody Robert."

"Did he stop speaking to you, just like that?"

"He went north, to Amblethorpe to break the news to his father. When he came back to London he took up with the government set."

How tragic for both young men. Damian had been the greater loser, but she sensed that the loss of their friendship had been hard for Julian too. She'd always felt deep waters flowed beneath Denford's brittle cynicism. His hurt must have been deep indeed that he would seduce his former friend's wife in revenge. In fact, the retaliation seemed excessive to the offense.

"What did he do to you?" she asked.

"I was in discussions about a collection of pictures. It was the most important purchase I'd ever made and vital to my future as a dealer in Old Masters. I had patrons ready to fight over the most important works. Damian ruined it for me."

"Are you certain? Would he have been so petty?"

"Ask Sir Richard Radcliffe about the Poussins that hang in his gilded Grosvenor Square saloon. Ask Radcliffe how he found out about a collection that belonged to a friend of the late Lord Windermere. Damian and I were the only ones that knew about them until somehow, by a strange coincidence, his new patron made a better offer. Ask Radcliffe how he was able to buy them from under my nose."

"I'd rather ask Damian."

"You want to believe him and not me?" Julian was showing ragged edges that were new to her.

"All I *want* is to hear both sides of the story," she said sharply. "Don't you think I have the right since I've been brought into your quarrel like a bone between a pair of snapping dogs?"

"An infelicitous image, not least because you, my dear Cynthia, are the farthest thing imaginable from a dry bone. You are a much more luscious prize." His cynical façade was back in place and his drawl made her want to slap him.

She struggled up from the low seat. "I must find Hamble and conclude today's business. Then I'm going home."

He tugged at her wrist and she tumbled back, almost landing in his lap. "Don't go off in a huff. I apologize for calling you luscious, though I refuse to take it back."

"You're impossible."

"I don't have so many friends that I can afford to quarrel with you."

"Are we friends?" she asked, twisting free of him.

"Apparently it's what I have to settle for."

She stared at him. Never for a moment had she thought Julian had any feelings for her beyond a mild affection. She had no illusions about his motives in pursuing her. Her fear had always been that she would fall in love with him, never the other way around. Yet he looked at her as though he really cared.

"I'm sorry there can be nothing more." she said. "You are a much better man than you pretend to be."

He turned his head and addressed a plant stand sitting next to their sofa. "Next she's going to tell me that one day I will find a woman I can truly love."

"I wish I could fall in love with you. Or I would if I wasn't married. But only because you always make me laugh."

"Does he make you laugh?"

She thought about the bhang and giggled.

"He doesn't deserve you."

"No, but I wish he did."

The confrontation with his wife ran through Damian's mind as he sat in the library waiting for Bingham. Nothing seemed amiss with the latest batch of reports from his London agent, beyond the excessive amounts Cynthia spent on clothes and furnishings. Her household decorative purchases made him shudder. He must tell her not to buy any more furniture or pictures without consulting him first.

However, he couldn't quarrel with her efforts at the dressmaker. She bore almost no resemblance to the young woman he had wed. The fact that he'd failed to recognize her at Drury Lane bore testament to her transformation from dowdy provincial to ravishing London beauty. Too bad that her morals had made the same journey.

The hypocrisy of the thought scratched his conscience. Did he not wish for a fashionable wife who would help advance his career? There had never been a chance that his marriage would become a love match like that of his parents, an ill-matched but curiously happy pair. He would settle for shared ambitions and compatibility in the bedchamber.

His breath shortened. Why wouldn't she agree to give up Denford? All she had to do was admit her sin, accept his forgiveness, and they could be perfectly happy together.

Bingham, a partner in a respected firm that had handled the Lewis family affairs for half a century, was announced "Tell me," Damian asked, once the formalities had been observed and a new series of reports delivered, "how did it come about that Lady Windermere occupies this house? I expected it would be let once I left the country."

"In the hurry of your departure, you forgot to leave instructions. When Lord Morton inquired as to its availability this spring, I wrote to Markham at Beaulieu to see if you had mentioned the matter to him and he asked Her Ladyship. I understand she decided to come to London to visit the warehouses for the redecoration of the manor, and to consult a physician." He looked anxiously at his employer. "I saw no reason why she shouldn't use the house under the circumstances."

"No reason at all, Bingham." He wished she'd remained in the country, however. Julian Fortescue would never have encountered her had she been safe in Oxfordshire. "Is there anything else?"

"I hesitate to bring this up, but there is an oddity that bears investigation with regard to Lady Windermere's expenditures. She has bought a good many pieces from a warehouse in Long Acre."

"Hamble & Stoke. Never heard of it." Damian leafed through a sheaf of bills, recognizing some of the more egregious examples of Cynthia's bad taste. "Fifty guineas seems high for a miserably uncomfortable sofa, and I wouldn't take the still life in the hall at any price. Still, I won't complain. Her extravagance doesn't threaten to outrun the constable, does it?"

"No indeed. Mr. Chorley's settlement was generous and will be more so when a happy event should occur." Bingham cleared his throat. "Now that Your Lordship has returned," he added delicately.

Not as things stood at present. If he couldn't get back into Cynthia's bed there was no chance of reaping the greater benefit of the dynastic alliance. Also he would explode from frustration.

It wasn't just the lovemaking he'd regret either. A smile played on his lips as he thought about her kindness to Oliver and Pudge, the way her brow creased when she was thinking seriously, even her surprising sarcastic edge when he displeased her. Somehow he had to make up their quarrel.

"Just pay the bills and don't worry about it, Bingham."

"I have done so, my lord. Also the account from a carrier for transporting Lady Windermere's purchases from Long Acre to Hanover Square. Nothing seemed out of order until the last submission from the latter. For some reason the carrier's bill was attached to copies of invoices from Hamble & Stoke. A clerk in my office noticed that the sums are different from those submitted to us for payment."

He laid two sheets of paper side by side on the table. The bill from Hamble & Stoke, signed by William Hamble, listed half a dozen items, including "A pair of bronze and gilt incense burners, French. 35 guineas." The entire figure came to just under two hundred guineas. The list attached to the carrier's invoice was the same, though written by a different hand, a neat copperplate typical of a professional clerk. The same except for the prices. The incense burners were fifteen guineas and the total one hundred and ten.

"Are the invoices usually attached to the carrier's bill?"

"No. It must have been an aberration."

"Or a mistake." Damian lifted his eyebrows at his employee and the two men shook their head in unison. "Or a fraud."

"I am afraid so, my lord. I fear Her Ladyship has fallen among thieves, as the saying goes."

"She isn't used to London ways."

"Shall I pursue the matter further and prepare a suit?" Bingham asked.

"No. Leave these with me for the moment."

Half an hour later, he was in a hackney heading for Covent Garden, pondering what happened to the difference between the true price of the furnishings and that paid out by Bingham. The money went to Hamble but what did he do with it? Damian didn't know if Bingham had been tactful, or whether he had really failed to notice that there was no reason for Hamble to establish a complicated system of false invoices if he was merely overcharging a wealthy customer. He had to wonder if the wealthy customer was a party to the scheme.

Why would Cynthia steal from her own husband? Her pin money was fair and he'd given her virtual carte blanche for household improvements. Uneasy doubts swelled into full-blown suspicion when he recognized his own coach being walked up and down the street by his own coachman. She certainly wasn't at her dressmaker's. He had to hope that Cynthia was indeed the victim of Hamble's fraud, for the alternative was far worse. She must need the money for someone else.

Among Cynthia's friends, Caro had wed a duke and Anne Brotherton was rich as Midas. She might be slipping a little aid to Oliver Bream. Patronizing the arts was an acceptable activity for a lady, but nothing gave Damian the impression that Oliver had access to the kind of sums involved in this particular scheme.

That left the Duke of Denford. Ryland had told him Julian's title brought him little money, yet he seemed to be living comfortably. He would no doubt find it a huge joke and delicious revenge to steal hundreds of guineas, thousands even, from his enemy, along with his wife.

Paying off his driver, Damian pushed open the door of a shabby building with Hamble & Stoke painted in red on a scratched fascia board, and entered an ill-lit hall containing a staircase, a couple of doors on either side, and a tall desk at which a scrawny clerk was intently writing. He looked up indifferently, jerked his head in the direction of a door on his right, then continued to ply his quill. Damian wondered what manner of accounts the man was concocting. But he lost interest in the subject when a low chuckle he'd recognize anywhere wafted in from an adjacent room. Damian slipped into the shadow of the stairs to listen.

"Hamble, you old villain. I'll take twice that sum and you should be grateful."

"Now, now, Your Grace. If you don't want these pictures, why would anyone else?"

"Because most people don't have my discriminating taste. You can sell the lot wholesale to an Oxford Street gallery catering to the vulgar rich."

"Why don't you do it yourself?"

"Because I'm a damn duke, now, curses. I'm fighting a pack of snarling Fortescues over every penny of the family fortune, and my supposed dignity is an arrow in my quiver. I can no longer be seen to conduct trade except in the discreetest fashion."

"I'd say you 'ave a problem, then, Your Grace." The elderly Cockney voice was replete with the pleasure of a good bargaining session. The conduct of trade had much in common with diplomacy, save for being socially unacceptable at the higher levels of society. Damian spared a moment's sympathy, quickly squashed, for his former friend's dilemma.

"I suppose," Julian said, "I could offer them to Isaac Bridges. He'd take them off my hands as a favor."

How Hamble would respond to this move was to remain a mystery. Light footsteps sounded at the top of the stairs and a whiff of rosewater cut through the musty atmosphere. A beam of winter sunlight filtered through a panel of glass over the front door, catching motes of dust in the air. Damian craned his neck, and through the spindled banister he saw his wife, exquisite in blue velvet, walk down the stars bearing some kind of urn, like the Queen of Sheba bringing gifts to Solomon.

"Mr. Hamble!" she called. "How much do you

think we can bill my husband's man of business for this vase?"

"I do not think, madam," Damian said, stepping out to block her final descent, "that it is possible to put a price on such an egregious act of cuckoldry."

Her jaw dropped. He felt worse than on any day since the morning after his twenty-first birthday.

Chapter 15

Cynthia stared out of the window of her bedchamber at the muted browns and grays of the winter garden. It was Christmas Day and she was alone again, as forlorn as the few sad snowflakes that had managed to penetrate the coal-fueled heat of London and lay disconsolately on the gravel paths. No merry Christmas for her, this year. But there was one silver lining to the relentless weight of clouds. She didn't have to attend Lady Belinda Radcliffe's Christmas party.

The door from the passage opened behind her.

"I don't need anything," she said. "Go downstairs and enjoy your Christmas dinner."

"I am not your maid. All the servants are below stairs."

She swung to face Windermere, whom she hadn't set eyes on since he'd hustled her out of the shop and into her carriage in Long Acre, ordering her to go home and stay there. She'd heard him in his room, late at night, but he hadn't made use of the communicating door: no mattress complaints, no offer of bhang. Also no scolding or threats of retaliation.

"You haven't eaten," he said from the doorway, with an air of concern she found spurious. The diplomatic Earl of Windermere was back in force, not a hair out of place. Even his complexion seemed paler.

"I thought perhaps I was to be starved to death in my prison cell."

"Don't be absurd. You could have gone downstairs at any time, or ordered a meal in your room."

She knew that. Her door wasn't locked and her maid had tried to ply her with food. She had accepted only bread and butter and tea for supper. "I didn't feel like eating until I knew my fate."

"Now you're being melodramatic. I asked only that you remain in the house until I had attended to matters."

She had waited on tenterhooks, dwelling on her supreme ignorance of the law. She worried about poor Mr. Hamble, who, although he'd made a fair profit from her purchases, risked the ruin of his livelihood should Lord Windermere decide to prosecute. She worried about the inhabitants of the house in Flowers Street when she no longer had anything except her pin money.

Julian she didn't worry about, much. She doubted there was much the law could do to a duke, however newly minted. Besides, although he had come up with the scheme by which Hamble submitted inflated invoices and paid her the difference, he wasn't otherwise a party to the fraud.

"Did you summon a magistrate or a Bow Street Runner?" she asked. "Will you send me away?"

"I don't wish for a scandal so your conspirators are safe. For now."

"It wasn't their fault. I wish you would let me explain."

"There is nothing I want to hear from you about the Duke of Denford."

"Did you call him out?" One of her greatest fears had been that they would duel. If things were to be resolved in a fight, she was afraid for her husband's safety. More so than Denford's. Julian had never struck her as a man likely to be caught at a disadvantage.

"Concerned for the fate of your lover, I see. Or do you hope he will make you a widow? I'm afraid I have no wish to accommodate you." His temper was showing beneath the smooth marble façade.

"My greatest desire is that no one will come to any harm, including certain innocents involved in this business." She took a deep breath and ventured to cross the space that separated them. "Please Damian! You must let me explain."

He ignored both her plea and her proffered hand. "Not now."

"Why not? What else is there to do?"

"You must get ready for Lady Belinda Radcliffe's

Christmas dinner. We are summoned for one o'clock and you need time to dress in your best."

"I won't go." She was appalled. It was intimidating enough to face a fashionable gathering for the first time. To do it when her nerves were rubbed raw and she couldn't expect any support from her husband was terrifying.

"I am afraid, my lady, that I must insist. I believe under the circumstances you owe me your graceful acquiescence."

He had a point and she should acquiesce, though she wasn't sure if she was capable of grace. "Will we be out late?"

"How long we stay depends on how enjoyable we find the party."

"I expect I will wish to leave before the end of the first course."

"Please restrain yourself," he said. "We have spoken before of the importance of my relationship with Sir Richard. He is anxious to meet my wife and I expect you to behave yourself with all the decorum of which you are capable."

His manners were slipping, his ire now undisguised. Cynthia found it preferable to the iceberg who had entered the room five minutes earlier.

Until she set eyes on Lady Belinda Radcliffe, Cynthia hadn't been certain how she would behave. Windermere had spent the short carriage journey giving her such basic advice about how to go on in society that he must have intended to be insulting.

"Don't tell me any more," she said finally. "I know how to correctly address a baronet and his wife, even if she is the daughter of a duke. And if I didn't, I know now because I am not deaf. Let me also inform you that the Birmingham Academy for Young Ladies is, indeed, for *ladies*. We were not permitted to eat beef with our fingers or spit at our dinner partners. I can get through a meal without embarrassing you."

Her feelings as she ascended the massive staircase from the towering hall were torn between the certainty that she would make a fool of herself and a desire to do so, and make a fool of her husband.

"Good Lord," she said, gripping his arm and forgetting that she had sent him to Coventry about halfway along Brook Street and refused to utter another word in response to his pompous instructions. "I've never seen such a huge house in London." She gawked like an ignorant rustic.

"Radcliffe bought it a few years ago," he replied. "It's one of the biggest houses in the square."

"He must be very rich." All around her she saw signs of wealth that made Windermere House seem quite a modest residence. "I suppose that was a vulgar remark," she added.

"Given the lavishness of our surroundings I believe the observation is justified. Our host has succeeded in turning a handsome fortune into a splendid one."

To her ear there was a faint note of disapproval in his comment. He'd found Mr. Chorley's conspicuous wealth cause for scorn too, but it hadn't stopped him from wedding her for it.

At the top of the stairs they were directed into a vast saloon, but Cynthia had only an impression of serried pilasters, profuse gilt, and royal blue silk hangings. Her attention was riveted on a woman she had no trouble recognizing from Drury Lane. Close up, Lady Belinda was stunning.

She appeared to favor red, this time a deep crimson crepe that clung to her slender but luscious figure. The trimmings were gold lace, and matched the setting of a splendid ruby and pearl tiara that set off dark hair, flawlessly arranged in the most fashionable Grecian style. Her skin was white, her eyes large and almost as dark as her hair, her lips painted carmine to match her gown.

"My dearest Damian," she cried in an odiously affected lisp at odds with her empresslike beauty. "It makes me so very, very happy that you are sharing our little Christmas feast." She smiled warmly, revealing straight white teeth.

Satisfied with her appearance when she left her room, standing next to her magnificent hostess Cynthia felt like an undersized and overdressed snowball, or maybe a kitten. White satin with a gauze tunic threaded with silver seemed the sort of thing a provincial would choose, and perhaps it was. A dumpy little blonde from Birmingham could never compete with a woman who was born to the cream of society and bestrode it like a Colossus. And she was just about as tall as one too. Cynthia hated her on sight.

Her husband was no better. An inch or two shorter and a good twenty years older than his wife, he was as beautifully dressed, if less gorgeously. Cynthia couldn't define why she found him immediately repulsive, or why she had to hold back a shudder when he kissed her hand. "My very dear Lady Windermere," he said. "I have keenly looked forward to meeting Damian's bride and I am not disappointed. Exquisite, quite exquisite. But I should expect nothing but the best from my dear boy."

Cynthia wondered waspishly if her husband was embarrassed by this fulsome praise, since he'd made little secret that he'd found his bride less than lovely and certainly hadn't wed her for her fashionable appearance. A sideways glance showed him predictably unabashed.

"My lady does indeed look very beautiful tonight," he said, with a tender glance. "As does Lady Belinda." He kissed that lady's hand with what the successful graduate of the Birmingham Academy judged to be excessive, even unmannerly enthusiasm.

"Dear, dear Lady Windermere," Lady Belinda

said. "I am so happy to have met you at last. Damian is such a *dear* friend. You should have told us you were in town and we'd have invited you to dine during his long absence."

Cynthia refrained from remarking that since she had no idea of the Radcliffes' existence, she was unable to call on them. She doubted they'd been in a state of equal ignorance. She might not rub shoulders with the *ton*, but she'd learned enough of the narrow society of the London great to know that little happened in Mayfair that wasn't spread by the servants. The Radcliffes would have known within a week that she occupied Windermere House. She hadn't been *dear* enough to merit their attention before her husband's return.

The studied nonchalance with which Lady Belinda kept a hand on Windermere's arm as she delivered her condescending speech roused Cynthia's courage. Whatever the future of her relationship with Damian—and at this moment she wouldn't wager more than sixpence on the chance of reconciliation—she wasn't going to let this gaudy siren intimidate her.

"Dear Lady Belinda," she said. "It's a great privilege to be invited to celebrate the feast at your magnificent house. I notice that you haven't any Christmas greenery, but with such splendid furnishings I suppose simple decorations would be overwhelmed."

"Oh, country customs," the other replied with

a dismissive wave of her satin-covered hand. "One reason we prefer to spend Christmas in town is to avoid such crude rusticity."

"I don't believe anyone would accuse you of rusticity, my lady." Cynthia smiled sweetly.

Lady Belinda looked Cynthia up and down with an assessing eye. "I see that the impression you like to give is that of unvarnished innocence."

"I am a simple woman. I have no pretensions to be what I am not." She sensed Damian stiffen at her side.

"I hope that isn't true, Lady Windermere."

"What can you mean, Lady Belinda?"

"Only that simplicity is quite overrated. It's the kind of thing gentlemen say they like in a woman and become tired of in five minutes."

Recognizing that she was out of her depth, Cynthia bared her teeth and beat a temporary retreat. "I defer to your greater experience." She curtseyed again and Damian, perhaps anxious to escape from an exchange that was aimed at him as much as at her, led her away from the reception line.

A fair and slightly stout young man had been hovering nearby and spoke to Damian in a language she didn't understand.

"Allow me to present Count Becker from the Bavarian embassy," Damian said.

"My lady," Becker said with a stiff bow and a click of the heels. Cynthia gathered her wits for her first conversation with a foreign diplomat. She didn't know a word of German, but the blatant admiration in his wide blue eyes boosted her courage. Still, she'd like to make an impression for more than her looks. If Lady Belinda was watching, and she'd wager on it, she wanted to appear a success. And emphatically not simple.

"*Gnaedige Frau*," he began, and thankfully continued in accented English. "I heard you speak of Christmas greens. I miss the customs of my native land." He looked at the unadorned magnificence of the Radcliffe's saloon with undiplomatic disapproval.

"How would you decorate your rooms in Bavaria?" Cynthia asked, and Damian gave her a quick nod of encouragement. "I have never traveled out of England but I am most interested in foreign customs."

The count was easy to talk to, and she enjoyed hearing about fir trees festooned with cakes and sweetmeats. If she could only avoid Lady Belinda and other more alarming company, she would be able to get through the evening. It pleased her that Damian remained at her side, contributing an occasional reminiscence of a Christmas spent in Berlin. She had rather expected him to leave her to sink or swim. Of course, he wouldn't want her to embarrass him. He was probably terrified she'd make a faux pas and damage his standing in the Foreign Office.

The undemanding charms of Count Becker afforded only a short respite. Her host came over to lead her into dinner. As he seated her on his right, at the head of a long, lavish board gleaming with silver, crystal, and hothouse flowers, she tried to suppress her instinctive dislike. While the fact of him being her husband's mentor wasn't a recommendation, it was her duty to be on good terms with him. Wondering if she had anything in common with this worldly man, the only thing she could think of did not make her feel better: Their spouses had once been intimately involved and might very well still be.

Lady Belinda sat at the other end of the table, apparently greatly amusing all within earshot, including Windermere seated a couple of seats to her right, diagonally across the table from Cynthia. It reminded her of spotting him at the theater, completely oblivious to the presence and even the existence of his wife. Did Sir Richard know? Of course he did. Surely there was little those shrewd eyes missed.

"Do I gather that you prefer country life, Lady Windermere?"

"I spent my early childhood in a country village but most of my life I lived in Birmingham. Though some call it provincial, it is scarcely rustic."

"Not when so much of the wealth of the nation is generated there. I believe Joseph Chorley is your uncle."

"Indeed. Are you acquainted with him? I would think you inhabited different circles."

"A wise man has many interests."

The lavishness of Sir Richard's home and hospitality spoke of great wealth. They dined off priceless Sevres plates, which were replaced by another set for anyone who turned down turtle soup in favor of lobster in a butter sauce. A large turkey and a haunch of venison dominated the sideboard, but she suspected they were only nods to the traditions of the season. The Radcliffes' kitchen was undoubtedly overseen by a French cook, or several.

To ask about the source of her host's income was out of the question, so she pretended to misunderstand him. "I see that you are a connoisseur of painting. Is that not a Rubens?"

"Unmistakable, isn't it."

"Has it been in your family for long? Is collecting a Radcliffe tradition?"

"Not at all. Everything in this house is my own acquisition. I've been lucky enough to have a number of fine works fall in my way."

"I noticed a pair of mythological scenes that I believe must be the work of Poussin."

"You are quite the *cognoscenta* yourself, Lady Windermere. I would assume Damian had taught you, had he not been absent. But there is no one with a better eye for a painting than the Duke of Denford."

She put down her fork and fussed with her napkin for a few seconds. When she looked up, Radcliffe's pale eyes with small pupils regarded her beadily. His eyelashes were so light as to appear nonexistent, and she wondered if that was why she found him sinister. Certain that nothing he had or would say was insignificant or without motive, she tried to keep her wits about her. Talking to Sir Richard reminded her of dealing with her uncle. She felt she had been thrown into a game in which she did not know the rules.

"I am acquainted with Denford. In fact he was the one who told me about your Poussins," she continued boldly. "Otherwise I might not have recognized the artist. What is their history?"

Radcliffe smiled thinly, as though well aware of the reason for her interrogation. "They belonged to Lord Maddox. Fortescue, as he then was, wanted them but they came to me instead."

So far he had confirmed Julian's story. She stole a glance at Damian, as she had throughout the meal. He was in his element: sleek and self-contained, his face giving nothing away, the perfect diplomat. In this mode she believed him capable of anything.

She turned back to Sir Richard. "You were fortunate to have heard about them."

"News of great pictures for sale always spreads. Denford may have lost the Poussins, but he has bought and sold many fine works. I hear he has an especially important collection on hand now."

"If so, he hasn't said anything to me. You should ask him yourself."

"Sometimes these things require a certain delicacy. If you should hear anything, Lady Windermere, it would be a favor to me if you sent word of it."

Remembering Julian's bitterness, she doubted he'd wish to sell anything to Radcliffe, however much he needed the money. Nor did he ever discuss his business with her. It wasn't part of their friendship, a friendship that seemed likely to end.

Sir Richard beckoned to one of the army of footmen to fill their wineglasses. "I prefer a burgundy with game," he said. She sipped the red wine cautiously, not wishing to face Sir Richard—or his wife, for that matter—without a full and unclouded set of wits.

The topic of the burgundy carried them though the ragout of pheasant, then Radcliffe abandoned wine talk as they switched to claret. "You wish to assist Damian in his work, do you not?" he asked.

"My husband has told me of the duties of a diplomat's spouse. I gather," she continued, "the first rule is never to say what one means." Perhaps a sip or two from each glass of wine had rendered her indiscreet, or maybe she was tired of Radcliffe's polite intrusions.

"Very good. You are obviously born to the role, and also wise enough to know you may be frank with me." He gazed down the length of the table toward his wife. "I am blessed with a spouse who spares no effort on my behalf. If you will do the same, there is no limit to the heights Damian may attain."

"I'm sure his talents will take him as far as he wishes to go, with or without my interference."

He ignored her modest disclaimer. "There are times, Lady Windermere, that you may have to do things against his wishes, even without his knowledge. For his own good, you understand."

"I fear I do not understand."

"You will. I am so glad we can speak bluntly to each other. I foresee a long and fruitful partnership."

"I didn't know we were on such terms," Cynthia said, swallowing a growing unease.

"We have the mutual goal of dear Damian's advancement."

She was really beginning to dislike the word *dear*. "What do you mean?"

"Maintain your . . . friendship with Denford."

"I am sure you are aware, Sir Richard, that Denford and Windermere quarreled."

"That is why it is so important you stay on terms with the duke. Continue to see him, and if you discover anything along the lines I mentioned before, be sure to let me know."

"Let me get this clear. Telling you about some paintings Denford may or may not own will assist my husband? I fear the world of diplomacy is far too convoluted for my poor brain."

"You can ask Damian, if you wish. But should you prefer not to raise the subject of Denford with him, I offer my services as a conduit for any intelligence you gather."

If Radcliffe believed that she was having an affair with Denford, and quite likely he did, he was encouraging her to continue it. The man possessed nothing that she would recognize as morality, and she wondered if her husband did either. Would he be so indignant about her perceived infidelity if it hadn't been with Julian? Her mouth went suddenly dry and she reached for the famous Radcliffe claret. What she wouldn't give for a glass of water.

Suppose her husband expected her to bestow her favors in pursuit of his career? She had always assumed his first priority from her would be an heir, but he showed no great urgency.

"Do you have any children, Sir Richard?" she asked.

He took her abrupt change of subject in his stride. "Lady Belinda and I have not been so lucky. I have a son and a daughter by my first wife, both well settled."

"Did you know that the vast majority of my uncle's fortune is to be settled on my son? If I do not give my husband an heir, Windermere will not reap the full benefit of his marriage."

She didn't have the impression the news came as any surprise to Radcliffe. Doubtless Damian had discussed it with him before he agreed to the bargain. "An unusual if not unprecedented arrangement," he said, waving it aside.

"I'm breaking the rules again, but we are speaking bluntly to each other, aren't we, *dear* sir. My priority as a wife must be to do my duty to secure the Chorley fortune. I shall not have . . . time . . . to pursue other interests, such as the Duke of Denford's art collection."

Chapter 16

After leaving the premises of Hamble & Stoke the previous day without drawing blood, Damian had taken a hackney to Grosvenor Square and demanded he be excused from any further involvement in the Alt-Brandenburg affair. All he wanted to do was put a bullet through Denford's black heart. Sir Richard had not proved sympathetic to his thinly veiled pleas. Finally Damian came out into the open about his wife's relationship with the duke.

"Naturally I heard about it," Radcliffe said. "And you will just have to swallow your finer feelings until you've completed your task. Only a weak man allows personal considerations to get in the way of his duty. You, my dear Damian, are not weak."

"Perhaps I can choke the information out of Denford," he said.

Sir Richard's thin lips stretched into a sympathetic smile. "That's the spirit, my dear boy, although I trust it won't come to that. Wouldn't be very diplomatic, would it? These things happen when a young woman is left alone," he added. "I'm afraid it's your own fault for dashing off to Persia like that instead of taking care of your new bride. You shouldn't have ignored my advice. I expect to see both of you at our Christmas dinner tomorrow, and no more of this nonsense."

As a result, Damian now watched his wife and Sir Richard Radcliffe deep in conversation at the other end of the table and wondered what the latter was saying to her. Never had he felt less in sympathy with his mentor. He didn't like to think of his innocent wife under the influence of Sir Richard's devious worldliness. A ridiculous thought since Cynthia had proven to be the farthest thing from an innocent. Damian just didn't seem to be able to keep that fact from slipping his mind.

As the covers were changed for the next course, Sir Richard turned to the lady on his other side and Damian's heart leaped into his mouth. Cynthia's new partner was Prince Rostrov, an attaché at the Russian embassy, who, as far as he knew, spoke not one word of English. The Russians, of course, all spoke French better than they spoke their own language. Poor Cynthia was going to endure a difficult hour.

He had to pay a little attention to his own neighbor now that Belinda, thank God, had stopped dominating the conversation. A few minutes later he glanced up the room to see Cynthia and the prince chatting. Rostrov's English must have made huge strides in the past year, unless she was laughing at his accent and bad grammar, which wouldn't be at all like his kindly wife. Rostrov, he now remembered, had an eye for a beautiful woman and was probably paying her all sorts of compliments. She blushed prettily at something he whispered. Damian felt the urge to do violence that was becoming distressingly common.

The day stretched into twilight; candles were lit, curtains drawn, and course after rich course paraded from the kitchen; glasses emptied, faces grew redder, conversation more desultory; even the most stiff-backed European aristocrats slumped in their chairs. Damian wished he could get away from the overheated luxurious confines of the Radcliffes' palace and breathe fresh air. When Lady Belinda arose and announced that, since it was Christmas Day, the entire party, gentlemen as well as ladies, would proceed to the drawing room, there wasn't a single male complaint. Even the most dedicated toper had sated himself on the contents of Sir Richard's famous cellar.

One of the last to leave the dining room, Damian joined the rearguard of the party in time to see Prince Rostrov presenting Cynthia to the Grand Duchess Olga, sister-in-law to the Russian ambassador. Since there was absolutely no chance that Her Serene Highness, on a brief visit to London, had troubled to learn English, Damian hastened forward to assist his wife with a difficult encounter. To his utter amazement, he discovered them in animated discussion about the best linen drapers in London. Lady Windermere spoke fluent and almost flawless French, in accents that would not have disgraced a duchess at the late court of Versailles.

He stood back and listened as Cynthia had one of the most difficult women in Europe eating out of her pretty little hands. She was incredible: beautiful, clever, and an asset such as he had never expected.

When Lady Belinda joined the discussion, it appeared that the distinguished Russian guest had taken a dislike to her hostess. Belinda, in excellent French but no better than Cynthia's, extolled the offerings of a particular merchant. The grand duchess, having visited neither establishment, insisted that the one recommended by Lady Windermere was preferable.

"I am sure, Your Serene Highness, that the linens in your own land are superior to anything you can find in England." Cynthia's tactful speech failed to soothe, but succeeded in diverting the grand duchess's ire. "Russians make *ordures*," she said, consigning the products of her countrymen to the dust heap. "Only the French are any good, and they have all gone mad. *Mon marchand favori* in Paris was sent to the guillotine by the barbarians, therefore I must shop in London. So uncivilized, the English. They expect me to visit their establishments instead of coming to the embassy."

"You see," Cynthia explained, "the selection of merchandise is so great that they could not transport it all to you. It is more convenient if we go to them." She smiled winningly. "And it's much more enjoyable to be able to explore an entire shop. I often find things I didn't even know I wanted."

"Very well. We shall manage." She turned her back on Belinda in a pointed manner. "And Lady Windermere will accompany me."

Bravo, Cynthia!

"I should be delighted, Highness. There is nothing I enjoy more than shopping."

"Your dear little wife has made a success with odious Olga," Lady Belinda said, maneuvering Damian away. "I wish her joy of the impossible woman."

"Lady Windermere is not little," Damian said curtly.

"I am far taller."

Damian said nothing and thought about his wife's ideal proportions, and how well they'd fit together if he ever got the chance again.

Belinda lowered her eyelids and smiled seductively. "You never brought me those Persian illustrations."

"Somehow they didn't seem an appropriate gift for my hostess on Christmas Day."

"I can't think of anything I'd like better. I expect to see them no later than Twelfth Night."

He'd decided not to give them to her, until this morning. Despairing of sharing the poses with his wife, he'd ordered them placed in the carriage because they were entirely appropriate for this particular hostess, at any time of year.

Now Belinda had annoyed him and he didn't feel like indulging her. "I'll send them around when I can lay hands on them."

"I'd rather you brought them yourself."

"I don't think that is a good idea."

"And yet I get a notion all is not blissful in the Windermere wedding bower."

A notion! Sir Richard would have told her everything. He was sure they'd thoroughly discussed the situation and drawn all sorts of conclusions, most of them correct. It made him angry that his relations with Cynthia should be a subject for their gossip. What lay between them was no one else's damn business.

Removing her hand from his arm and himself from her perfumed proximity, he accepted a cup of coffee, hoping to shake off his postdinner stupor. Unlike every other guest, Cynthia looked fresh and sweet. Her white gown suited her perfectly and made all the other ladies look garish and overdressed. Dismissed by her new best friend the grand duchess, she stood alone for a minute or two, peering at one of Radcliffe's famous Poussins.

His stomach clenched. He didn't want to think about the pictures because it was impossible to do so without thinking of Julian.

He wanted to walk over and talk to her, except he didn't know what to say, certainly not in a crowded room. At least he could bring her coffee and then he'd think of something. "A cup for Her Ladyship," he said. "I will deliver it."

"Sugar, my lord?" asked the footman who manned the coffee urn. He had no idea if his own wife preferred her coffee sweetened, and that was exactly the kind of commonplace, intimate information he ought to possess. He stirred in a spoonful and hoped he was right. When he turned around she was no longer alone. He groaned at the sight of the Countess of Ashfield, an established pillar of the beau monde and an old friend of Damian's father. The harangue was her normal method of address, but what she said to Cynthia must have been more than usually high-handed. Whatever he might think of his wife, he wasn't about to let anyone else distress her.

"I brought you this," he said, handing her the cup, which she accepted with an avid thank-you. "Lady Ashfield. What a pleasure to see you."

The countess looked at him through a bejeweled lorgnette. "About time you came home, Windermere."

"I think so too. I didn't know you were acquainted with Lady Ashfield, my dear."

"She was kind enough to invite me to a dinner at her house," Cynthia said. "Quite the grandest event I attended in London before today."

"Thank you for your kindness to my wife," Damian said, surprised and touched. It occurred to him that the Radcliffes, for all their vaunted friendship, had never taken the trouble. They should have done so, for his sake.

"Don't thank me, young man," she said scornfully. "I invited her as Anne Brotherton's chaperone."

Cynthia gulped her coffee and set the cup down with a shudder. Apparently she did not like it sweet. Add it to the list of things he had wrong about her. Damian took her hand and rested it on his arm. "Quite absurd to think of her as a chaperone, isn't it. She is much too young and pretty."

"Absurd because she has no idea how to behave! She let Miss Brotherton run around town with that rogue Marcus Lithgow and then, against her guardian's express wishes, took her off to the country. I'd like to know where Anne is. You can't just misplace an heiress. It simply isn't done." The old witch's gray curls quivered beneath her turban. "What have you done with Anne and why did you abandon her?"

Cynthia gripped his arm. "She is spending Christmas in Hampshire with the Duke and Duchess of Castleton. I had planned to do so also, but I came back to town to greet Windermere."

"Hm. There's something fishy going on here."

Lady Ashfield might be right. Cynthia seemed uneasy and Damian didn't think it was just the presence of the old countess, unnerving as anyone might find her. "I am quite sure there is not. Didn't you just receive a letter from Caro, my dear?"

She cast him a grateful look, grasped the rope he offered, and lied like a diplomat. "Caro and the duke are both in excellent health and delighted to have Anne with them."

"And Marcus Lithgow?"

"I have no idea."

Lady Ashfield harrumphed again but there wasn't much she could do, short of shaking the truth out of Cynthia. To do that she'd have to go through him. "I don't know what your father would have had to say. Or your poor sainted mother."

"I can't see why either would have an opinion either way on the whereabouts of Miss Brotherton. I have no doubt that my mother would have found my wife as delightful as I do."

"Thank you," Cynthia said, after Lady Ashfield had sailed off, thoroughly routed.

"You looked in need of rescue." He held on to her arm when she tried to move away. "I'm just curious; is the heiress really missing?"

"She planned to go to Castleton. I just haven't heard that she arrived." Her mouth pursed into the little rosebud he recognized as mischievous. "Yet."

"What about Lithgow?"

"I don't know exactly where he is," she said evasively.

"If the pair of them have eloped to Scotland, Lady Ashfield will never speak to me again."

"I doubt you'll be so lucky. Anne would never do anything as scandalous."

"Marcus would." Though he had no particular grievance with Lithgow, who had not been present the night of the great disaster, he'd cast him off as a matter of principle. Viscount Lithgow was not a respectable member of society. "You seem to have made a habit of tangling with my disreputable former companions."

He intended the remark idly, but it cooled the temperature by several degrees and killed their lighthearted badinage. She pulled away from him and would have stalked off had it not been for Lady Ashfield, who had sailed around the room, changed her tack, and was coming in to launch another broadside. Cynthia stepped back to his side and they stood arm in arm like the comfortable married couple they weren't.

"That woman terrifies me," she said.

"She terrifies everyone."

"Either you're very brave, or good at hiding your fright."

"I've tangled with worse. The courts of Europe are home to many grand duchesses. Lady Ashfield isn't a bad old thing at heart. She merely thinks she knows everything and that she is always right."

"Why are there so many people like that?" she said with feeling. "*I* try to keep an open mind."

"**L**et's leave," Damian said. "I don't think I can stand this place a minute longer."

"Don't you want to stay longer with your *dear* friends?" Cynthia said, then realized it was foolish to argue with a suggestion that so exactly matched her own fervent desire. Though the demands of the day had challenged her self-assurance and social graces, she thought she had done well with the Radcliffes and the other guests. Her husband was responsible for buffeting her emotions and making her testy. He'd bewildered her with his mixture of consideration and disdain.

"I will be glad to go home," she said, "if you don't think it unmannerly to leave so early."

"Frankly, I don't care."

As he talked his way smoothly through the obvious displeasure of their hostess, Cynthia maintained an unyielding smile and wondered what was coming next, scolding or fence-mending. The atmosphere within the dark confines of the carriage seemed thick and tense.

"Your French is excellent," he said. Goodness gracious! He had actually noticed.

"You ordered me to work on the language. It was one of the reasons I came to London, to find a teacher for French conversation."

"I commend your obedience to my wishes." His tone was dry. She braced herself for the scolding that was surely imminent. "You did well today," he continued in a softer tone. "Very well indeed. I would venture to say that no lady could have handled herself better, even those with far more experience that yourself. Your management of the grand duchess was masterly."

"Truly?" she said, surprised at his praise. "All I did was have a very ordinary conversation with her, such as I might enjoy with any new acquaintance."

"If it always works this well, I suggest you continue to treat imperious members of royal families as though they were ordinary people."

"I was quite nervous about meeting her," she admitted. "Luckily Prince Rostrov coached me in the proper method of address. I don't generally call people Your Serene Highness."

"Grand Duchess Olga might be able to forgive London merchants for failing to bring the entire contents of their warehouses to her hotel, but failing to adequately Serene her might have led to war."

The word *warehouse* put her nerves on edge. If he intended to torment her with his silence, he achieved his goal. "I had no idea I was so important."

"I was joking, you know."

"So was I."

"You seem nervous, but there is no need. To-night I am proud of my choice of bride. You would be an ornament to any embassy."

"How gratifying. For you."

Was he never going to bring up what had happened yesterday? He sat so still, as perfectly turned out as when he'd left his valet's hands, unruffled by the stresses of the evening, the swaying of the carriage, or, apparently, the perceived peccadilloes of his wife.

Instead of giving her a chance to explain, he was congratulating himself for choosing her, the bride he'd taken virtually sight unseen as the price of an estate. He hadn't thought much of her a year ago but she now passed muster and he was *proud of his choice*, as though the credit was all his. He didn't care that it had taken hours of painstaking reading of French texts, as well as long conversations with her tutor, to reach her current fluency. He hadn't even asked how she'd done it. Did he think she'd gone from dowdy companion to fashionable countess with a wave of the magic wand? It took *work* to look this good. He hadn't said a word about Beaulieu and had no idea of the care she'd lavished on the place. Even Windermere House had been spruced up.

True, she'd introduced a few ugly and overpriced objects to the London house. All right, many extremely ugly and shockingly expensive items. But Damian Lewis, Earl of Windermere deserved a little teasing for his horrible treatment. And it had been in a good cause.

The time had come to tell the truth. And if he didn't like it, too bad. She refused to be ashamed.

"Damian," she said. "I didn't steal your money for myself."

"No," he said. "I guessed as much. I may not have been an ideal husband, but I don't believe I have been a miserly one. I left orders that you could spend what you wished."

"On gowns and furnishings, yes. But not on other things."

His voice hardened. "Not on your lover."

"He is not . . ." What was the use? He wouldn't believe her. "Julian introduced me, but the arrangement was between Hamble and me alone."

"I don't know what to believe anymore."

She sensed weariness in him, perhaps a softening of his stance. "I would like to explain myself, but I'd rather show you. First we need to go home and collect something. I think a couple of stout footmen wouldn't be a bad idea either."

"Why?"

"We are going to an insalubrious part of town."

Chapter 17

To Damian's certain knowledge, London was the biggest and noisiest metropolis in the world. It wasn't quiet on the evening of Christmas Day, but the traffic that usually clogged the thoroughfares of the west end of town and the City was light and their progress brisk. Damian gave up trying to interrogate his wife about their destination, or the contents of the hampers strapped onto the back of the carriage. The whole errand seemed remarkably unwise but he was in the mood to humor her. And he wanted an explanation for her fraudulent ruse. Past Bishopsgate the streets became darker, narrower, and meaner.

"Don't worry," Cynthia said. "We're almost there and I've never had any trouble at Flowers Street. The people who live there look out for each other."

Damian hoped so. The street was so narrow the coach barely fit and a fast escape would be out of the question. His coachman, he noted, knew the way and stopped at the right house without being told the address. Other than helping her down from the coach, he let Cynthia direct the operation. One of the footmen held up a lantern while she knocked on the freshly painted door of a house in markedly smarter condition than its neighbors.

"Merry Christmas, Aggie," Cynthia said to a young woman with a babe in her arms.

The girl, barely more than a child herself, beamed. "Merry Christmas, my lady! We didn't expect to see you today."

"I meant to come tomorrow but decided to bring your gifts now. His Lordship has offered me company. Let me present Aggie Smith, my lord. And this little angel is her daughter, Hannah. May I?" She took the little bundle from the girl and kissed the infant's nose. "I believe she has grown since last week, Aggie. And become even prettier."

"How do you do, Mrs. Smith," Damian said with a nod.

The girl managed a wobbly bob of a curtsey and a noise something between a choke and a giggle, the latter perhaps inspired by his use of the honorary missus. He'd be very surprised if Aggie Smith, who wore no ring, was married.

"Will you ask the men to bring in the hampers, my lord?" Cynthia asked. "Put them on the floor in here." She walked into a room in which a chorus of female and childish voices arose, along with the cry of another baby.

The inhabitants of Flowers Street might look after their own, but Damian wasn't going to trust them, after dark, with the Earl of Windermere's coach and horses. Leaving the driver and one of the footmen to guard his property, he helped the other haul in the hampers. Landing on the floor with a pair of thumps, they were at once engulfed by a mass of shrieking bodies while his wife, still holding Aggie's baby, laughingly protested.

Damian decided to enforce the protest. "Stop! Let's have a little order."

The seething mass withdrew and resolved itself into half a dozen children ranging from a couple barely toddling to a skinny boy on the verge of adolescence. They gazed at him with open mouths and an appropriate hint of alarm. "Tha's right," yelled another young woman, slightly older than Aggie but also burdened with an infant. "You wait for 'Er Ladyship."

"Thank you, my lord," Cynthia said. "I know you are all anxious to see what I have brought, but first you must be introduced to His Lordship and wish him a merry Christmas."

"Merry Christmas, 'Is Lordship," the youngsters cried in dutiful unison, their eyes never shifting from the baskets.

Damian tried to follow the introductions. In addition to Aggie, there were five grown women, though two of them were sadly young to be mothers, and another, younger still, was pregnant. The eldest was presented as Mrs. Finsbury, a widow with four children. No other husbands, dead or alive, were mentioned. As the children named themselves he noted that the room, which occupied most of the ground floor, was clean and freshly painted, simply but comfortably appointed with strong, practical furniture.

"Very good, children," Cynthia said, once the formalities were concluded. "Did you all have your supper already?"

"Yes, but I'm still hungry," said the oldest boy. "I'm always hungry."

"I wonder if there's anything to eat in here. What do you think?"

"Look inside!"

"Open it!"

"If someone will take Hannah from me, I'll see if there's something in here that will help those hunger pangs." Aggie retrieved the baby, and Cynthia blew the little creature a kiss. Falling to her knees and throwing aside the lid of the first basket, she looked as adorably excited as the others and almost as young. She lifted out a cloth-covered dish and took a deep breath. "Mm. This smells good. What do you think it is?"

The children shrieked with joy.

"Cake!"

"Roast beef!"

"Pie!"

Pretending it was so heavy she could barely lift

it, she carried it over to a table at the far side of the room and removed the cover. "Pie it is. Mince-meat, I think. Is it big enough to fill you up, Tom?"

"I never seen one so big," the boy replied, "but I bet I could eat it all."

"Let's see what else we have." She produced bread, cakes, jellies, sweetmeats, cheese, and a huge ham. She continued to tease the youngsters, showing unabashed delight at their reactions and a playfulness that enchanted him. He wanted to snatch her up, twirl her around, and kiss her until neither of them could breathe. His heart expanded with a spirit of Christmas that had been singularly absent at the Radcliffes' lavish dinner.

Soon the table groaned with enough food, in Damian's inexpert estimation, to feed the household for several days. The children, though eager to fall on the feast, held back. None was plump but they appeared to be well fed and decently dressed. Thanks to the machinations of Lady Windermere and Mr. Hamble, he assumed.

The former, having consulted the mothers, bade each choose one thing to eat. "We'll keep the rest until tomorrow when you will enjoy a big dinner."

Under the watchful eye of one designated mother, they made their selections. Damian began to distinguish between them, and find them interesting. Tom was jealous of his prerogatives as the eldest and kept the middle ones in order, while making sure that the youngest got their due. The two middle ones, both girls, seemed to be the same age, perhaps twins though they didn't look alike. They whispered and giggled a lot, drawing the scorn of Tom. All were united in adoration for plump little Pudding, a child of indeterminate sex who waddled about with an infectious toothy grin. To a boy and girl they wore expressions of ecstatic bliss as they tasted their carefully chosen sweetmeats, savoring each morsel as though they might never eat again. Damian tried to remember when he'd been happy about something so simple.

If the children had temporarily forgotten the second hamper, Cynthia had not. She produced some greenery and a bright sprig of holly, which she arranged on the mantelpiece over the small fireplace. By this time the children were ready to take an interest in what else would emerge from the casket of wonders.

He watched the ceremony from the fringe, as his wife distributed her largesse with unaffected grace and obvious pleasure. She'd taken trouble to select gifts that were both useful and suited to each individual. All ages received warm clothing, and cloth to make more. For the children there were small toys and books, received with more cries of rapture.

For Cynthia, he observed, charity was not only about giving money. It was warm and personal. She cared deeply about these waifs and strays she'd taken under her wing. She hadn't merely spent the last year shopping and visiting and consorting with the Duke of Denford. His wife had a whole life he knew nothing about and wished he did.

She seemed to have a particular bond with Aggie and her baby. When everyone else had received their gifts, Cynthia unwrapped a silver tissue package to reveal a blob of fine lace.

"It's for Hannah," she said with a rueful smile, placing the tiny cap on the baby's head. "I know it's impractical, Aggie, but the minute I saw it I had to buy it. I couldn't resist. Doesn't she look perfect?"

Damian stepped closer to look at the little red face in its white frill and at his wife's tender gaze. "She looks like Lady Ashfield," he whispered in Cynthia's ear. She gave a repressed snort at the private joke and elbowed him in the ribs.

Aggie fingered the lace with reverence. "It's too fine for the streets around here, my lady. She'll only wear it at home."

"You and the other Spitalfields weavers make the finest silks in the world," Cynthia argued. "Why should you not enjoy wearing beautiful things too?"

"Thank you, my lady. You are very good to us. You too, my lord." Aggie was grateful but he thought he detected a skepticism she kept hidden from her benefactress. He strongly suspected the piece of lace would find its way to a pawnbroker as soon as the infant grew out of it. And why not? He appreciated Aggie's practicality as much as his wife's frivolity and the sentiment behind it. Life was always better for a little pure beauty, and it was likely that the denizens of East London had little enough of it in theirs. Cynthia had brought great joy to her household of women and children this Christmas Day. Later he would discover how far her charity extended beyond the provision of the life's unnecessary but delightful frills. Very far indeed, he suspected.

She should have children of her own. For the first time he felt an inkling of interest in procreation beyond the duty to produce an heir. This visit to these humble premises made him think of a family life with Cynthia. It occurred to him that since her fraudulent dealing had been in a good cause, there was no reason not to forgive her. Yes, certain matters needed to be settled. Julian Fortescue still cast his shadow. But they were back where they had been the night of the bhang.

A broad smile stretched his lips. He was suddenly *very* interested in procreation.

Young Tom stood beside him with an air of distaste while the others cooed over the lace-bedecked infant.

"It must be hard to be the only man in the house among all these girls," Damian said quietly. "It's a good thing they have you to keep an eye on the little ones."

Tom puffed out his chest. "I'm the only boy except Puddin' and 'e's too small to be much help."

"The ladies like to make a fuss about things, don't they?"

Puzzled for a moment by the use of a term of gentility, he grasped that Damian meant the other inhabitants of the house. "Aye, m'lord. That they do."

"See those greens over the fireplace? There's one branch with white berries. That's mistletoe, you know."

Tom extracted the branch in question from a clump of fir. "Can I eat them?"

"I don't recommend it. They'd taste bitter and give you a pain in the stomach. "

"What's it for then?"

"At Yuletide anyone is permitted to kiss anyone else if they stand beneath a sprig of the stuff."

"I can think of a few fellows that'd pay me for this. And some others who don't need it to get what they want." The boy's canny look said that while he might not know much about traditions, his surroundings hadn't left him ignorant of the basic facts of life. The infants in the house weren't products of divine intervention.

"I was thinking the ladies here would like to exchange Christmas kisses."

"Not me," Tom said firmly.

"Of course not. But we must humor them. Why don't you hop up on that chair and invite them? You can hold the mistletoe up high *and* avoid danger of having to participate."

Laughing, Tom scrambled onto the seat. "It's kissing time," he piped, arousing a chorus of laughter.

The mothers all knew what to do. A squealing

exchange of feminine bussing ensued, with Lady Windermere taking fervent part. The shy older girls won smiles and hugs from their patroness but Cynthia's greatest enthusiasm was reserved for the babes in arms. He'd give her an infant of her own to cuddle and coo over. But before that blessed event another one (or dozen or hundred) must occur.

Soon.

Tom proved an admirable lieutenant, not even requiring the half-crown bribe Damian had planned. "What about you, guv? Ain't you going to kiss 'Er Ladyship too?" The boy was going to get his money honestly. "The nippers expect it. They've never seen a lord before. Seein' a lord and lady kissin' would be a rare treat."

"Never let it be said I failed in my duty. My lady?" He held out his hand. Blushing, she met his eye over the lace-capped head of Aggie's baby. While he could admit that the infant was endearing, she was also very much *de trop*. "Give her to me," he said firmly. The child seemed absurdly light in his arms and terrifyingly fragile. He handed her quickly to her mother, who winked at him. Good girl, that Aggie. "My lady?"

The assembly of women smirked. Grinning like a Cheshire cat, Tom brandished the mistletoe. With a martyrish air Cynthia took up position. "I wouldn't want to disappoint the children."

Damian smiled wolfishly. "Let us not do so then." Her shoulders stiffened beneath his hands.

"Relax," he whispered, stroking her tender collarbones with his thumbs. "We've done this before. Forget that we have an audience." The perfect mouth formed a mesmerizing O of surprise.

"I thought the only reason we are doing this is to please our audience." The warm scent of roses flooded his senses. He wished they were somewhere else and alone together. His head buzzed with desire and he couldn't for the life of him remember why they hadn't spent the last twenty-four hours in bed, making love. All suspicions, accusations, and quarrels seemed unimportant in the face of his need to possess his wife. She was his and he intended to keep her. Her eyes reflected vulnerability and fear but his throat was tight with longing. He couldn't form the words to reassure her.

"It will please me too," he said on a breath. The feeble phrase gave no sense of the brew of resentment, forgiveness, and tenderness he wished to convey. Those emotions were for examination at a calmer time when he wasn't overwhelmed by bone-deep, searing lust. But for now . . .

His fingers skimmed over her gauze sleeves, too fine to disguise the warmth of her skin. Taking one tight fist in both hands he carefully unfurled her fingers. Soft, pretty hands with pearly pink nails. His thumbs traced the lines crossing her palms, another detail about his wife that he intended to explore at length and at leisure. He dropped a lingering kiss into the very center. At her sharp intake of breath he raised his eyes to hers, still wary but softer. Damn their audience.

Keeping the hand in one of his, his other descended to her waist, following the curves beneath their layers of silk, to the sweetest rounded bottom in the history of the world. Lowering his eyelids for a moment, he recalled her naked. *Pray God, soon.*

"Kiss 'er, guv!"

The sooner he did his duty, the sooner they could leave. It wasn't as though he didn't wish to, hadn't been planning it for the past half hour. He let her go, but only to frame her heart-shaped face between his palms, closed his eyes, and brought their mouths together. Her sweet, pliant lips invited him to invade with all his pent-up desire. But they weren't alone and there were children present, so he kept it shallow, little more than an exchange of breath. Though it drove him to the brink of losing control, he didn't want their tenuous contact to end. He held her head still, until it dawned on him that she wasn't trying to escape him but to kiss him back. A bold dart of her tongue along his inner lip sent blood roaring into his already lively cock. Abruptly he let her go and she swayed. Her eyes were big and dreamy.

"It's time we took our leave, Cynthia," he said.

By the time they had said their good-byes and entered the carriage, the dizziness that had possessed Cynthia's brain when Damian kissed her under the mistletoe had abated. Her body still thrummed and her legs felt weak but her head had cleared enough to remind her that she needed to speak with him before anything else happened. Confident now that he would understand her financial ruse, and certain that he intended to take her home to bed, she determined to press for a more perfect reconciliation.

Damian appeared to wish to omit the explanations. As soon as the carriage lurched forward he pulled her into his arms. "Cynthia," he whispered, "I want you so much." That his voice was ragged, his words blunt and unadorned, pleased her. She loved to see her husband's sleek veneer crack.

His hand slipping through the front of her cloak to seek her breast, his lips hot against her neck, tempted her to yield without delay. Her pulses sped and heat bloomed in her lower belly. She managed to wrench herself away and put a foot of plush seat between them.

"Not now, not here," she said in response to his incoherent protest.

"Why not?"

"There are footmen."

"Riding on the box."

"We are in the streets of London."

"I need to introduce you to new ways of passing the time on a journey. It's dark and there's nothing else to do."

His caressing voice conjured up the possibilities of their situation. The carriage was still warm from the hot bricks provided by their efficient servants. If she extinguished the small lantern they'd be enclosed in a cozy refuge from the chilled world outside, just the pair of them, like a couple of nesting creatures. In the swaying light she could see Damian's face filled with raw desire that matched his lusty pleas.

"Another time," she said with genuine regret. "When we have settled other matters between us."

"Right now the only matter between us is my wish to kiss you."

"Stop, Damian. You refused to listen to my explanation so I showed you instead what I did with the money I made through Hamble. Every penny has gone to buying that house and maintaining it. Mrs. Finsbury looks after all the children while the other women go to work at the factory."

He sighed, evidently resigned to conversation. "I have nothing against charitable endeavors. But why this one in particular?"

"Mrs. Finsbury's husband was killed in an accident at the Finch Street factory. It belongs to my uncle." She fingered the silk covering her knee. "This material was woven there. But more importantly, every penny that you gained through marrying me comes from the profits of Finch Street and other places like it."

"There's nothing to be ashamed of in successful commerce."

"Of course not."

"I am sorry about Finsbury's death. What of the others? Are they also the widows of weavers?"

"None of them are married."

"I see."

"I don't think you do. They didn't intend to bear children out of wedlock. Each one is a victim of Wilfred Maxwell, my uncle's partner and the manager of his London factories. He makes a habit of violating the young females in his employ and there is nothing they can do without losing their jobs and livelihood. Maxwell allows the girls to keep their positions as long as they don't make a fuss, or miss too many days of work when they give birth. So far I have given a home to five. The most recent addition only arrived last week."

"What does your uncle say to this?"

"I wrote to him but he doesn't care. He told me to leave Maxwell alone."

"Such irresponsibility is appalling."

"Maxwell is a villain and my uncle not much better," she said. "I feel a duty to Maxwell's victims, but I would wish to help them in any case. There are too many young women in the world at the mercy of unscrupulous men, and so little I can do."

"I applaud your efforts," he said warmly. "I understand your sense of responsibility to these particular women and admire you for taking action. I am curious, though. Why do the women not send the infants to the Foundling Hospital? They can have little affection for the products of their rape."

"You are wrong. Women love their children, no matter who the father is."

"I see," he said after a pause. "They seem like fine children."

"If they are it is because they have loving mothers and a good home. I've learned much about the hardships the poor face. It's made me realize how fortunate I was when my parents died. I cannot now have much respect for my uncle, but at least he didn't leave me to starve or sell myself on the streets." The blunt reference to prostitution shocked him, she could see, but she never felt particularly ladylike after a visit to Spitalfields. She also wanted Damian to share her feelings because he was in a position to do more about the problem than she. "I can't bear to think about those little girls, and the babies like Hannah, living such a precarious existence."

"Young Tom is a good lad," Damian said. She had noted his interest in the boy. How gratifying it would be if he would share her endeavors.

"A wonderful boy. His mother relies on him to help and protect the younger children. But she worries too. There are some bad influences on the streets of Spitalfields."

"He needs male company."

"How like a man to think that," she said teasingly.

"I have no objection to the company of women." His voice dropped. "I envy Tom his mother and sisters."

"I'm sorry." She reached out and took his hand. "I wouldn't imply otherwise."

"But to do well in life, and perhaps provide for his family himself, he needs an education and the example of other men."

"He would like to train as a weaver, like his father. I intend to provide the apprenticeship fee."

"Good. He at least won't be in danger from Maxwell and his ilk. It's better if men go to work and women stick to the domestic realm."

"No doubt that is so, except that women are sometimes left to fend for themselves. From what I have learned, one of the good things about the silk business is that it pays well, even for women."

"I remember we spoke of this at dinner not long ago."

"And we spoke of the efforts of many in Parliament to do away with the laws that ensure that the weavers earn high wages." She squeezed his hand and took a deep breath. "I hope to persuade you to change your mind and support the Spitalfields Act."

"I can't do that. I gave my word to your uncle."

"My uncle! After what you have seen and heard tonight do you believe you owe him your support in this?"

"A gentleman does not go against his word. And it's not just Mr. Chorley. Others, men I respect, think the same way." He slid along the seat and put an arm about her shoulders. "Let's not speak of dull politics now."

Cynthia wavered. Her inclination was to melt into his arms now and argue later. Like women throughout history, she could influence events through her powers of seduction. That's what Lady Belinda Radcliffe would do.

She did not, under any circumstance, wish to be like Lady Belinda.

She slid back to her own corner and folded her arms. "At least hear me. Let me try to change your mind."

"You may continue to support your own little household on Flowers Street with my blessing and admiration."

"But what of the hundreds, perhaps thousands of others who will see their wages lowered? I can't support them all. Besides, they don't want charity but the ability to make their own living."

"I know you mean well and I honor you for your impulses," he said. "It's a complicated issue, and not one that should be decided according to your sentimental response to the cases of certain individuals, deserving as they may be."

"You believe me incapable of thinking rationally?"

"No," he said impatiently, "but neither do I think you are the best judge of the wider consequences of the Spitalfields policy. Sir Richard Radcliffe supports repeal."

She was about to decry the fact that he would listen to Sir Richard over his own wife, then stopped because of the absurdity. Of course he would. At no point in their acquaintance had Damian given her reason to believe he valued her opinion about anything. Certainly not more than that of his revered mentor, a man Cynthia would like to see tossed into the Thames. And his lovely wife too.

The optimism kindled by the spirit of Christmas at Flowers Street and their sweet mistletoe kiss had dissipated, to be replaced by a dull depression. For whatever reason, Damian had decided to overlook her supposed liaison with Julian, but he had no real respect for her and certainly no love. He wanted to bed her, that was all.

While once she would have settled for a small measure of affection, she had changed. "You believe me an adulteress who is too simple to be trusted with an opinion on a political matter. I cannot imagine why you would wish to consort with such a creature."

Her husband completely failed to grasp the opportunity to make amends she'd served him on a silver platter. All he had to do was deny that he believed her an unfaithful fool. Instead he reached for her hand. "Can we talk about this another time? We're almost home and I am ready for bed."

"I am afraid . . ." she said, haughty as Lady Ashfield, and why not? She was a countess too. " . . . I must beg you to excuse me, my lord. I have a headache."

Chapter 18

Dealing with his wife, Damian decided, was a bit like a game of Chowgan, where each time he took a good shot with his mallet, he found someone had moved the goal. They should send her to manage Prince Heinrich of Alt-Brandenburg. She'd have him in such a muddle he'd sign the treaty just to stop the ache—in his head and elsewhere.

During a brisk morning walk around Hanover Square, Damian tried to make sense of her attitude toward him, the way each time he thought they were becoming close she would find a reason to back away. While admitting his own role in their quarrels, he couldn't get away from the nagging feeling that he didn't have the whole picture. Something lay behind her anger, something that had happened in his absence. Returning home, he resolved to take the radical course of asking her a direct question and followed the sound of clinking china to the morning room. She was up early.

Or perhaps not. Oliver Bream sat at the breakfast table, teacup in one hand, applying charcoal to a leaf of a small sketchbook as he drank. Even from a sideways perspective and a few feet's distance, the artist demonstrated a deftness that came only with hard work. Damian's unpracticed fingers itched.

"Oh, good morning, Windermere," Bream said vaguely, waving his cup. Without any perturbation at being found eating breakfast by the master of the house, he made an adjustment to his drawing, nodded with satisfaction, and put down his stick of charcoal. "More tea please, John. And a slice of that ham."

"I'll have the same," Damian said. "And a couple of eggs and some buttered toast. Thank you—er—John." The servant, hired during his absence, probably knew Bream better than he knew the man who paid his wages.

"Do you often breakfast here?" Damian asked.

To Damian's amusement, Bream blinked, surprised at being interrupted, but graciously tolerating the inconvenience. "Quite often," he said. "The servants know to feed me if Cynthia isn't down yet. It was hard while she was away," he added wistfully.

"You live in the mews behind the Duchess of Castleton's old house, I believe."

"It's not the same now that Caro lives in Hampshire," Bream said gloomily. "I used to eat all my meals with her, if I hadn't sold anything lately."

"Caro maintained her salon after her husband died?"

"There was always something going on at Conduit Street. Some fellows I didn't see again." He stopped and thought about it. "Caro didn't keep up with Robert's gaming friends, but most of the crowd still gathered there."

Damian was filled with sudden regret for the loss of the old times and old companionship. Robert had been a dazzling conversationalist with a discerning eye for a fine work of art, counterbalanced by his unfortunate passion for gaming. He and the seventeen-year-old Caro had eloped as soon as Robert came into his majority and control of his fortune. Rather than spoil the original quartet of Robert, Julian, Marcus, and Damian, Caro had fit in perfectly, a wild child always up for a lark. How angry Damian's father had been when he'd lent the eloping couple a carriage from Beaulieu for their dash to Gretna Green.

That had also been his last visit to the estate before his own majority a few months later. The recollection dowsed the spark of regret.

They munched ham in comfortable silence for a few minutes. Damian began to see why Cynthia liked the artist. His utter absorption in his own concerns made him a soothing companion. No need to exert oneself to amuse Oliver Bream; the occasional application of nourishment was all he needed to be perfectly content.

Bream abruptly picked up the thread of their conversation. "Caro didn't buy our pictures anymore after Robert died because he lost all his money. But she still fed us."

Damian hadn't grasped quite how much Robert had continued to lose after the fateful night. Somehow it didn't make him feel better. Julian, almost as much to blame, hadn't been punished for his part. Instead he'd fallen into a dukedom.

"I suppose Denford was at Conduit Street a lot."

"Yes," Bream replied. "I could go to Julian's for breakfast, but there's no cook at Fortescue House and he's out of town a lot. When he wasn't traveling he was always at Caro's."

"How much in the last year?"

The artist, who had reopened his sketchbook, tilted his curly head and considered the question. "Well, he was in town in the spring. I remember seeing him often at Conduit Street with Cynthia and Anne. We all went to a masquerade at the Pantheon. Or perhaps Cynthia and Julian went together and the rest of us met them there. I don't remember. After Caro married Castleton, Julian was away for a few months. Something to do with a collection of pictures."

The news about a picture collection was interesting, but paled in importance compared to the other item of gossip. His breakfast turned sour in his stomach. He recalled only too well the kind of licentious no-good one could get up to at a masquerade ball. "Did he take my wife around town a great deal?"

He failed to disguise the urgency behind his question, for Bream jerked his head up in alarm and relapsed into discretion. "We often went out in a group. I don't pay much attention to the niceties, but I don't think there's anything wrong about a married lady accepting a gentleman's escort when her husband is away. Cynthia doesn't mean any harm. She's the kindest person in the world."

Damian's pulse slowed. He was beginning to see the futility of dwelling on the past. "I think you may be right about that, Bream. She cares for everyone." If he could only resolve what trouble lay between them, she might care for him too. Lady Windermere's affection would be worth winning.

By the time he'd finished his meal, his wife had not appeared and his uninvited guest showed no sign of departing. He stamped out into the hall just in time to see Ellis open the front door to the devil himself. Julian Fortescue had always possessed unmitigated gall. Tossing him into the street unfortunately wasn't an option with the butler looking on. Sometimes the demands of discretion were damn annoying.

"Denford," he said, cloaking his fury in ice. "Come with me back to the library. Please."

The duke raised a black eyebrow and followed him down the back passage.

Once out of earshot of the servants, Damian

crowded his unwelcome visitor. They were much of a height, Julian having an advantage of barely an inch. Damian scowled, thrusting his head forward so they were almost nose to nose. "I told you to leave her alone."

Denford didn't flinch. "Where is Cynthia?"

"Lady Windermere to you, Duke."

"Don't be an ass, Damian. We may be at odds, but let's not pretend we don't know each other."

"At odds! Is that what we are? My wife is upstairs. There is no reason for you to see her. Ever."

"I want to make sure she is well."

"Why wouldn't she be?"

"You tell me, Damian."

With incredulous fury he understood what Denford implied. "I have never a hit a woman in my life and I never will."

"I'm relieved to hear your years among the dirty machinations of government haven't changed you in that respect. But there are ways of hurting a woman without striking a blow. The Damian I once knew would never have behaved with so little courtesy and gentleness. The way you hustled her out of Hamble's and into the carriage was brutal."

He hadn't been physically rough with Cynthia, he was certain, though perhaps intimidating in his anger. He must make sure she wasn't afraid of him, once he'd got rid of bloody Denford. "It's none of your business. There's no point revisiting the past again."

"None at all. Let us look to the future, which is my business."

"The only thing I have to say about your future is this: Keep away from my wife."

"That's not what I had in mind."

"I'm warning you."

Denford's lips stretched into the sneer he used to find amusing when its goal was the taunting of the Oxford proctors, an outraged hostess, or a stiff-backed pillar of the House of Lords, especially the late Lord Windermere. Now Damian understood exactly why those worthies had all wanted to kill Julian Fortescue. "Stop looking as though you'd like to throttle me. You wouldn't succeed if you tried and you will wish to hear my proposition. I called to see you, so the least you can do is offer me a seat."

"To see *me*?" Damian stepped back. Curiosity fought with the urge to commit violence and emerged the victor. Beating Denford to pulp was an option he kept in reserve. He waved at the pair of wing chairs on either side of the hearth and they took their seats, like the civil acquaintances they weren't.

"Last time we spoke tête-à-tête," Denford began, "you were uncommonly interested in the Falleron collection."

"You *do* have it!"

"Let's just say that I can lay my hands on certain pictures in exchange for a consideration."

Damian felt the rush of anticipation that always accompanied a diplomatic breakthrough. He wasn't even going to negotiate much. The Foreign Office could afford it, and all he wanted was to complete his mission and get rid of Denford forever. "Name your price."

Blue eyes flashed in the hawkish face. "Cynthia. I want Cynthia."

Damian shook his head, doubting he had heard correctly. "Is this a jest?"

"Do sit down again and let us discuss it reasonably. The country gets its alliance, Prince Heinrich the Dreadful gets his pictures, and I get Cynthia."

"No." Damian couldn't believe they were having this conversation. Julian expected him to wink at his wife's continued infidelity in return for certain considerations. Depressingly, it was the kind of arrangement he might not have found unacceptable if the woman in question were someone else's wife. It was also the arrangement that Radcliffe had hinted at.

"You can't have her," he said, returning to his seat with a stiff spine that matched his determination. "Once you helped me lose the thing that mattered to me most. I won't let you besmirch my wife with your squalid morals."

If Denford were capable of sincerity, that's how Damian would have read his softened gaze. "You mistake me. My intentions are entirely honorable. I wish to marry your wife."

"You can't. She's already married to me."

"Obviously. That's why she's your wife. That can be changed. Divorce her. I'll give you cause— God knows I've been trying hard enough—then you can bring your plea to Parliament. Given your connections in the cabinet, there should be no difficulty persuading that coterie of rogues and extortionists." Denford spoke of His Majesty's government with the scorn of a bishop sermonizing on the denizens of hell.

"You are mad. I understand you wanted to seduce Cynthia to get back at me. But why would you go to all the trouble to wed her?"

"I may be mad, Damian, but you are a horse's arse. I used to feel guilty about what happened at Cruikshank's, but no more. You marry a lady who not only brings you a fortune, but is also beautiful, clever, and kind, and you have no idea how lucky you are. Instead of appreciating your treasure, you neglect her."

Damian stared at Julian in amazement. He really meant what he said. "Are you in love with my wife?"

"I'm not even sure I know what love is. I doubt if I am capable of feeling it and I'm quite sure I don't deserve it. But I have a fancy to settle down and the scandal of a divorce doesn't trouble me. I've never been respectable and I don't care if I am now. Some people will fawn over me because I'm a duke, others will shun me. Either way, I don't give a damn."

"You never did." At first this carelessness of convention had strongly attracted Damian. Invited to Julian's rooms in Christ Church College, he'd discovered an Aladdin's cave of drawings and watercolors pinned on walls, propped on the mantelpiece, and littering every flat surface. Drunk with aesthetic stimulation, Damian had tripped over a stray copy of Aristotle's *Politics* that lay abandoned on the floor. When he apologized for damaging the book, Julian opened the window and flung it out into the quadrangle. "Dreadfully dull book," he said. Damian, who had dutifully plowed through the Latin and Greek texts that Eton required for university preparation, was alarmed and thrilled. Shortly afterward he discovered how little was required of a nobleman at Oxford and took full advantage of the laxity. But it was Julian who had showed him the way.

It was Julian who had led him down the primrose path of wild behavior and cocking a snook at his father. Julian who had opened his world to a dizzying variety of sensations and experiences outside the ken of a naïve and sheltered boy. Julian who had ultimately driven him back to embrace the straight and narrow with all the zeal of the convert.

Julian, the most important influence in his earlier life, had stolen the woman who should be the central figure of his future, and wanted to make the theft permanent. Except, he hadn't. Damian was so shocked by his proposition, he'd missed the careless admission of Julian's failure to seduce Cynthia.

He'd refused to believe her when she swore she'd never been with Julian, but she'd been telling the truth. Of course she had. Cynthia, Lady Windermere, his wife, was an honest woman, as anyone but a consummate fool would know after half an hour in her company. A dozen times, as he'd come to know his wife, he'd found himself thinking of her as innocent, and he'd been right all along. If only he'd listened to his instinct instead of his reason. She was true blue and incorruptible.

"You never bedded her," he stated. The question that had haunted him was settled in his mind without a shadow of doubt. He didn't even need confirmation.

Julian shrugged. "Lady Windermere proved a tough nut to crack. I did my best from the first day I met her at Caro's. A worthy punishment for you, I thought."

"Because of the Maddox business." The exploitation of an innocent in their strife turned his mouth sour. His desire for revenge had set off the exchange but it was Julian who had brought Cynthia into their conflict. "You should be ashamed of yourself," he said. "My wife had nothing to do with what happened between us."

"Believe it or not, I am ashamed." They looked

at each other across the endless two-yard width of the marble hearth, and Damian wondered if he imagined the regret and anger in the other's eyes, or whether he was still reading his own mind. Then Julian shook his ridiculous long hair, ran a long thumb over the silver tip of his affected ebony walking stick, and smiled his taunting smile. "Not that being seduced by me wouldn't have been thoroughly enjoyable for her."

Damian's fists clenched, not least because *he* was ashamed. Cynthia would have had a better time in bed with her lover than she'd had with her husband. But he intended to remain her husband and make sure she never regretted the loss of the Duke of Denford. He summoned the reserves of patience and calm he'd cultivated in years of diplomacy to keep himself planted in his chair. But he was a coiled spring, a jack-in-the-box ready to launch itself at the least provocation, straight for Julian Fortescue's traitorous face.

"Back to business," Julian said. "If I'm to be wed, I'd prefer a wife I like and admire. I cannot imagine a woman I'd rather spend my life with than Cynthia. She only married you because her uncle bullied her. I'll make her happier than you do."

Julian, with his unerring eye for quality, had seen the remarkable woman behind the gentle exterior. He was right about Cynthia and about Damian too. Where his wife was concerned Damian had been an utter arse, so caught up in his own concerns he'd had little thought for her. He'd arrogantly assumed from the start that she had wished to wed him, been honored by the match and its advantages. But she'd never given any sign of worldly ambition and might very well prefer life with Denford, even with the accompanying scandal.

"Come, let us make an agreement," the duke said. "Your wife in exchange for the Falleron collection."

Sleeping late and drinking chocolate in bed was one benefit of marriage Cynthia had never regretted. She would sip her hot drink, mixed precisely to her taste, and remember waking at dawn in the spartan accommodations of the Birmingham Academy for Young Ladies. Then she would sink back into her plump, soft pillows and think about negotiating Aunt Lavinia's nerves and Uncle Chorley's alarming demands. There was a letter from Birmingham that morning. Chorley had learned of Windermere's return and ordered his niece, in blunt terms, to get herself with child immediately, since she couldn't be relied upon to keep him in her bed for long before he wandered off to another part of the world. That she'd denied Damian last night gave her a certain satisfaction, as far as Chorley was concerned. She'd go about the conception of a little Chorley-Lewis heir when she was ready.

While taking her side against her uncle's on the Spitalfields Acts wasn't a prerequisite for intimacy, giving her a serious hearing was. Sir Richard Radcliffe, she remembered, was acquainted with Joseph Chorley and they had much in common. Neither exercised a benign influence over her life and marriage.

On her way downstairs Cynthia glanced into the drawing room and her eye caught the gargantuan French buffet, for which Hamble had billed three hundred guineas, in all its overgilded, overwrought glory. She didn't regret the ruse that financed her Flowers Street household. Choosing only the ugliest objects least suited to the classic elegance of Windermere House was another matter. It had been done for revenge, and wasn't revenge always petty? She'd seen Damian wince when he laid eyes (and his behind) on the cerise sofa and avoid looking at the gruesome still life in the hall. He did seem to enjoy the pair of censers, though for their use rather than their beauty. Thinking about that evening, the happiest of her married life, made her blush.

With a newfound determination to forge a marriage on her own terms, it seemed fair to begin with a gesture toward his. She would make a list of all the most dubious purchases and replace them with items in good taste. No, it would be better to consult Damian. They would do it together and learn more about each other in the process.

The morning room was empty but for a servant clearing away two used places. "Mr. Bream just left," the footman informed her. "I believe His Lordship is in the library."

She hoped they'd got on well together, Damian and Oliver. It would be agreeable to have friends in common. Not much chance of him making up with Julian. Yet those were Denford's deep tones wafting down the back passage from the partly open door of her husband's sanctum. Apprehension knotted her stomach as she stopped at the door.

"Come, let us make an agreement. Your wife in exchange for the Falleron collection. You don't want Cynthia. You only married her for Beaulieu."

The wickedness of Julian's brazen request scarcely registered. All she cared about was the answer. She held her breath, waiting for her husband to deny it, at least the part about not wanting her. Julian's claim had once been true, but surely no longer. They'd come so far in the days since his return.

"She's mine," Damian said in a voice like a growl.

The two possessive words send a thrill down her spine. Her fists clenched as she waited for him to elaborate. *She's mine and she will stay mine because I care for her.* Those were the words she longed to hear.

"She's mine and you can't have her."

You can't have her.

Hope fizzled like a snowflakes on a bonfire and turned into steam.

They were Lysander and Demetrius, always wanting the same women. Or a pair of dogs growling over a bone. She, Cynthia, a living breathing human, was merely the latest object in the long rivalry between Damian and Julian. She stepped into the room and slammed the door behind her. Had she been in the mood, the two men's gaping surprise would have been comical. They stood side by side on the hearth, frozen in attack position.

"Lower your fists, Windermere," she snapped. "And you, Denford. I will not have any fighting in my house."

Damian did as he was bid, though his stance remained tense. He pierced her with a bright, unwavering regard. She was glad to see him tense and emotionally overwrought with not a hint of unnatural calm.

"Now sit down like civilized creatures," she said, "instead of a pair of snarling hounds leaping for each other's throats, and you can tell me what this is about."

Julian relaxed onto his heels, hands behind his back, a faint smile twisting his mouth. "By all means. Why not ring for tea and cakes while we are at it?"

Damian took her elbow and turned her toward

the door. "Please leave us, my lady. I shall deal with Denford, and then we will talk. In private."

"No," she said, shaking him off. "You were discussing me when I came in and I have a right to hear it."

"Certainly you do," Julian said. "It concerns you intimately." What mischief had he caused before he made his outrageous offer? "I want to marry you."

"What?" She backed away from both men. "That's absurd. In case you haven't noticed, I am already wed."

"That's why I need to speak to your husband about a divorce."

Divorce! Typical of Julian, he spoke as though he'd asked for nothing so very unusual. She'd only ever *heard* of anything so shocking and had no idea how a marriage could be dissolved. It was the kind of thing ladies whispered about in horror.

"Do you want to ruin me?" she asked furiously.

"On the contrary. I want to take you away from your ungrateful lout of a husband and cherish you as you deserve. We'll go abroad." Julian's blue eyes flashed. He was enjoying the confrontation.

She scowled at him and turned to Damian, who was red in the face as though about to have a seizure. "And you, my lord? What do you think of this proposal?"

"There has never been a divorce in my family and there never will be."

Wrong answer. "I see. You married me for an estate and want to keep me to prevent a scandal. And because another man wants me. You're nothing but a dog in the manger."

"You're very busy with the canine metaphors today," Julian remarked.

"Be quiet," she said through clenched teeth. "You've caused quite enough trouble. I think you should leave."

"I'll leave if you come with me," Julian said. His dark, sardonic presence intimidated some, but to her, today, he was merely annoying.

She turned to the man who could make her bones melt with a look or a touch. "Well, my lord. What do you have to say?" Silently she begged him to ask her to stay, to show that she was more than a piece of property he refused to give up. Julian was right about one thing: She did deserve to be cherished. But the wrong man had offered.

Damian wasn't getting the message. Once again he steered her toward the door. "Please, my lady. Leave us so that I can get on with giving Denford the beating he's been asking for these last seven years." Without waiting for an answer, he left her standing and launched himself at the duke, knocking over a fire screen on the way and catching Julian by surprise. The two of them landed on the carpet in a tangle of limbs, accompanied by grunts, bangs, and a good deal of swearing.

She had had enough. "I'm leaving," she said, though she doubted they heard her. "I was invited to spend Christmas at Castleton House and I have decided, belatedly, to accept the invitation." She didn't care if she never saw either of them again.

Chapter 19

By the time they fought each other to a standstill, everything hurt. Damian sat on the floor, inhaling great gulping breaths, sure that every inch of his body was bruised. Julian was in the same condition, panting heavily, his long hair, which Damian remembered pulling in violation of all gentlemanly rules, failing to disguise one eye swollen shut. He put a hand to his own aching nose and found blood.

It had been a messy fight. They used to fence together but neither had been fond of boxing.

"Why did you do it?" Damian asked. He didn't have to explain the question. Kicks, bites, gouges, and flailing fists had cut through the accumulating detritus of seven years of enmity and brought them back to the evening at Cruikshank's gaming house. "You urged me to wager Beaulieu."

"No one forced you." A fat lip muffled Julian's words.

"You took me home."

"That's what a friend does. Should I have left you passed out in a corner?"

Damian closed his eyes and relived the fetid atmosphere of the Pall Mall hell, the odor of tallow, sweat, vomit, and desperation. "Better than leaving Robert alone. You could have guessed what he would do. I trusted you."

Julian avoided his eye, as he had the day after when he delivered the news that Robert had lost the deed to Beaulieu to a well-known cardsharp. "I didn't think Robert would wager your property. I'm sorry." And Damian didn't believe him now, any more than he had at the time.

"Admit it, Julian. You *knew* there was a chance he'd lose it. Damnation, even drunk as a wheelbarrow I would have known it. The only reason I didn't was that I was unconscious. No friend of mine would have left Robert alone."

"I've committed many sins. Believe it or not, Damian, failing to protect your handsome little inheritance from the depredations of our demented friend is not the worst thing I've done, or the worst thing I've seen, by a very long way."

"What kind of an excuse is that? I ask you one more time, why did you do it?" The question had hovered at the back of his mind for years, tormenting him whenever he thought of his loss, the loss of Beaulieu and of friendship. "Did you resent me? That's it, isn't it? You were jealous because I came into my fortune and you had nothing. And yet," he added bitterly, "I would have shared it with you. You had only to ask. We were like brothers."

"Were you going to give me half your estate? I don't think so. The world doesn't work like that. You and Robert were born with everything, you especially. Marcus and I had nothing. Every penny in our purses, every thread on our backs, had to be begged or earned. I'm sorry about Beaulieu because I know it was important to you, but its loss didn't ruin you. You still had your title and Amblethorpe and the connections to succeed as a diplomat. When you took away the Maddox collection you set me back years. I failed you, Damian, but you failed me too. I returned from France and found you and Robert still playing at being rich boys. And why not? That's what you were. But I had seen terrible things in Paris and I was no longer in the mood for playing."

"What happened? We knew you must have seen the Terror and the public executions by guillotine. When I asked you about it you put me off with satirical jests. If you were so troubled, why didn't you tell me?"

"Because talking changes nothing. Look at us now. We've spoken about our differences but it hasn't made them go away."

"Talking may not have. Perhaps fighting helped. You're going to have a hell of a black eye tomorrow." Damian shifted again, trying to find a way to rest that didn't hurt. Gingerly he used his handkerchief to dab at his nose, which seemed to have stopped bleeding. "I think you may have broken my nose."

"We are an insult to the noble art of pugilism," Julian said.

On one level Damian wanted to laugh, but while the fight had drained his poisonous rage, it left him with a new anxiety. When Cynthia left the room she'd said something he'd been too drunk on bloodlust to comprehend. He pulled himself onto his knees. "Can you walk?"

"Can you?"

Swaying, Damian managed to get onto his feet. "Yes. I'll send a servant to show you out, if you need help."

"What, no lovely lady to tenderly bathe my wounds?"

The fight hadn't made Julian less provocative. "If that's a reference to my wife, you are right. Talking makes no difference."

"I assume that means you are rejecting my offer."

"You assume correctly."

"So dear Prince Heinrich won't be getting his pictures."

"Prince Heinrich can go drown himself in the North Sea for all I care."

"Tsk, tsk. Such lack of regard for the future of Great Britain, let alone your own future with the Foreign Office." Julian, who had also risen, retrieved his ebony walking stick from the floor behind a chair. For once, he genuinely needed its support. "So lucky you have a good estate and a rich wife and can afford to kiss a career good-bye."

Damian discovered that even grinding his teeth hurt. "If you know what's good for you, you won't be seeing my wife again."

"Which is where we came in. You know I don't respond well to threats, my dear Damian."

"Fine. Let me try a statement of fact. Cynthia is my wife, and I am keeping her."

"You may certainly try. If she hasn't already left you. But you still have Beaulieu and that's all you care about."

Cynthia had said something about Beaulieu too, before she left. *You married me for an estate.* Everyone thought so because it was, of course, true. But not anymore. If he lost Beaulieu tomorrow, along with every penny of Chorley's fortune, he'd still want her. As Julian was intelligent enough to notice, his wife was beautiful, clever, and kind. Damian was supremely fortunate to have married her, but instead of telling her so, he'd lost his temper and ranted about scandal.

Damian tore out into the hall, where Ellis was in the act of closing the front door.

The butler stared at him. "Ahem, my lord. I had thought it better not to interrupt the—er—contretemps in the library but perhaps I was wrong. Should I summon a physician?"

"Where is Her Ladyship?" Damian shouted.

"I just handed her into the traveling chaise, my lord. She said you were aware that the Duchess of Castleton had summoned her suddenly."

He hobbled through the door and stood on the front steps clutching his bruised ribs as he watched Cynthia's carriage disappear into Brook Street. A worse pain afflicted his heart at the thought of losing her.

"I'm going to join Her Ladyship," he told Ellis. "I'll travel post. Send a footman to the inn. No, never mind, I'll ride. Organize a horse and send my valet up to me."

"Are you well enough, my lord?" Ellis asked. He must look like a savage with hair awry and a bloody nose.

"I'm fine. I am also in a hurry." He stopped on the stairs. "Did Her Ladyship travel alone?"

"Of course not, my lord. She took a footman and her maid. And the kitten, Pudge." Damian's heart sank. If she intended to leave him for good she wouldn't abandon her pet.

As he washed his face, which had survived the battle unmarred aside from the nosebleed, his valet fussed.

"Never mind that. Put my shaving gear and a change of linen into a saddlebag. If I'm not back with Her Ladyship tomorrow, I'll send for you and my trunks."

When he even thought about failing to change

her mind he suffered a panic that numbed all physical pain and left a single, bright truth. He burned for his wife with a passion that excluded any other concern. Nothing else mattered.

It was bitter cold and starting to drizzle but with luck he ought to overtake the carriage before she'd covered even half of the thirty-mile journey. Dame Fortune teased but did not abandon him. An overturned cart, an argumentative toll keeper, and a flock of sheep delayed him a little. On the other hand he learned that Cynthia's chaise had passed the tollgate at Hounslow. He was on the right road and not far behind.

As the miles passed, his aches and pains became harder to ignore. He vowed never again to undertake a lengthy journey on horseback after a hard fight. Or maybe he should avoid fighting, though that might prove difficult while Julian, Duke of Denford, remained on earth. Their conversation had solved nothing between them. His one consolation was that Cynthia, in fleeing London, had left Denford too. As the countryside opened up and the traffic grew lighter, he was able to progress from a trot to a canter, much easier on his bruises. But away from the heat of the metropolis, a light rain turned to sleet and then a steady snowfall. Passing an abandoned coach that had slid off the slippery road, he prayed she'd had the good sense to stop at an inn.

He inquired at every inn in Staines but to no avail, wasting precious minutes. Snow coated his hat and shoulders; his sore nose risked the added indignity of frostbite. He was forced to slow his mount to a walk as the road disappeared in a coating of white, so that he could no longer see ruts or holes. The beast would need to be rested soon, even if the early winter dusk wasn't looming. Surely Cynthia couldn't be too far ahead, and if she was he'd have to speak sharply to his coachman for putting his mistress in danger.

Blinded by the swirling snow, he didn't see the smart blue carriage before he almost rode into it. He'd ordered the new vehicle when he'd become betrothed, thinking then that he would stay in England and settle down with his new bride, before he'd escaped to Persia in dismay. How he wished he'd stayed, for many reasons, one of which was that he would not now be dealing with a wife, servants, and equipage in a snowstorm that looked fit to rival a Russian buran.

Drawing his mount alongside the stalled chaise, he pulled open the door. "What do you mean, going out in this weather?" he demanded, relief making him surly. He addressed the sole occupant of the carriage, who was not, he realized with stark horror, his wife. "Where is Her Ladyship?" The maid gaped and pointed to the open door on the other side. "What the devil? Are you mad, Cynthia?" he called. "Get back in immediately." There was no sight or sound of her.

"Is that you, my lord?" The coachman, on foot, looked up at him.

"Yes, Harrison, it is. Why did you stop? I would have hoped you had the sense to take shelter by now."

"Yes, my lord. I wanted to stop at Staines but Her Ladyship said to go a little farther. With the snow getting deeper I reckoned I'd better lead the horses. We're less than a mile from Egham now."

"Very good. Now where *is* Her Ladyship?"

"Excuse me, my lord," said the maid. "A minute ago, when we stopped, my lady opened the door and the kitten escaped. She went after it and I was about to go after her."

The encounter was degenerating into farce and Damian was not amused. He dismounted, handed the reins to Harrison, and strode around the carriage in the direction the maid had indicated. "Cynthia!" he shouted over wind whistling through trees invisible in the swirling white fury. Nothing. He yelled louder and thought he heard a faint cry. Following the sound he swore under his breath as his boots slid on the grassy edge, almost casting him into the ditch. Only a dozen feet away he found her sprawled on the ground. "Are you hurt?"

"Damian! What are you doing here?" At least she wasn't unconscious. "I slipped."

"Not surprising when you go walking in the snow. Can you get up?"

"Not without dropping Pudge. She won't stop wriggling."

"Give her to me." He leaned over and took the creature, who protested piteously when he thrust her into the capacious side pocket of his greatcoat, and reached down a hand to pull Pudge's owner upright.

"I'm not hurt," she said. "Just wet and cold."

"That's your own fault. Now hurry. You can ride with me to the inn."

He settled into the saddle with Cynthia secure in his arms, took the reins, and headed forward, praying to make it to safety without wandering off the road or laming the horse. It seemed likely to be the longest less-than-a-mile of his life.

He'd come after her. She didn't know why. But if he was going to be so unpleasant, he would have done better to remain in London.

As she lay winded in the road, his voice had called through the freezing misery and she'd thought for a minute that she'd died, which was odd because things hadn't seemed to have reached such a desperate state in the short time since she'd left the carriage. But while a soul on the spiritual plane might imagine her husband's voice, being clawed by a kitten was a distinctly living experience. So was snow down the back of her neck.

"You're a fool to set out on a journey in this kind of weather," he said brusquely, after he and the coachman bundled her onto his horse without so much as a by-your-leave. She felt helpless, little stronger than her kitten. Her cloak, warm enough for a carriage, was not designed for rescues in the snow and was soaked through.

"I didn't know it was going to snow, did I?" she complained through chattering teeth. "How convenient it would be if the newspaper printed a daily forecasting of climatic conditions in different parts of the country."

"It's the middle of winter. You should have guessed."

"It hasn't snowed a single flake all month."

They were arguing about the weather.

She stiffened when he tried to draw her closer against his chest. "Keep still. This will be warmer." He adjusted his heavy coat to protect her from the wind.

"Why did you follow me?" she asked sullenly.

"Why did you bring the kitten? A carriage journey is no place for a cat."

"She was perfectly good."

"Until she escaped and nearly killed you."

"She thought we'd arrived. And I was fine." Her shivers belied the claim.

"Oh yes, fine indeed. Lying in the ditch where you might have frozen to death if I hadn't turned up."

"Harrison would have helped me."

"You have no business endangering yourself and my servants."

"I suppose you're worried about the carriage too." The anger that had driven her out of London lingered although he had responded the way she wanted. He'd come after her. Nevertheless, she couldn't stop the pointless sniping.

"Certainly. It's only a year old."

"What have you done with my cat?"

"Warm and snug in my pocket. She's probably fallen asleep." His voice turned gentle, with a note of humor, and her indignation slipped away. She'd left because she wanted him to want her. Wasn't chasing her on horseback through a storm a step in the right direction? She relaxed and rested her cheek against his chest "We'll get you warm and snug too, very soon," he promised.

"Thank you," she replied softly, feeling safe and protected.

She had no idea sharing a horse was such an intimate thing. While his hands were busy with the reins, his arms enclosed her, holding her firm. Her legs rested across his thighs and she grew ever more aware of their sinewy strength beneath his breeches, and of the distinct bulge of what lay in between. The slow jogging of the horse had her thinking of a different rhythm. She nuzzled his neckcloth, inhaling the refined scent of the soap he favored together with the earthier notes of leather and horse, and provoked a slight, almost imperceptible hitch of breath in reaction. Threading one hand inside his coat, she felt the beat of his heart.

"What?" he asked.

"My hand is cold," she lied.

He urged the horse forward. She would be sorry when the journey ended and also glad. For the inn would provide bedchambers. Perhaps only one.

"I see light up ahead," he said. "We'll have you in a warm bed soon."

She was already beginning to feel quite warm, thank you.

Reaching the inn yard, he dismounted, then lifted her down, keeping her in his arms. It turned out that the The Swan at Egham was a small place that didn't see many travelers. The innkeeper, once convinced that he had a pair of noble guests on his hands, was all smiles, promising accommodations for the entire party. He dispatched the ostler to help with the carriage and a maid to prepare bedchambers for my lord and my lady. Bedchambers. Two of them. One each.

"I haven't seen snow like this in years," the innkeeper remarked. "I reckon most travelers stopped at Staines."

"Sensible ones did," Damian agreed, giving her a significant look. She uttered a faint squawk of protest at his needling. "My wife had a slight accident and I need to get her warm at once."

"I can walk," she said.

"She's delirious."

There were worse things than being carried. It kept her in Damian's arms.

Damian bore her up to the inn's best bedchamber where a servant was plying a warming pan between the sheets of the bed.

"Here you are," he said, putting her down next to the already glowing fire. "A room this size will warm up soon. Would you like something to drink?"

"Tea would be agreeable."

"Bring some tea for my lady."

The servant departed, leaving an awkward silence. Damian held his hands out to the heat. His practiced glibness had deserted him, leaving him staring at his wife in frustrated longing. Holding the woman he adored so close had been a delicious torture. In the course of the short ride, outright hostility had softened to silly bickering and ended in a silent harmony he hadn't wanted to end.

"I should leave you." He didn't want to. "The fire is beginning to take hold. It'll warm up soon."

"You just said that." She tugged at her bonnet and tossed it aside to reveal golden hair incongruously dry. He reached out a hand to touch the shining locks that swept back from her forehead, then pulled back. Clamping his arms firmly to his sides before they got any ideas, he felt a lump in his pocket. "Here," he said, extracting a yawning kitten. "Here's your cat."

"Thank you." Not for the first time he envied the creature clasped to her bosom. She dropped a kiss on its tiny gray head and settled it on a pillow, where it yawned again, turned over, and went back to sleep.

He stared at the bed. It was a good size and looked comfortable. "You'll have to disturb her when you get into bed."

"Pudge won't mind. She doesn't mind anything, even lumpy mattresses." He might have read an invitation in the remark, but he was humble and unsure of himself. He didn't trust himself to interpret the widening of her blue eyes, the faint curve of her pink mouth. His intention was to subject his wife to a prolonged campaign of wooing before he tried his luck again.

"I'll leave you to undress."

"I have nothing to change into until the carriage arrives but I need to remove this wet gown." She tossed aside her cloak and presented her back. "I have no maid either. Will you undo me, please?"

Now this was torture. There was nothing in the world he wanted more than to undress his wife yet he couldn't believe things would end up according to his deepest, most fervent desires.

Focusing on the immediate task, he examined the back of her gown.

As she visualized Damian's long fingers seeking the fastenings of her sensible but stylish traveling gown, Cynthia's skin tingled. Waves of longing shot down to her belly. Closing her eyes, she heard the faint click as the hooks were loosened, felt the chill on the exposed back of her neck, his cool hands through the linen of her shift. The minute the gown slackened she swayed backward, finding nothing but air and space. He'd stepped away.

"You are undone," he said in measured tones.

Shaking her shoulders, she let the gown slip to the ground and stepped out of the stiff woolen circle. Pivoting on the heels of her half boots, she faced him. He was beautiful and solemn, like an angel at the last judgment. Did angels have earthly desires? How could he stand there still as a graven image when her intimate core was empty and throbbing, aching to be filled by him. She chose to believe it wasn't her fancy that his gray eyes had turned dark, dark with need. Need for her.

Oh, she was indeed undone.

"Your shoes are wet." Never had mundane words sounded so fraught with sensual possibilities.

Without uttering a word, she sat on the edge of the mattress and extended a leg. He dropped to one knee, and worked off the damp jean boot. Then he took the stockinged foot between his palms and rubbed the soles with his thumbs. She let her linen shift rise up, her knees fall open, evoking flared nostrils and a hitch of breath. Nevertheless, he did nothing but continue his blissful ministrations until she removed her foot and offered the other. While he removed the boot she tried an experiment, opening her thighs so brazenly that her intention could not be mistaken. She felt herself grow hot and wet inside. He glanced up the inviting tunnel and smiled. The message had been received. With utter concentration he returned to the massage of her foot.

The curve of his mouth propelled her state of longing into the heavens. He too had delivered a message. He was hers, just as soon as she gave the signal.

"Damian," she said, stroking the dark hair back from his forehead. It was soft and disordered, unlike its usual impeccable state. She noticed a faint bruise on his left cheekbone and, when he looked up, a reddening and perhaps a trace of blood about the shapely nose. She didn't want to hear about his fight with Julian.

"What?"

"I want you."

"Are you sure?"

"I've never been so sure of anything in my life."

He swallowed. "Shall we undress?"

His blazing eyes sent her up in flames. "I want you now. Fast. I don't want to wait a minute. Not even a second."

Her husband knew what *fast* meant. He released her foot and pushed her firmly onto her back. Spread-eagled before him with arms extended, bare to her upper thighs aside from her stockings and garters, legs hanging over the end of the mattress, she felt shockingly, delectably open. The air, warmed by the fire but still with a little winter nip, cooled her private parts without in the least diminishing the burning heat inside. Tilting her head, she watched him watch her. Fully dressed in coat and waistcoat, breeches, and tall polished top boots, he offered a picture of masculine grace and strength that evoked a soft vulnerability in her that she could define only as a wish to be utterly possessed.

"I think you'll have to take at least one garment off." She cast a taunting little smile, lest he think anything had changed and he was in charge.

"There are so many areas in which your education needs to be improved." Without taking his eyes off her, he opened the buttons of his sober brown buckskin breeches.

"*Un, deux, trois . . .*" she counted. "*Quatre, cinq, six.*" All the way to eleven.

And the fall of leather descended.

"Your French really has improved, my lady."

His male member leaped out from a frame of white linen. Far from sober, it seemed unbridled and fierce, darker than the rest of his skin, thick and powerful-looking. This time she anticipated nothing but pleasure. She stretched her arms and legs wider and lifted her pelvis. "*Maintenant, s'il vous plait, monsieur.*"

He stood between her splayed legs and lifted her shift all the way to the waist. She felt no shyness, only exhilaration. "*Enchanté, madame,*" he replied, grasping her bottom with one hand to bring her to the right height. Her head lolled back onto the bed so she didn't see how he came in, only felt the quest at her entrance followed by a thrust and a smooth, gliding entry. "*Je veux te foutre.*"

Whatever he said sounded wicked and possessive; she felt wicked and possessed. Owned by him, utterly in his hands to take what he meted out with every confidence that the result would be her pleasure.

"Ooooh, yes," she crooned on a long breath.

Her very great pleasure.

"All right?" he asked in a strained voice.

"Oh my goodness, Damian," she shrieked.

Her extreme delight.

"I take it that's a yes. You are incredible."

"Don't stop."

"Not a chance."

Both hands held her at exactly the place he wanted, resisting her involuntary convulsions as he withdrew and returned again, and again. With each entrance her longing increased, building to the crescendo of sensation he'd given her with his mouth the night of the bhang. Now she knew what to expect and, as far as his controlling hands allowed, met him thrust for thrust and discovered inner muscles that could clench his marvelous, brilliant member, savagely demanding it remain within, even as each movement intensified her bliss. Her thighs closed about his hips, her legs wound about him, holding him tight.

"*Finalement, je te fous,*" he gasped between heavy breaths. Since she didn't know this particular French phrase, she guessed that it wasn't one she would encounter in polite society. Rightly so. There was nothing polite about their joining. It was crude and earthy. The motions were the same as the soulless couplings they had endured after their marriage, but there the resemblance ended. How the same motions could achieve so different a result, she had no idea. He was a silken hammer in her soft cradle and she loved every slick inward drive, each momentary retreat, each return more satisfying than the last. She couldn't stand the joy and never wanted it to end as she mounted to the same apex of ecstasy she'd enjoyed before. She felt that crest of joy, then the tumbling into delight, no less astonishing for being known.

"Oh, Damian," she keened, jerking her head from side to side on the counterpane.

"*Oui,*" she screamed. "Oh God, yes!"

As tremors seized her body, his movements sped

to a fever until they were wild and unrestrained. She expected the stiffening of his muscles, the arching of his neck, the cry of completion, and the rush of heat as he spilled his seed.

What happened next was different, though. Instead of removing himself from her body and her bed, he collapsed on her, still joined. As she became capable of sensations beyond what she dubbed the earthquake of delight, she registered the scratchiness of his coat rubbing her arms and neck and the tops of her breasts, rising above her stays. He took her mouth in a long, deep, wet kiss of the kind he'd never given her during their previous unions. For the first time she felt a *rightness* about this most intimate of actions, the strange congress of man and wife. More than that. It might just be the best thing the world had to offer.

Eventually, out of breath, they parted. They ended up sprawled on the bed, side by side with only the backs of their hands touching, a fleeting shadow of their devastating embrace.

"Sorry, Pudge," Damian said when the kitten squeaked and retreated to the hearth to continue her nap. "Was that fast enough for you?"

"Yes, thank you."

"Slow can be good too." He trailed his fingers over her breasts.

Would it be proper to say *I look forward to finding out*? She settled for "Oh." Her boldness had vanished, leaving her paralyzed by shyness. Etiquette offered no guidance as to what to say under these circumstances. She wasn't sure Lady Ashfield herself would be able to advise her on the correct behavior in this situation.

He tucked her head into the curve of his shoulder, making her wince. "Did I hurt you?"

"Just a hairpin. I can't believe my hair is still up after that agitation." He helped her rummage among her tousled locks, handing her the pins until they were all removed. The simple task seemed profoundly personal, more so than the energetic union of their bodies. That was a normal function of marriage while hair arranging was not. A strange and illogical truth.

"Why do you smile?"

"No reason. I just feel well." Discussing her peculiar insight was a further advance in intimacy she wasn't yet ready to pursue. The intensity of their congress had receded, leaving her physically replete but aware of the weighty issues that still lay between them.

Chapter 20

Damian awoke feeling sore all over and unsure of where he was. The bed was smaller than he was used to, though comfortable enough. The small chamber was well heated. The window revealed only that it was daylight and snowing. It all came back to him.

"Good morning!"

Now this was a sight worth waking up to. Cynthia, clad in blue with her golden hair neatly dressed, smiling at him from a seat near the fire.

"What time is it?"

"I'm not sure. I've been up a couple of hours but I decided to let you sleep." Pink roses suffused her creamy cheeks. "You had a long ride through the snow."

"It's still coming down, I see."

"I doubt we'll be going anywhere today."

Perhaps not tomorrow either. She couldn't escape him, and enforced proximity would give him the chance to woo her into staying with him willingly, joyously. Yesterday's lovemaking had been a good start.

"There's food in the next room. Since we shared a bed"—she blushed again—"and the inn doesn't have a private parlor, I ordered breakfast upstairs. There is bread and butter and cold meats. The tea is probably cold but I can ring for fresh, and something more substantial if you wish."

"I'm sure it will do very well. Uh, how did we come to share a room and why don't I remember?"

"You came with me upstairs after dinner, removed your coat, lay down on the bed, and fell asleep."

The sheer bliss of ending a long sexual drought, and in sensational fashion, had temporarily numbed the havoc wrought by a brutal fight followed by a long, hard ride in poor conditions. The triumphant charge had ebbed over dinner. Damian had much to say to Cynthia and no idea how to begin. Perhaps it was as well that they had dined in a public room, under the interested eye of the innkeeper and his wife and a stranded commercial traveler who was the only other guest.

"That wasn't very polite of me. Apparently I at least had the decency to remove my boots too."

"As a matter of fact I pulled them off. It was quite a struggle."

"I am obliged."

The pink roses turned to deep red as she fixed her attention on the large sketch pad she held on her lap. She'd been bold enough in the grip of passion, but he rather hoped her grasp of French didn't extend to the crudities he'd used in bed. In five minutes he returned, still wearing only his shirt and breeches.

"Since we're not going anywhere today, I don't see the point of dressing. I brought my breakfast in here, if you don't mind."

"Not at all."

With Cynthia occupying the only chair, he perched on the end of the mattress, the recent location of long-delayed satisfaction. Thinking about that incredible bout had him ready for a repetition. But she looked so ladylike and serene this morning that it was impossible to believe she'd opened her legs and demanded he take her. He bit into a sandwich of bread and ham, concentrated on chewing it thoroughly, and watched her draw.

"Another window view?" he asked.

"It wouldn't be very interesting since there's nothing to see but snow." She peeked at him from under her lashes. "I attempted to draw you while you slept. I hope you don't mind."

"Would you show it to me?"

Without a word she handed him the block. Remembering the less than flattering portrait she'd produced before, he looked with some trepidation. For a moment he scarcely recognized the face. He'd never seen himself with his eyes closed, but that wasn't the reason. He stared at a man he hadn't seen in years, one he'd once known well. A young face, innocent and carefree in repose, smiling faintly in his sleep, the only shadow a dusting of bristles on his chin. He couldn't quite define the difference from the earlier drawing. The features were the same.

"You're frowning," Cynthia said. "Do you think it very bad? I was quite pleased with the likeness."

"Is this how I always look when I am asleep?"

"I haven't enough experience to judge so I'll have to let you know."

"Do you think I look the same when awake?"

"Not always. You do today." As she studied him, he wanted nothing better than to kiss the gravity from her bewitching features and fluster her into blushing smiles. "Openness," she said, with a nod. "Ever since I've known you, you've been closed off, self-contained, giving away nothing. As I drew you sleeping I saw you without a mask."

"I am a diplomat. It is my job to be diplomatic."

"Do you have to be like that with me?"

He did not. He hadn't always been so with others either. Under the influence of Radcliffe, he had hidden his emotions and buried them so deep they'd almost ceased to exist. The lessons had fallen on fertile ground. Or frozen ground, rather. He'd come to Sir Richard in a state of shock and readily assimilated precepts that had numbed his pain. "I don't want to be."

"Tell me about yourself."

It would be easier to show her. "May I borrow your pencil?" She handed it over without any comment but a raised brow. "Would you mind standing? You have the only chair." He posed her at the end of the bed, the cheap worsted curtains providing a swirl of drapery to complement her graceful form. "Look at the window, please, to present a three-quarters profile."

"Oliver said you used to paint."

"Hm." He outlined the bedpost, curtain, and the sweep of her skirts in half a dozen deft strokes. "I don't suppose you have any charcoal."

"In the pencil case."

He rummaged in the utilitarian wooden box on the floor next to the chair. "I always found I could get a better effect with charcoal. For shading."

"Did your mother teach you to draw?" Cynthia asked.

"I think I told you my sister had no talent. It turned out that I did. I always wished I could be an artist."

"But you had to be an earl instead."

He shrugged and applied the fragile black stick to the outlined curtain and smudged it with his finger. He hadn't forgotten the technique, though he badly needed practice. With hands occupied, and half his mind too, he found it easier to talk about the past.

"My father insisted it was no profession for a nobleman, or any man for that matter. He had no interest in the works of man's creation, be they literature, music, or visual. He preferred the products of nature, especially when they could be cultivated for profit or killed for sport. He tolerated the habit in my mother, because he loved her. And because she was a woman." As he sketched the details of Cynthia's figure he remembered the late earl's reaction when he drew pictures of horses instead of riding them. "My enjoyment of drawing lessons was a source of strife between my mother and father. But they came to an accommodation. At Amblethorpe, for most of the year, I was my father's son. But we spent a few months each year at Beaulieu where I was allowed to do as I liked."

She turned her head to show eyes glistening with tears. "And after she died?"

"We didn't go to Beaulieu anymore."

Cynthia held her breath. Beaulieu loomed over his past and their marriage and she wanted to hear more. His dark head bent over his paper and she feared his confidences had come to an end. "Why not?"

"After Mama and Amelia died, my father couldn't bear to go there. But she had left it to me and on my twenty-first birthday it was mine. I intended to live there." His expression was flat again, not closed off so much as bleak.

"Oh God," she whispered. "And then you lost it."

"Julian told you, did he?"

"That's why you married me."

"The only reason. I don't care about the rest of your uncle's money. All I wanted was to get my mother's house back."

"I'm sorry." What else could she say?

"I was too, but not now. I am the one who should apologize. I thought when I had Beaulieu back, I would feel happy again, but it made no difference. I could win back the house, but not the people I loved." He spoke slowly as though the words were hard to summon. Her eyes prickled and she wondered if he was close to weeping himself. "In my anger I treated you unfairly." He looked up, and the candor in his expression sent her heart flying. "I hope you'll give me the chance to make amends. Might you be able to forgive me?" Hearing him own up to some of his past mistakes was a balm to her wounds.

"There's one thing I want to make clear," she said. "I never betrayed you with Julian."

"I know that now."

"I am not wholly innocent. I encouraged his attentions because I knew they would irk you. And I came near to surrender."

"I'm glad you didn't. I believe I could have forgiven you, but it would have been hard for me to forget." He sketched away for a minute then looked up with a steely glare. "I won't let you go to him."

Why? Her chest was tight and she couldn't

speak, even if she'd dared voice the question. *Tell me it's more than possessiveness and jealousy.* She groped in her pocket, seeking a handkerchief.

"You moved."

She had forgotten she was posing for him. "I beg your pardon." She hoped he'd say more but he was intent on his drawing. "May I look?"

"Very well," he said after a moment's hesitation. "It's very rough and I am sorely out of practice. I would only show my work at this stage to a fellow artist."

It was rough, but even this unfinished sketch amazed her. "You are good. But you've flattered me."

"On the contrary. I haven't begun to do you justice. You are a beautiful woman, Cynthia."

The simple statement meant more to her than any of Julian's clever compliments. "Thank you. Did you stop having lessons after your mother died?"

"I dismissed my drawing master out of deference to my father, though I resented it bitterly. The following year I went up to Oxford, determined to continue my studies along with Latin and Greek. The teacher I found recommended I copy the statues in the Ashmolean Museum."

"That's how you met Julian."

"The museum was located in the basement of the Bodleian Library. He laughed at my tutor's hidebound method and said I should travel to Europe and learn to paint like the Old Masters. A few months later, after we'd been summarily ejected from Christ Church College and ordered never to darken the precincts of the university again, that's what I did. We went to Paris."

"That must have been fun." Cynthia sat on the edge of the bed.

"Oh it was. And it vexed my father greatly. We spent the next four years having the time of our lives, in Italy, Germany, Holland, and above all France. I studied drawing in Amsterdam, oil painting in Rome, and both in Paris. We saw the Bastille fall and breathed the heady oxygen of La Liberté."

"Were you a revolutionary sympathizer, Damian? I find it hard to believe."

"I was," he replied stiffly, much more like his usual self. "Until it all went wrong. The revolution turned to cruelty and violence and we came home. The principles that sounded so fine in theory soon created chaos."

"What about the others? Julian and your friends. Did they feel the same?"

"Robert continued to mouth revolutionary platitudes while gambling away his inheritance. Marcus didn't much care."

"And Julian?"

Damian shrugged. "I thought I knew Julian as well as any living soul, but I can't tell you exactly what he thinks of the way Liberty, Equality, and Fraternity descended into mass murder. He went back to Paris alone after Robert and I came home for good. Something happened to him there. And then *it* happened. My towering folly and great disaster."

"I don't understand why you blame Julian. You lost to Robert, and it was he who lost Beaulieu again."

"We played all the time and lost to each other. Vast sums. Marcus makes his living from gaming and Robert was mad for cards and dice. It was an obsession with him. I didn't care for play, except in fun, and Julian, with no money to risk, only ever bet chicken stakes. Throwing the deed to Beaulieu onto the table was stupid. I was among friends and very drunk. Drunker than I realized. I passed out, and this is why I blame Julian. He encouraged me to make the bet and then he took me home, damn him. The next day I went to Robert to redeem the estate but it was too late. He'd never have lost Beaulieu to another gamester if Julian had been there to stop him."

"Julian meant it for the best."

"Did he? I doubt it. He pretended to apologize. And he had the gall to offer the consolation that I would still eventually inherit Amblethorpe. I hated Amblethorpe and he knew it. Robert at least was genuinely sorry."

"Did you speak to either of them again?"

"I went north to tell my father and decided I had to become an upstanding member of the nobility. I wrote to Robert and Julian and told them

I was changing my habits, that I couldn't continue the wild life I'd been leading since I was sixteen." He pulled a rueful face. "I daresay I was a bit pompous."

"I wouldn't be surprised, though under the circumstance you could be forgiven."

"Apparently not. I had been back in town a couple of weeks when Julian invited me to breakfast. I was actually pleased. I had missed him and thought we might make up our quarrel, even if we no longer did everything together." Throughout the recitation Damian had been wound up, intent on his tale of the painful past. She had never seen her husband blush but she was fairly sure that underneath his tan his cheekbones turned red. "I shouldn't tell you this next bit. Not suitable for a lady's ears."

"I believe I will survive." She couldn't imagine what he would say that was more shocking than those Persian paintings. Not to mention what they had done together yesterday in this very spot. "I am a married lady, after all."

"That's the trouble. The next bit concerns a female who was neither a lady nor married."

"You had a mistress? How shocking! I thought you had resolved to turn respectable."

"There's nothing untoward about a single man having— Never mind. I see you are teasing."

"I've spent hours in Caro's company."

"The lady in question was a dancer at the opera

and not my mistress, though I intended that she would be and was not without hope. Until I called at Julian's lodging and found him in bed with her."

"Oh dear! Did you love . . . her?"

"I was deeply enamored, though love may be overstating it."

"There seems to be a pattern to his revenge. So at this point you were the injured party. I suppose you had to get back at him." What was it about men, that they couldn't put wrongs aside and move on? "Something about a collection of pictures."

"I'm not proud of myself. Through my father, I had introduced Julian to Lord Maddox. I mentioned the affair to Radcliffe and his fatter purse prevailed. It was petty on my part, but I can't help thinking Julian deserved it."

"What happened to the dancer? What was her name?"

"I don't remember. I suppose she stayed with him for a while. Julian never had any difficulty attracting women, even without a fat purse."

"Whenever you mention him, there is an edge to your tone that's just like his when he speaks of you. Neither of you can leave the past alone."

"I've never had a friend like him, before or since."

"You miss him."

"I miss what we once had. And I suppose I regret that I can never have it back." He sighed. "Our friendship was like our youth, never to be recovered."

"You poor old man. Do you need me to carry

your charcoal?" She offered a hand with mockery he chose to ignore. Instead he followed her invitation and sat next to her on the bed.

"Now you know about my regrettable past."

"Regret is fruitless. Every experience helped make you the man you are."

"I daren't ask if that is a good thing." he said, looping an arm around her shoulders. "Thank you for listening to my long, dreary tale."

"No thanks are needed. I want to hear about your past, your thoughts, your plans for the future. Part of the trouble with our early marriage was that we didn't talk, or rather you didn't, except in French. The only place you didn't speak French was in the bedchamber." She leaned against his chest, covered only by his shirt. His body warmed her cheek; she felt his breathing and heard the beat of his heart. "You turned things about," she said, slipping her arms about his torso. She'd never held a man like this before and it was lovely. "Yesterday you spoke French in here."

"So I did. I suppose you understood every word."

"I confess that I am uncertain of the meaning of the verb *foutre*."

"It's idiomatic, very hard to translate. In some uses it means 'to put.'"

"*Je veux te foutre*." She remembered the phrase. "'I want to put you' doesn't make sense."

"I told you it was an idiom. *Je veux beaucoup te foutre*. I don't think I can translate it. There's an

English word beginning with the same letter and quite unacceptable in polite society."

"You fiend! I would never say that word."

"You appear to know it, however. One wonders what they teach at the Birmingham Academy for Young Ladies." A low chuckle rippled through him.

"I heard it in London. No one would dare use it in respectable Birmingham."

"Sounds deadly dull."

"It is."

"Since your education in excitement was inadequate, I shall have to take you in hand."

"Teach me something else."

He whispered, sending warm breath and delicious shivers into her ear. "*Je veux descendre à la cave et te baiser là.*"

A hum of sensation shot through her to the area she assumed he meant. "If kissing me in the cellar means what I think it does, you already did that."

"I wasn't sure you remembered. Under the influence of bhang you came quickly and departed into oblivion."

"Tell me more."

"I'm talking myself into a state unsuitable for the forenoon."

"It's not as though we have anywhere to go." She rolled her eyes at the window.

With an exaggerated sigh he pushed her away and returned to the chair. "Stand up, my lady. I have a drawing to finish."

Disappointed, Cynthia resumed her pose. Damian worked away at his charcoal with profound concentration. Only the occasional mutter, of satisfaction or disgust, broke a silence rendered complete by the snow, which muffled the usual noise of an inn yard. It was like being on an island.

"Don't smile. I'm working on your face now. It's hard enough without you twitching."

"What is it like drawing after so many years?"

"Like getting back a missing limb."

"Goodness. I have always enjoyed sketching, and I like to paint in watercolors, but not like that."

"Perhaps because you never lost it." He raised his head, his absurdly perfect features set and grave, but not closed off. "I realize now I did myself a great disservice by giving it up. I must have been mad." Then his mouth curved, very slowly, and his cheeks developed dimples. "But it doesn't mean there aren't other things I enjoy just as much."

"Is it your favorite thing in the world?"

"No. There is something I love better."

Chapter 21

Making a portrait required intense focus on the subject. Every aspect of Cynthia's form and features had to be transmitted from the eye to the hand. As never before, Damian studied the nuances of her appearance: the indentation of her neck above the lace ruffle of her modest gown; pearly oval fingernails; faint blue veins showing through the pale skin at the wrist. His palms imagined the contours of shoulders and bosom, the latter lightly heaving when she laughed. And her face. He knew the curve of the brows descending to the shapely nose and the pink rosebud mouth, the smooth cheeks and jawline given character by the assertive little chin. Now he discovered the faintest shadows beneath each wide eye, thick lashes several shades darker than her hair, a little dip below the plump lower lip.

With every stroke and smudge of charcoal and fingers he felt his rusty skills return. While his work wasn't as polished as it used to be, he had never applied himself to a portrait with greater fervor. The connection between subject and artist, Cynthia and himself, deepened as he drew. As he traced thin lines to define the quirk at each end of her mouth, she smiled.

"You moved just as I was drawing your mouth," he complained.

"I'm sorry. You smiled and it made me respond."

"I didn't realize I had done so."

"I wondered what you were thinking. You've been very quiet."

"I was thinking that portraiture is like love-making."

"Oh." She blushed and bit her lip. "How so?"

"Stop moving your mouth. It is done best with complete concentration and, preferably, great knowledge of the subject."

"Do you know me?"

"I am making it my business to do so better."

"Can you not learn more from listening than looking?"

"Every sense conveys knowledge."

"I'm not sure I want to smell anyone." She wrinkled her nose. "It doesn't seem very romantic."

"What of perfumes? You yourself favor a light rosewater."

"I don't like heavy aromatics."

"A good thing. It would be a pity to mask your sweet natural scent. As for taste and touch, I wouldn't wish to make the acquaintance of everyone through such sensual exploration, but their uses in amorous congress must be evident."

Since he'd been staring at her fixedly for more than an hour, he detected the light flush that he suspected descended beneath her garments, the barely perceptible acceleration of her breathing. What a very fine thing it would be if she were to be as aroused by hearing talk of lovemaking as he was by delivering it. She didn't seem to be unduly shocked. While he finished the drawing, he described out loud each minute detail of her face and the stroke of his fingers that conveyed it to paper. No word was spoken that could not have been uttered in a drawing room full of maiden aunts, but he aimed to spin a seductive web to ensnare the two of them. It wasn't as though there was anything else to do. With luck they'd be caught in the snow for days.

"**I** think that's finished," Damian said, dropping the stick of charcoal into the pencil box. "Stop me before I spoil it."

Cynthia stretched her arms and rotated her neck. "I'm the opposite. I despair of improving my work and give up in disgust."

"Do you wish to see it?"

Happy to move after holding the pose for half an hour, she stood beside him while he held the sketch pad at arm's length. Once again, his talent astonished her "The way you have provided texture with the charcoal is marvelous. I can't seem to get the shadows right, try as I may with cross-hatching or by smearing the pencil."

"I had some great teachers but I need practice. Shall we take lessons together?"

Nothing he said could have pleased her more. "I'm a mere dabbler compared to you, but I would enjoy it very much. May I have the drawing?"

"If you wish. As long as I have the original."

The glow that had warmed her blood while he drew and talked, bloomed to full heat. Peeking sideways, she found him looking at her with unabashed hunger. Whatever else her husband felt, he desired her.

They were alone in a bedchamber with nothing else to do. Did it matter that it was barely noon?

She took a deep breath, then cursed the door and whatever servant had decided to knock on it.

"Come in," Damian said.

It was Harrison, the coachman. "Excuse me, my lord and my lady. It has stopped snowing and it's warming up fast." So it was. She had been too absorbed to notice the change in the quality of the daylight. "Will you be wishing to travel today? One of the wheels got knocked about a bit in the storm last night. The ostler here thinks it's safe, but I'd like you to have a look at it, my lord."

"I? I know nothing of wheels."

"I'd as soon not travel without your agreeing."

Damian raised his eyebrows and shrugged. "Assuming that the carriage is, in my expert judgment, ready for use, I'll return shortly and we can discuss our movements." His smoldering gaze suggested that his immediate plan was very much in line with her own.

"And my lady," Harrison went on.

"Yes?" Cynthia trusted she wasn't expected to render an opinion on the soundness of the horses.

"I found some items of yours when I cleaned the carriage this morning. I gave them to Miss Matthews and I believe she brought them up with your bags."

While Damian performed his unwelcome errand, Cynthia wandered into the other room to see if the things Harrison had found included her favorite shawl, which she hadn't been able to find when they packed in a hurry. She discovered a pair of lace mittens, her silver needle case, and a familiar portfolio.

How did *that* come to be in the carriage? It must have been stowed under the seat on Damian's orders sometime in the last few days. With guilty excitement she carried it into the larger bedchamber and spread the pictures on the bed. Should she lock the door? No need. Matthews wouldn't enter without knocking and if Damian came back? Well, she wouldn't mind being surprised by him in the act of examining his portfolio. It would save her from bringing up the subject.

There were a dozen of them, just as beautiful and outlandish as she recalled, glowing with gilt and rich vibrant colors. Like Oliver she pondered the technique, but only in a passing thought. Her attention settled on a painting she hadn't looked at in detail before. A sloe-eyed lady, entirely naked save for a pair of bracelets, lay on a pile of pillows. No one was putting anything into anything in this particular view. What shocked her was that there were *two* men with her. Turbaned and robed, they sat cross-legged and impassive, just looking at her, avidly and with utmost concentration, as though she were the most fascinating thing in the world.

Thus had Damian regarded her while he drew her portrait and she had glowed under the intensity of his gaze. Supposing, instead of being swathed to the neck in wool, she had undressed for him. Her breathing deepened.

Two men! Did women actually consort with two men at the same time? The idea amazed, appalled, and on a deep level attracted her. What if she were that reclining beauty? It was a thought that would have her thrown out of Birmingham forever, if she dared voice it, which she never would. For a moment she let herself dwell on the notion of sharing a bed with two men at the same time, but there was only one she wanted. However, it didn't do any harm to let her fancy toy with a little foreign wickedness. She'd never act on it and no one would ever know what went on in her head. Imagining herself in the position of the Persian lady, she felt silk cushions under her skin, heard the distant song of a fountain, inhaled the scent of strange flowers. Two pairs of eyes seized every inch of her revealed flesh, admiring and wanting her. She was all powerful and utterly vulnerable.

Moaning, she leaned against the stout bedpost and clasped her hand to her aching secret place. Pressing and rubbing relieved her ache for a moment, and then her desire mounted and the intervention of wool and linen was an unsupportable barrier to pleasure. She clawed at her skirts, burrowed beneath the layers, and found herself wet and wanting. It was easy, she discovered, to pleasure herself, and she regretted all the years she had done without. She didn't even have to look at the picture. It was etched on her mind when she closed her eyes and imagined lustful gazes devouring her. Her middle finger found the place that, when agitated, brought her to the height of joy. She tumbled into bliss and feared her legs would collapse under her. A pair of strong arms and a hard body saved her from falling.

Oh God.

She tried to pull away, shamed to her toes that she had been discovered like this, her hand up her skirts.

"Don't," Damian said softly against her temple. "Stay."

Face on fire, she hung her head. "I don't . . ." She couldn't even complete a sentence.

"Watching you pleasure yourself was beautiful. And exciting." Because she was looking down she saw the proof of it, straining against the fall of his breeches. "I take it you like my pictures."

"Why are they here?" She dwelled on an inessential.

"I was going to give them to a friend and I am glad I did not. I thought you would be shocked."

"I am, but . . ." Daring to look at him she found that his gaze, hot and steady, rekindled her heat.

"That makes me very happy. Tell me what you think when you look at them." Keeping an arm around her, he pointed at the one with the two men. "At that one, say."

"She likes to be looked at."

He tilted his head and regarded the miniature with his artist's eye. "So she does. By two men at once, no less. Would you like that?"

"Not really. But I like it in the drawing." She spoke barely above a whisper. "I like it when you look at me."

"And I want to oblige you." His smile was wide and his dimples pronounced. "With fewer clothes, I think."

Fever rippled through her. "Yes, please," she said.

He set about undressing her with the quiet competence of a well-trained maid, except that it was nothing like being disrobed by Matthews. When her maid got her ready for bed her breasts didn't swell or her belly throb. When Matthews loosened the drawstring of her shift she didn't have strong, masculine hands, artist's hands, to slide the garment off her shoulders. Matthews didn't leave her naked and she did not stare at her mistress.

"Stay there," he commanded. "Put your hands behind your neck and hold on to the bedpost." The posture raised her bosom and left her body exposed, without a hand to offer a fig leaf to her sex. Stepping back a couple of feet, he surveyed her slowly, starting with her bare toes and moving up her legs, lingering over the fair curls, her curved hips and belly, the prominent breasts. As his eyes passed each place, she fancied he touched her with a feather's caress. Her skin tingled, her nipples tightened, and her private place grew wetter. She clenched her inner muscles and swiveled her hips.

"Don't move," he said. "See how excited you can become just from me looking at you."

She'd often felt invisible, starved for notice and attention. Never had she envisioned this delicious scrutiny. "Do many people enjoy being looked at?"

He considered his answer with the same calm deliberation with which he continued to examine her body. "I don't know if it's common, but you aren't alone. Some people have special things that arouse them. Can you guess what mine is?"

Wide-eyed, she shook her head. He came over

to her, casually tweaked her hard nipples with his fingertips, and whispered in her ear. Something in French she didn't understand except for that one word.

"I see," she said. "You like to use the kind of words they don't use in Birmingham."

"Dreadfully dull place."

"Do you always speak in French?"

"Sometimes German or Italian. I shall have to tutor you."

"I would like to learn words for certain things." She touched her sex and, greatly daring, the bulge of his, through the soft doeskin of his breeches. "Also, I should like to look at you."

"While I undress, look at the drawings and tell me what you see."

Turning her back on him, not without a sway of her hips for his benefit, she picked up one of the miniatures. "The man is lying back on his elbows. The woman straddles him and is about to lower herself onto his . . . male member. There must be a better word for it?" She heard rustling cloth and a heavy garment tossed aside.

"There are dozens. I prefer *cock*. Short and sweet."

"In this picture the lady seems to think so. Or sweet, anyway, since she is about to taste it. I would estimate that the gentleman's cock is not especially short, though I don't have a frame of reference for comparison."

"You have quite a talent for dirty speaking yourself, my lady." More rustling and a boot lying on its side, visible from the corner of her eye.

"Thank you, my lord." She dropped a curtsey, which ought to give him a splendid view of her bare bottom. Feeling his heated eyes on her behind made up for not watching him remove his clothes. She visualized the emergence of his . . . cock. *Cock.* It was good to know its name since she intended to think about it a lot henceforth.

"Describe another." His voice was muffled so he must be removing his shirt.

"Goodness, this one is very peculiar. The man is lying on his back with knees against his shoulders. His cock is sticking up and the lady has her back to him and seems to be about to sit on it. I should think it would be quite uncomfortable."

"In that case we won't try that one." His voice shook with laughter.

She turned and discovered him almost as naked as she. "Are we going to try any of them?"

He stepped out of his breeches and flung them over the back of a chair. "Only if you would like."

He was a magnificent specimen, her husband, firm and muscled and proportioned like a statue of a god. His cock looked long, hard, and ready. "I would like to try them all. Though maybe not that backward one."

"Make your choice."

Making herself return to the array of miniatures

now that they had a rival for attention in Damian's bare flesh, she put her imagination to work. "I am torn. This one is interesting. The woman is on her hands and knees and the man is taking her from behind."

"How does it make you feel?"

"They *all* make me feel like that thing we don't say in Birmingham."

"You want me to fuck you?"

He was snickering at her and she couldn't let him get away with it. She spun around and gave a good push to his solid, very shapely chest. Taken by surprise, he landed on the hearthrug, knees apart and supported by his elbows. "I think I shall fuck *you*," she said, and followed him to the floor, settling herself with a knee on either side of his thighs. Nice thighs. She tested one with her palm. Powerful.

"It would be my very great pleasure, Lady Windermere."

Hands on his shoulders, she lowered herself until his stiff cock brushed her privates. "What is my sex part called?"

"Some men of a poetic bent have been moved to title it the 'cradle of Venus.'"

"Very poetic and quite a mouthful."

"A wonderful mouthful."

"Is there anything shorter?"

"*Cunny* or *quim* are possibilities. The words are generally thought crude—"

"—and *cock* isn't?" she interrupted with a snort, letting the cock stroke to and fro along her quim. "I understand. Not in front of Lady Ashfield."

"Unless you wish to give her an apoplexy."

Seeking a rhythm and not getting enough purchase, she took it in her fist and rubbed it where she was slick and wanting. It was like pleasuring herself, but better. A cock was more satisfying than her finger, not least because next—soon—it would fill her and deliver sensations she couldn't achieve alone.

"I hope the good people at the Birmingham Academy for Young Ladies appreciated what a diligent student they had," he said, breathing hard.

"Both my understanding and application," she replied, positioning herself carefully and descending until his long, thick cock was firmly lodged in her quim, "were greatly appreciated." A gusty sigh marked the satisfaction of feeling him fill her, echoed by his own groan of pleasure. Much better than a finger because it was part of Damian and they were joined together in a way that made her heart flutter like a mad thing, even though that particular organ wasn't involved in the physical transaction.

He tilted his head back and his groin forward. "I think I must be the luckiest man in the world. Now, *fous-moi*."

Chapter 22

She was, quite simply, extraordinary. Once she worked out what to do, she rode him like a golden angel with muscles of steel, coming twice before sending him over the top and wringing out every drop of seed he had in him. She sprawled on top of him on the floor of this shabby inn. The Swan at Egham would always hold a special place in his heart as the place where he had known he was in love.

When had it happened? When had his wife, Cynthia, become the most important thing in his world? He knew exactly the moment when he first wanted her: seated at dinner laughing at Julian, whom he then believed to be her lover. He did not know when desire turned to love, only that it had happened between then and now. She had all he would have chosen in a bride and thought he would never have when he married her: beauty, intelligence, and excellent French. But those qualities of the perfect diplomatic partner were admirable, not lovable. Humor, strength, generosity, and a deep-rooted kindness that he would never have had the sense to search for in a wife, those were what he loved. And something else that might take a lifetime to define. A lifetime of talking and painting and laughing and lovemaking. A lifetime for him to defend her against the depredations of other men and her own foolish generous impulses, like rescuing kittens in the snow.

Stroking her silken back, he found gooseflesh. "It's growing cool. We should go to bed."

"It's barely afternoon," she objected, all rosy and tousled.

"You need to lose this obsession with time. The right hour to do anything is when we say it is."

"Is this the immensely correct Lord Windermere speaking? The doyen of the diplomatic service? What would the grand duchess think of such disregard for propriety?"

"She'd be envious," he said. "Help me put away the miniatures and we'll get under the covers."

Bustling about, he found her nightgown and his shirt. He would have preferred to keep her naked and suspected she would have been happy to oblige him in the matter. But he had a faint recollection that she was susceptible to chills and wouldn't risk her catching cold. How on earth had he been so lucky, undeserving bastard that he was? He'd managed to fall into a marriage that fulfilled every dream he might have conceived, had he ever dared aspire to such glory. Now he must see if there was a chance she could ever love him as he loved her.

He wasn't above using her new sensual tastes to bind her to him. He drew up the covers slowly, worshipping her with his eyes as inch by inch her gorgeous flesh disappeared into her nightgown and beneath the blankets. His mind wandered to the science of improved heating, so that he could keep her naked all the time.

First he had to ensure their future. Even gripped by extreme lust, he had noticed her interest in the picture of one woman and two men. While he was ready to indulge any sensual desire she could think of, and doubtless many she could not, sharing her with another man was not on the table. Not Julian, or any other.

He got into bed beside her and sat upright. He wanted to be able to read her face as they talked. What he'd learned about Cynthia since his return from Persia would fill a litany of praise, but he wanted to know everything.

"Why did you choose to marry me?" he asked. "I was so bound up in my need to regain Beaulieu that I scarcely gave your feelings a second thought."

"Choose? I wouldn't say I chose the marriage, though I did consent to it. In theory I could have said no."

So much for any slight hope that she had been attracted to him. "Why did you say yes?"

"My uncle would not let me stay in his household if I refused you. The alternatives were worse."

"What were they?

"I could have become a governess, not a good prospect without a recommendation. Or I could have married Mr. Maxwell."

"Your uncle's business partner?"

"The man responsible for raping Aggie and others. Though I was not yet aware of his worst habits, I knew I would do anything to avoid him."

So she preferred him only to a life of drudgery or marriage to a villain. And he had thought her lucky to get him. "Did you even care that I was an earl?" Surely he'd had something to offer her?

"I hardly knew what an earl was when you called on us in Birmingham at Old Square, and certainly never dreamed of wedding such an exalted creature. I had no notion of any future beyond remaining as my Aunt Lavinia's companion."

"I thought you were getting something from the marriage as I was. I got Beaulieu, you got a titled husband." He couldn't disguise his pique. "It seemed like a fair exchange, but now you say you gained nothing you wanted from our marriage."

She patted his hand. "Not having to marry Maxwell was certainly something."

"I suppose I should be flattered that I rated higher."

"Much higher. If you had seemed a cruel man I would have defied my uncle and taken my chances as a governess. When you called on us you were kind to Aunt Lavinia."

"Kind? I treated her with normal courtesy." He remembered Mrs. Chorley as a nervous little woman, cowed by her domineering husband. "You forget that it is my job to put people at ease. What did you think of me?"

"I was completely overcome by your appearance. My aunt had chosen a new gown for me. While I didn't know enough to realize that it was overtrimmed and lacked elegance, I knew it did not suit me. And her maid had set my curls with sugar water so my hair felt brittle and uncomfortable. I felt like a complete dowd compared to you, so handsome and debonair. And so unreadable."

"Closed off was how you described it. I suppose I was. I think I have been for years. My training for the diplomatic service completed the process, but I shut down my feelings when I lost Beaulieu. I was bitter and angry and resented you because you were the only path back there. I didn't want a wife."

It was an uncomfortable admission but the truth, and one she must have realized by now. "I'm sorry," he said, clutching his forehead. "I am making a sad hash of trying to persuade you to stay with me. I hoped you would forgive me, that we would forgive each other. I'll willingly take the lion's share of the blame."

Her reaction surprised him. She sat bolt upright and shrank away as far from him as the narrow bed would allow. "Good," she said, rejecting his effort to take her hand. "You deserve it."

She had tried to put it behind her it and thought she had succeeded. She didn't want to spoil their Swan Inn idyll with the painful subject. But when he spoke of them forgiving each other, Cynthia needed to explain exactly why she had behaved the way she had. And Damian needed to acknowledge that the lion's share was more like an elephant's.

"Last winter—" she began. Then broke off. She wanted to tell the whole story so that he'd understand. "Last year at Beaulieu, when you suddenly announced you were going to Persia for an unspecified length of time, possibly years, you left me instructions." He had the grace to look abashed. "Quite a list of them, like improving my appearance and my French. You also told me the house needed refurbishment." She remembered the way his gaze had swept over the threadbare upholstery and light-streaked curtains, then rested on her ugly, frilly, sage green gown. "You told me to stick with your mother's original scheme and replace the materials exactly."

"Did I?"

"Naturally I was sympathetic to such a sentimental request, until you spoiled it by implying that I hadn't the taste to make my own choices."

"Are you sure that's what I meant?"

She fixed him with a beady eye. "I had no doubt."

He capitulated without a fight. "I didn't trust your taste and I showed no respect for your position as my wife. Even if our tastes didn't match, you had the right as the mistress of the house to choose your surroundings. I am sorry." He tried to take her hand again but she shook him off. "I freely admit that I was an unfeeling brute. Let me make it perfectly clear that you performed impeccably in my absence. You are the picture of elegance, a superb French speaker, and a brilliant manager of my household, both here and in the country. The steward at Beaulieu sings your praises by every post, and I have every faith that you will even be able to make Amblethorpe habitable. I also completely understand why you thought it amusing to introduce some very ugly pieces into the house. Please, my dear Cynthia, now you've had your revenge, can we get rid of the pink settee and the dead birds in the hall? Next time you commit fraud in a good cause, buy a Titian or a set of Hepplewhite chairs."

"You find it amusing."

"Don't you? As revenge goes, it's a witty one. That explains the furnishings, but it's mere mischief. Nothing like taking up with Julian." The humor faded from his eyes. "Now that I know you, it surprises me you'd even consider an affair. Not only are you the kindest and most forgiving lady in the world, you are a woman of principle."

She swallowed hard. She had tried to forget the pain, to accept her erring husband back without further recriminations. She feared that if he made light of her feelings now he would be beyond pardon and there could be no happy future.

"For weeks I refused to have anything to do with Julian. I did my best to be a faithful and obedient wife." Tears gathered, as they often did when she remembered the long awaited letter, responding to several of hers, happy ones during her pregnancy and the heartbroken conclusion. She got down from the bed to find a handkerchief.

Clutching the linen square like a lifeline, she stood in her nightgown and bare feet at the foot of the bed. Damian stared back at her with his blankest expression.

"I would never have encouraged Julian had it not been for your cruel indifference to losing our child."

"You were with child?" he said, his voice hoarse with disbelief. He jumped out of bed and took her by the elbows.

Her immediate thought was that he'd forgotten an event that meant so little to him. "Our marital duties were almost immediately rewarded," she said.

"You said nothing of it."

"I can assure you it wasn't a secret. Do you expect me to believe half a dozen letters went astray?"

"It's possible. Between the weather and the French, communications in the Mediterranean were troublesome last year." He shook his head and his hands tightened to the brink of hurting her arms. "Didn't you guess when I said nothing in response to your news?"

"But you did. You dismissed my miscarriage in two short sentences." All her bitterness and grief welled up. "I remember the words. How could I forget them? *I am sorry to hear of your indisposition. You must be more careful of your health. Yours etc. Windermere.*"

His forehead creased as he appeared to search his memory. "You had a cold." This time his grip did hurt her and she pulled away. "You were caught in the rain walking home from church. You told me you were susceptible to chills." He spoke like a man in a daze. "I had forgotten, but now it comes back to me."

The wet walk had happened soon after he sailed and the report of a minor chill had taken up a major portion of her first dutiful letter to her husband, because she couldn't think of anything else to write. She hadn't thought of it since.

"I never knew you were with child," he said slowly, as though unable to assimilate the news. "You came to London to consult a doctor."

"He didn't make any difference. I lost the baby. I wanted the child so badly because I had nobody else." She buried her face in her hands and felt scalding tears soak her fingers. "And all these months I've resented you for nothing," she cried before being overcome by sobs.

He put his arms around her and let her weep out her misery and remorse. Especially the latter. The grief was an old story, still present but dulled by endurance and the passage of time. In the here and now she had to face the fact that she'd taken revenge and almost betrayed her vows in retaliation for an injury that had never existed. Worst of all, she might have lost the chance of winning her husband's love.

"I'm sorry," she said, sniffing as the crying subsided. He continued to hold her, rubbing her back. "I'm so sorry," she said, pulling away and retreating to the window. She saw the inn yard through a blur and wiped her eyes. "Can you ever forgive me?"

"Forgive you! What do *I* have to forgive? I may be innocent of this particular sin of callousness but there are plenty more. Let's not speak of your fault. I am sorry that you went through the experience alone and without comfort. Was it very bad?"

Believing in his regret, she didn't want to talk about it further. The details were painful and not such as a man could understand, or want to hear about. "I recovered," she said, and started to look for her clothes. She felt cold and strange and uncertain of her feelings now that the lump of resentment she'd carried for months had dissolved. "Are we going back to town this afternoon?"

"Unless you want to stay here another night."

"It's a small inn and not very comfortable."

"I like it here," he said. "But the decision is yours. What about Castleton?"

"I was only going there because I was angry. They don't expect me. I'd prefer to go back to town. I left without giving the servants their Christmas boxes."

This raised a smile. "That's my little philanthropist. I'll summon your maid."

Chapter 23

That Damian would never have been as cruel in his response as Cynthia had believed was cold comfort. Suppose he had received the report of her pregnancy. What would he have done?

The truth was, he wouldn't have much cared. Consumed by work so that he could forget the wife he had so rashly married, the thought of a child would have been another unwelcome burden. And an infant Chorley-Lewis, son or daughter, would be a victory for Joseph Chorley, who had blackmailed him into marriage so that he could have connections to the aristocracy. Eventually Damian would want an heir, but in an undisclosed, theoretical future that had little to do with his present concerns.

The intensity of her grief surprised him at first. He tried to see it from a woman's point of view. From Cynthia's. He'd left her alone, married but not really wed. A child would have given her the affection she certainly couldn't expect from her husband, and an object for her own devotion. He remembered her saying vis-à-vis her charitable endeavors that women loved their children even if they hated the father.

Now that he knew the truth he could think of a dozen hints she'd dropped that had gone over his head. While he wished he had understood sooner, perhaps it was for the best. Loving her as he did, he could now share her disappointment and grief. That he had caused her pain wrenched his guts, and the loss of a child who had barely existed hurt him too, in retrospect. Family duty and the future of the Lewises mattered a little. Having children, a real family, with Cynthia mattered a lot.

On the journey to London significant conversation hadn't been possible in the presence of the maid. At Windermere House he'd told her about the Falleron collection and she had laughed at his dilemma, ordered to negotiate with Julian when he believed him to be her lover. He'd seen precious few of her smiles since her revelation. Tense and subdued, he couldn't tell what she was thinking.

He conceived a plan: Take her to Beaulieu where their marriage had begun so badly and make a fresh start; shower her with gifts to celebrate the season; get her naked as much as possible. And, above all, tell her how much he loved her and convince her it was true.

He set off the next day to the Foreign Office to break the bad news to the foreign secretary. He had failed to persuade Denford to let go of the Falleron collection and would no longer make the attempt.

On the way to see if Grenville could give him an audience, he hesitated at the door to Radcliffe's rooms and grimaced. Damian wasn't merely reluctant to deliver unwelcome news. He didn't want to see Radcliffe, or hear what he had to say, or share his thoughts with him. Gritting his teeth and remembering all he owed Sir Richard, he entered and prayed his mentor wasn't in.

Of course he was.

He heard Damian's resignation with his usual calm, then regarded his protégé over steepled fingers with a pale, unblinking stare.

"You've disappointed me, Damian."

"I'm sorry, sir, but in this case I must decide what is best."

Sir Richard continued to look inscrutable, but for some reason Damian didn't think he was particularly upset. Or perhaps the news didn't surprise him. "Lady Windermere failed to come through for us."

"My wife? What has she to do with it?"

"I rather thought everything, since it is her liaison with Denford that caused your regrettable decision."

"Lady Windermere," Damian said, "is not the Duke of Denford's lover."

"I'm sure you know best, dear boy, but it seems a waste of a promising relationship. I had a feeling she wasn't going to be helpful."

"What do you mean?"

"Merely that I spoke to her about her duty to your future career and the ways she could help. One way, in particular. She became quite provincial at my very reasonable suggestion. Apparently you can take a young woman out of Birmingham, but you can't polish base metal. Did she complain to you?"

"She didn't mention the matter." His head spun. Bad enough that Radcliffe suggested Damian pimp his wife. Treating Cynthia to the same insult made him absolutely furious. He clenched his hands together and summoned every ounce of control he possessed. He had never in his life felt less diplomatic.

"I am glad she had that much tact, at least. I confess I thought I'd done rather well by you. She's a pretty little thing with a good deal of charm. With time, experience, and a little less Birmingham she can still be quite an asset."

Damian fastened on one part of this maddening speech. "What had you to do with my marriage?"

"Didn't you know? You could say I arranged the whole thing. I knew you wanted to gain back your mother's estate and I knew Chorley was looking for a title in the family. So I suggested that he acquire it as his niece's dowry. No need to thank me. I'm always pleased to help."

There wasn't any point reminding Radcliffe that he'd been ready to buy Beaulieu when Chorley bought it from under his nose and blackmailed him into an alliance. Rather he ought to thank him for bringing him Cynthia. He refused to do that either.

Perhaps Radcliffe had once been his friend. Or he might have used Damian entirely for his own ends. Though Damian would wager on the latter, it all came to the same. His affection for Sir Richard was at an end, as was any obligation to the man.

"Thank you for clearing that up, sir. I always like to know where I stand. I'm sorry about the Denford business but I'm sure you understand."

Sir Richard nodded. "Can't be helped. We'll have to think of something else."

"Please convey my thanks to Lady Belinda for a most delightful entertainment on Christmas Day. Lady Windermere and I look forward to seeing you soon."

Sir Richard Radcliffe had taught him well. He could lie like a diplomat and never let his opponent see him sweat. He left the room with a straight back, an insouciant air, and a sour stomach that the man he'd respected for so long had turned out to be a cold-blooded manipulator.

He'd admired Radcliffe's ruthlessness, he realized, but perhaps Julian had been right when he equated patriotism with scoundrelry. At least in some cases.

Glancing at the *Morning Post* while he waited

in an anteroom to the foreign secretary's office, he was joined by a familiar figure.

"Good morning, my lord," John Ryland said.

"How are you, Ryland?" It was hard to believe that only two weeks had passed since they'd met. It seemed like another era.

"You must be satisfied with the outcome of the affair."

He had no idea what he meant and settled for replying "Indeed" with a hint of a question that Ryland picked up.

"But of course, you haven't heard."

"If the news is recent, I know nothing. I returned this morning from a brief trip out of London."

"The foreign secretary heard on Christmas Day that Prince Heinrich of Alt-Brandenburg has seen the wisdom of an alliance with Britain and signed the treaty."

"Without the pictures?"

"I'm sure he would still be pleased to buy them from the Duke of Denford directly, though perhaps not at the price His Majesty's government would have offered."

"When did this happen?" Damian asked with a mixture of irritation and curiosity. "It takes a week or two for dispatches to come from Germany. Whatever argument convinced him must have been applied some time ago."

"You likely feel you were withdrawn from Persia unnecessarily. The matter was so vital we needed several contingency plans. We are sorry you were inconvenienced."

Ryland wasn't remotely sorry, and neither was Damian, though not for the same reason. The whole business with Julian and the bloody pictures that he hoped never to hear of again had been a nuisance. But he couldn't regret coming back to England. A few weeks longer and Cynthia might have succumbed to Denford's seduction.

"Thank you for telling me. I had come to report my lack of progress, but there is no reason now for me to take up Lord Grenville's time."

Ryland frowned. "I don't need to tell you to keep this to yourself, my lord. Since you were involved I thought you should know the outcome, but it's not common knowledge yet, by any means."

Damian felt a spurt of irritation at the knotted intricacies of his business. Once he would have been idealistic enough to believe discretion was required by a further move in the diplomatic chess game. Sadly, it was more likely because some official in some department was guarding his ground against a rival. He was mildly intrigued that Radcliffe hadn't been told, or perhaps he had and elected not to tell Damian so he could scold him anyway. It wasn't important enough to waste time worrying about it.

Then he smiled. He'd forgotten to confess to Radcliffe that he had changed his mind about the Spitalfields Act. As Radcliffe, and Chorley too, would discover when the matter came up in Parliament, they hadn't got themselves the bargain they hoped for when they purchased the Earl of Windermere.

Lady Windermere, on the other hand, would be pleased. The gentlemen could go hang. It would be another gift for her on their second honeymoon.

The sight of the Duke of Denford coming down the steps of Windermere House dowsed his sparkling mood. Denford waited for him to alight from the carriage and seized him by the arm.

"What do you want?" Damian asked.

"I was looking for Cynthia?" Julian asked without a trace of urbanity.

She must have refused to see him, thank God. "If she isn't at home to you, the polite thing to do is leave."

"She is not at home to anyone. I am very afraid that she's been abducted."

Damian stared at him. "You're mad!"

"God, I really hope so. I'd like to think this note I received ten minutes ago, demanding the Falleron collection in exchange for her safety, was nothing but a remarkably bad joke."

"It has to be." He tore up the steps, with Denford at his heels. "Harrison!" he called over his shoulder. "Walk the horses. I may need the carriage again right away."

The butler, hovering in the hall, confirmed that shortly after Damian left the house, a message had been delivered to Her Ladyship and she had left the house.

"On foot? I had the carriage."

"She took John with her and he summoned a hackney."

At least she had a footman with her, but he didn't like the sound of the message.

"There seem to have been a lot of messages turning up on this side of the square," Julian said, reflecting his own thought.

"Do you know where she went, Ellis?"

"Her Ladyship didn't inform me, but her maid may know."

"Send her to me in the library and hurry. Come, Denford." The last time he'd been in the room, he and Denford had nearly destroyed the furniture and each other. His excellent servants had removed all signs of the fracas. "What the hell is going on?"

The duke appeared ready to explode. "It's your bloody rotten government that's responsible, of course. Those bully boys in the Foreign Office will stop at nothing. Apparently *diplomat* is another word for *criminal*. Read this."

"*We need the whereabouts and sleutel of the Falleron collection. If not, Lady Windermere will suffer. Someone will be in touch.*"

"If Grenville's ruffians so much as scratch her . . ." Damian couldn't ever remember seeing Julian so agitated.

He stared at the note, written on a nondescript

scrap of paper in no hand he recognized. "It doesn't make any sense. We don't even want the pictures. The prince came to terms without them. It has to be someone else."

"Someone forgot to call off the hounds."

Damian made himself stop and think. Tearing out of the house with no idea where to go would be futile. "I'll grant that occasions sometimes call for unofficial action," he said, thinking aloud, "though such operations are certainly not the common method of diplomacy." This drew a derisive snort from Julian, and Damian wasn't overly confident of the truth either. He'd heard rumors about some of the skulduggery undertaken by men like Ryland. "But the man who would certainly know about something like this is the one who informed me the prince had given in. Not an hour ago he told me I need no longer try to persuade you to sell the collection. If Cynthia is in danger it's not from that quarter."

"Then who? Why? Have you a better suggestion?"

He tried to apply logical processes to the cryptic ransom note. "What do they mean by the *sleutel*? Is that Dutch? Not one of my languages."

"It's Flemish and it means 'key.' Whoever wrote that note knows that the pictures are in the southern Netherlands and that their guardian will hand them over on hearing a key phrase, a password, that only I know."

"Good God! No wonder you haven't been able to get the collection out." This was no time to discuss the political situation in Belgium. "Who knows about the sleutel?"

"Aside from my man there? No one, or so I thought. The only other is dead."

"You wanted to see me, my lord?" Cynthia's maid spoke from the doorway.

"Come in, Matthews. Did Her Ladyship tell you where she was going this morning?"

"She had a message from that nasty Spitalfields place," she replied with deep disapproval. "Very upset, she was. Said she had to go at once. She never takes me there, not after the first time, that is."

Damian could imagine that the Flowers Street household would not sit well with the ladies' maid, very conscious of her status as a senior servant. "Thank you, Matthews. You may go. I assume," he said to Julian, "that you know about Flowers Street."

"Of course. In a sense I helped finance it."

"If Cynthia heard she was needed there, because one of the children was hurt or something like that, she wouldn't wait. At least she has a footman with her. I'll take the carriage and my other man and follow her there. I just pray I'll find her there, safe and sound, and it'll turn out someone is playing a game with you." He hesitated for a moment. "Will you come too? If there is trouble, an extra man would be useful and you are a fair fighter."

"You mean an unfair one. The best kind." The set of Denford's face, combined with his black top-coat, reaching almost to his booted ankles, made Damian very glad that in this battle Julian and he were on the same side. The duke fingered the knob of his cane but turned aside. "Much as I would prefer to take action, I had better stay at home and await instructions from the abductor. He's either mad or ruthless, or both, and I'm not going to risk annoying him. The only thing that matters is to get Cynthia back safely. Will you be able to do what's needed?"

"The art of diplomacy includes knowing when to apply force."

Damian made himself remain calm while he loaded his pistols. Suppose some rogue element of the government was responsible, operatives more secret and more ruthless than Ryland. The idea made his skin crawl and he was impatient to get to Spitalfields. If she wasn't at Flowers Street, the trail began there. Causing a most undiplomatic furor at the Foreign Office was also an option, one reason he didn't believe it would be necessary.

Through the rising panic the thought intruded that only Julian would be involved in something so outlandish. He had always possessed a flair for the dramatic. "If they get in touch—assuming *they* are serious—what do you intend to do?"

"I shall tell them where the pictures are and give them the sleutel." Julian looked utterly weary.

"Enough people have died because of the Falleron art collection. I don't want Cynthia's life on my conscience too. Especially not hers."

Damian realized that he had been embroiled in a sequence of events that extended far beyond the relatively simple business of satisfying the whim of a princeling. And there was at least one man he could think of who could be quite unscrupulous when it came to acquiring paintings.

"James," Damian said to the second footman on his way through the hall, "you come with me. Run out and make sure Harrison has the carriage pistols loaded. You'd better come too, Ellis."

"Me, my lord?" asked the scandalized butler.

"Yes, you. I'll explain in the carriage."

Julian spoke to him through the window as the coachman prepared to head to the east of London. "Take care of her, Damian. She's worth too much to be sacrificed to this damnable mess of mine." His narrow face looked gaunt, emphasizing the hawkish nose, the brilliant blue eyes dulled by unease.

"You would really give up the greatest collection of pictures you will ever lay hands on, for Cynthia?"

"In some ways it would be a relief. They have been nothing but trouble to me. If I were a fanciful man, I might think they were cursed."

Chapter 24

The door closed with a thud and a click of the lock without Cynthia getting a look at her abductors. There had been two: one to knock poor John into the gutter, the other to throw a sack over her head, cast her over his shoulder, and carry her to this place. The hackney driver had been part of the conspiracy. He had stopped, unbidden, at an unsavory corner on the way to Flowers Street, and driven off once the villains had pulled Cynthia and John from the carriage. Before the fetid sackcloth blinded her, she'd glimpsed the group of idle men who frequented this particular street turn away and go about their business of being idle, and very likely criminal. No help to be expected from that quarter.

Sparing a thought to hope her poor footman wasn't dead, she studied her prison. Judging by the small amount of light that came in through a narrow window close to the ceiling, she was in a cellar. In the gloom she made out a number of bulky sacks, perhaps two dozen in all, arranged in tidy piles. Untying one sack, she found a pale, chalky powder. It was no surprise to find a storeroom for fuller's earth in Spitalfields. The weaving factories would need vast amounts of the substance, used for treating and cleaning cloth.

Thankful not to be bound or blindfolded, she perched on a sack and considered her plight. Her first thought was of Wilfred Maxwell, the only man she knew who both managed a factory and had a grudge against her. Yet she couldn't see why abducting and imprisoning her here would serve his purposes. If he demanded a ransom, Damian would doubtless pay it. But after that, if Maxwell wasn't arrested, he would be ruined in the eyes of his employer. Even her uncle would surely draw the line at kidnapping. Of his niece. Given his attitude to rape, the abduction of an *unknown* woman probably wouldn't bother Joseph Chorley one jot.

In a dark corner she found a spade. Not much protection, but if Maxwell laid hands on her she wasn't going down without a fight and inflicting some damage of her own. Eventually she'd be missed at home and Matthews knew where she'd been going. Surely someone would be able to set searchers on the right path. Meanwhile she practiced swinging the heavy tool.

A scratching made her jump, but it came from the window, not the door. Someone was out there, obscuring the light so she could hardly see a thing.

The unmistakable sound of breaking glass was followed by a boyish whisper. "My lady. Are you there?"

"Tom! How did you find me? Are you in the street? Can anyone see you?"

"I'm in the alley aside of Finch Street. I was there when they nabbed you out of your carriage and followed the culls that did it." This was not the moment to scold Tom for loitering on the streets with bad company.

"You must go to Hanover Square and Lord Windermere. Go home first and Mrs. Finsbury will give you money for a hackney. Quickly. I don't know how long they will keep me here."

Damian missed Tom, who was heading west in a hackney, but Mrs. Finsbury at Flowers Street conveyed his message. He hoped he and James were intimidating enough to gain entrance to the impressive premises of the Finch Street Silk Weavers without having to draw their weapons. Ellis, six inches shorter, attempted to look dangerous, but Damian could tell that the butler's dignity was sorely tried by the effort.

In the event it was easy. Mrs. Finsbury, who had begged a neighbor to watch over the children, knew one of the porters and Damian slipped him a guinea. She went off to speak to the workers in the loom rooms while the porter led Damian and his servants down a back staircase into the basement level of the building. "This is where the fuller's earth is kept," he said.

"Do you have the key?"

"Only the master has keys to the storage rooms. I need to be getting back to the door. Don't break anything."

"Cynthia!" Damian called. "Can you hear me?"

"Damian?" she said faintly. The door must be a thick one.

He breathed a sigh of relief and proceeded to disregard the advice of the departed porter. Alas, the combined efforts of James and himself proved fruitless against the stout door. Maxwell had chosen his prison well. He was about to try shooting off the lock when Ellis intervened.

"Excuse me, sir."

"Yes, Ellis." Damian was hot and bothered. "Do you have any special knowledge of how to break a door?"

"No, my lord, but I believe I could open the lock." He pulled a set of skeleton keys from his pocket and knelt down. "It seems quite a simple device."

"What use does a respectable butler have for such tools?" Damian asked.

Ellis selected one of the slender pieces of metal and probed the lock. "A good butler dislikes damage and I have observed that locksmiths are not as careful as one would wish when called in to assist with a missing key. I decided to study the art myself."

"You are a pattern card of your profession, Ellis. Remind me to increase your wages."

"Thank you, my lord. Now, if you don't mind, this is a delicate business and better done in silence. It shouldn't be long now."

A minute later Cynthia was in Damian's arms. "Thank God! What did you do to Mr. Maxwell? Why did he do this?"

"I don't know and it's time to find out. Let's beard him in his office."

The first thing that struck Cynthia about Maxwell was his waistcoat of embroidered crimson silk, surely too fine for a day's work, even in a silk factory. The fellow had always been something of a dandy, but judging by his current appearance, he had prospered since she last saw him.

He blanched at the sight of her, shooting up from his seat behind a new desk that could have been one of the gaudiest excesses from Hamble & Stoke. He flared his nostrils, blinked rapidly, and summoned all his swagger. "Lady Windermere! What a pleasure. I take it you are Lord Windermere. We never had the pleasure of meeting."

Damian, at his most opaque, flicked his eyes over the man as though he were beneath his notice, then patted Cynthia's hand resting on his arm. "Will you speak, my dear, or shall I?"

"Thank you, my lord," she said. "I believe I am

the most directly concerned. I should like to know, Mr. Maxwell, why I was abducted."

"Goodness me, my lady. I am shocked. Surely you don't think I had anything to do with such a thing?"

"Since I was imprisoned on your premises, you'll forgive me for doubting your denial. You never struck me as a man who allows activities in his factory that he does not control."

"You have made ugly accusations against me before, my lady."

"Ones you didn't trouble to refute since the victims were of no importance. I think you will find it harder to escape retribution when you prey on a lady with a powerful husband."

"Quite so," Damian murmured. She was grateful that he allowed her to confront Maxwell. It would be so like a man to charge in and hit the villain. Not that she had any objection should he wish to inflict some damage later, after she had said her piece.

Maxwell picked up a paper knife and pretended to clean his fingernails. "What can I say? I've often complained to the magistrates about the lawlessness rife in Spitalfields. Anyone could have taken you and used my premises to hold you. You can't prove I knew you were locked in the storeroom."

She couldn't hold back a triumphant grin. "Was that where I was? I don't think I mentioned it. You've given yourself away."

Maxwell continued to bluster until Damian cut him off with a frown and a raised hand. If she didn't have a thousand excellent reasons to be glad of their marriage, the sight of him so elegant and unruffled, in contrast to the wretched Maxwell, would have sealed the pact.

"Enough, Maxwell," he said. "Your reign of terror is over. My servant has gone to summon the constable and the magistrate, but I'm going to give you a chance. Answer my questions truthfully and you may escape the noose, which I am sure is the penalty for kidnapping a peeress. Who ordered you to seize Lady Windermere?" Cynthia regarded her husband sharply. He seemed to know that Maxwell hadn't acted alone. "Who tried to obtain her ransom by demanding certain information from the Duke of Denford?"

"I don't know anything about the Duke of Denford."

"That wasn't my question. It's obvious you are a minor cog in this machine."

"Is my uncle involved in this outrage?" Cynthia asked, still shocked by the unexplained involvement of Julian.

Maxwell shook his head. "Chorley's soft over you. Wants his grandnephew to be an earl. There's more than one behind this and I don't know 'em. Get my orders in writing. I swear it," he added when Damian took a pistol out of his pocket and examined it carefully.

"I think he's telling the truth, Damian. You'll have to ask Uncle Chorley. He should know whom Maxwell works for."

James came into the room. "The magistrate is on his way, my lord."

"You promised," Maxwell said.

"You weren't very helpful, were you?" Damian said. "Perhaps a few nights in jail will improve your memory. If it does, or even if you remain forgetful and somehow manage to escape the law, there's one thing you can count on. I shall make sure you are never employed again in any position where you can prey on innocents."

Cynthia beamed at him. "You couldn't make me happier, my lord."

"I think I can. There are some people who are anxious to see your fall, Maxwell. Open the door, James, and invite the ladies in."

Almost a dozen women crowded in from the passage. Among them Cynthia saw Mrs. Finsbury, Aggie, and the other women from the Flowers Street household, as well as several others she didn't know. All Maxwell's victims had been invited to witness his humiliation. Thinking of the terror and pain he had inflicted on these women, Cynthia knew it was unlikely he would receive the punishment he deserved. The punishment, sadly, would be for keeping a countess in a cellar for a few hours, not for the violation of numerous powerless women and girls. Each one of them regarded

the monster with a similar expression of fierce satisfaction. In a world where they had no expectation
of justice, a small measure of redress was enough
for them. Her husband couldn't have bought her
a better Christmas gift. She couldn't wish for a
better husband, or one she loved more.

The magistrate took Maxwell away, to the cheers
of the assembled women. James reported that
his fellow footman John had been found with a
sore head, stripped of his livery, but otherwise
unharmed. And Julian and the boy Tom alighted
from a hackney as they left the weaving factory.

The duke held Cynthia's hand to his chest. "You
are alive, thank God."

She smiled back at him with what appeared to
Damian great fondness. "Of course. I don't think
my murder was ever an issue."

"You don't know whom we are dealing with
here. These people stop at nothing."

"Did you hear from them?" Damian asked. "Do
you know who they are?"

"I don't know exactly who is behind Cynthia's
abduction, only that they are dangerous. I gave up
the sleutel as requested. I had just sent off the messenger when Tom arrived looking for you."

Cynthia demanded an explanation, which she
heard with a good many eager questions and ex-
clamations. "If only Tom had arrived a few min-

utes earlier you wouldn't have given in to their demands. Thank you, Julian, for what you gave up for me. Can't you get it back?"

"If I get there first I can change the sleutel. I thought of giving a false one, but I didn't want to take the risk."

Damian frowned, torn between gratitude and anxiety. Now certain that Denford was in love with Cynthia, he wanted to get her away. He trusted her, of course, but he wasn't entirely confident of her affection. Denford's sacrifice was enough to impress any woman.

But his suspicion about the mastermind behind the business had to be investigated. "Do you think it could be Radcliffe?"

"The good Sir Richard?" Julian sneered. "How can you possibly think he would do anything underhand when it came to the acquisition of an art collection?"

"Touché. Let me just say that various circumstances make him a possible candidate."

"I didn't know him then, but I believe he was already at the Foreign Office in 1793. That puts him on a list. There are others. And that's all I have to say."

"Should this mysterious figure obtain the Falleron pictures," Damian asked, "how could he admit that he has them? What's the point of a collection of art that you cannot display?"

Julian gave his twisted smile. "It's complicated, but I'm not in a position to make a claim. If a London dealer or collector were suddenly to be discovered in possession of the Falleron collection, there'd be no one to question his right to it. When it comes to this property, I would say possession is nine points in the law."

"In that case, don't you think you should hurry to get possession before the others? You could get to Belgium in a couple of days."

"Trying to get me to leave the country, Damian?"

Damn Julian. He could always read Damian like a book.

He squared his shoulders and looked at his old friend and enemy in the eye. "I could put you in contact with a man at the Foreign Office who might be able to assist you."

"Thank you, but I'd rather face the French."

Damian stood nose to nose with his adversary in the narrow Spitalfields street. Denford seemed thin and strained, as though under unbearable stress. An echo of their old friendship stirred in Damian's chest. What had happened to Julian over the years?

"You have put yourself out considerably on behalf of my wife. I would not like to see you suffer for it."

"I didn't only do it for her." Was this an overture of reconciliation? Julian gazed at Cynthia for a few moments with emotions Damian could only guess at. Love, desire, regret? Whatever the duke was feeling, it wasn't detachment or cynicism. Then he turned aside and shrugged. "A few days ago, I offered to give up the Falleron collection in exchange for something. My mind has not altered."

Chapter 25

Since their butler and a large, almost naked footman shared their carriage, Lord and Lady Windermere were constrained from exchanges, verbal or otherwise, of any intimacy on the way home. After her ordeal, Cynthia would have enjoyed a little intimacy. Damian seemed his old self, his face flat and shuttered. If Radcliffe was their villain, it would hit her husband hard.

Now that the exhilaration of defeating Maxwell had passed, the victory of the extortionist—whether Radcliffe or another—grated on her. He had got what he wanted and Julian had paid for it. It wasn't fair. She rather thought Damian agreed with her. Without knowing what had happened between them that morning, she'd sensed a shift in their relationship.

"I'm going up to change," she said, "then I think I'll rest for a while in my chamber. Join me when you can." She hoped for kisses and comfort and a long, interesting dissection of recent events. That was what marriage should be like.

He came in looking serious, and didn't even react to her best dressing robe in blue silk trimmed with French lace. He hadn't removed a single garment beyond his topcoat, hat, and gloves. She resolved to do something about it before another hour went by.

"Do you really believe Sir Richard is behind my abduction?" She patted the divan where she had been pretending to nap.

Instead of joining her, he paced. "It's a possibility. I will make inquiries but unless Maxwell or your uncle gives evidence, I doubt we'll find proof."

"Do you mind dreadfully?"

"I had already decided that I'd been mistaken in his character. We will never be on intimate terms again."

Cynthia wanted to cheer. No more celebrations with Lady Belinda. "I can't say I was taken with either of the Radcliffes."

"Which proves, my lady, that you have excellent taste," he said with a ghost of a smile. "But I already knew that."

The room was too small to contain his restless pacing. He bounced between the window and fireplace with increasing speed.

"What's the matter with you, Damian? You're making me dizzy." She regarded him fondly. Although unable to tell what had him so agitated, at least he was no longer closed off. Sooner or later he'd tell her what was on his mind.

Settling at last on the hearth, he stood with his hands clasped behind his back, like a man about to give a speech at a public meeting. He even cleared his throat. "Denford sacrificed one of the world's greatest art collections for your safety," he said abruptly.

"I was amazed as well as grateful. I also don't underestimate him. Whoever is after it, I'll back Julian to get the better of him."

"I hope so. Belgium has been occupied by the French for several years, which is presumably why he hasn't been able to bring the pictures to England before. Someone like Radcliffe, with useful connections, might have the advantage in retrieving them."

"Didn't Julian imply that he used to work for the Foreign Office? Did you have any idea?"

"It came as a complete surprise to me, though it certainly explains a few things." He cleared his throat. "You have a high opinion of Julian."

"He's a very able man. And a good one too, even if he does his best to hide the fact." How agreeable it would be if the two men could resolve their differences. She didn't wish to give up Julian's company. And both would be happier if they could regain a friendship that had been pivotal in their lives. "I know I've given you cause—"

He cut her off. "Never mind that now." He

started to pace again, then stopped abruptly, close to her seat. "I believe Julian loves you. Perhaps he even deserves you."

What was this about? Cynthia rose to her feet. Momentarily bereft of words by the sheer obtuseness of the man she loved, it was her turn to pace.

"In the time I've known you," she said shaking her head, "I've thought you insensitive and I've thought you cruel. I have never thought you stupid." That silenced him. "Julian has been a good friend to me and it means a lot that he cares for me, though I do not believe him in love. But I have *never* truly wanted him."

When she reached the end of the room and turned around she found him grinning at her. "Well, that's good," he said. "Because I'm not letting you go."

"You aren't?" It was her turn to feel stupid. "Well, that's good."

"What I was *going* to say is that whatever Julian's feelings, they cannot be as strong as mine. I love you, Cynthia."

Her heart was hammering so hard she wasn't sure she'd heard him. Did he say he loved her? She could hardly speak for trembling. "Say that again."

"I love you. Lord, how feeble I sound. All my vaunted powers of persuasion disappear with you, the most important person in my life."

"Damian," she said, standing close enough that she had to tilt her head to see his expression. "You are doing quite well." Seeing love and uncertainty written plainly on his features, she wanted to sing and dance.

His response to her smile was almost a grimace of pain. "What I want to say is that I love you but I fear I don't deserve you. I am sorry for all I've put you through."

"The worst wasn't your fault, even if I thought it was."

"I should have been there with you. It slays me that you went through such grief alone, and I didn't even know about it."

With two steps she was in the protective circle of his arms, held against his chest. They remained thus for a minute, not saying anything. There was no need for tears because finally she was no longer alone.

After a while she let out a gusty sigh into his waistcoat. "I could never love Julian, you know. My heart was already taken."

He pushed her away to arm's length. "But you couldn't have been in love with me. Even if you were, you didn't remain so." Nonetheless, his face was bright with hope.

She took both his hands, entwining their fingers. "Listen to me, Damian." It was hard to speak from the heart; she wasn't accustomed to it. "We must both forgive and forget everything that happened after our wedding, but I treasure the memory of the ceremony itself. When I walked up to the altar on my uncle's arm, Aunt Lavinia had been telling me about my unpleasant marital duty and Uncle Chorley talked about sons. I scarcely heard them, because all I could think of was you. When you placed the ring on my finger I realized we had never embraced or kissed, never even touched with ungloved hands." He returned her clasp and she found it easy to speak after all. "I didn't know that skin could tingle and glow on contact with another, as it does now. I was frightened and excited about what was to happen that night. But you were so very handsome, I felt sure it would be good. Not like poor Aunt Lavinia, having to do it with Uncle Chorley. I kept peering at your face, the most beautiful masculine features I ever saw."

"Handsome is as handsome does, goes the proverb. I quickly proved I was as bad as your uncle."

"Never that. And as you know perfectly well, you've made up for your neglect." She leaned into the strong body that caused her such bliss. In case he didn't receive the message, she ran her hand down his torso, enjoying the muscles beneath the layers of fine cloth. Lingering for a second at the waist, she proceeded downward. She was looking so she noticed the twitch. Two twitches, actually, one of the lips, one farther down. "You were a serious man, a man of substance and affairs. A man with responsibilities. I couldn't expect levity from a man like you, neither should I wish it. Yet I hoped. As the vicar pronounced us man and wife and the organ pealed, I swore to myself that if you smiled at me, I would love you."

"What a dreadful bridegroom I made! I wish I could claim to have been serious and substantial. The truth is I was merely irked." This came with a more prominent twitch. Or two.

"I took your arm, and looked up at you, and you smiled. Just a tiny movement of the lips. A mere twitch." She glanced down and the twitch had become a distinct bulge. "I didn't find out about your dimples until much later. Still, it was enough for me. That's when I fell in love with you."

He came up with one last line of defense against her inexorable declaration. "But you didn't know me. And when you found out what I was like, you hated me."

"In a hidden place of my heart, that spark of love remained."

"It's a miracle it wasn't crushed by my indifference."

"A rescued kitten, a whiff of bhang, many small kindnesses, and the ability to send me to heaven with a look and a touch. Each of these fanned that little spark into a flame."

This time his mouth stretched into a wide, full-bodied, and completely dimpled smile. Recognizing that this was how Damian looked when he was happy, her heart swelled with joy. "Now my lord," she said softly. "I have a piece of advice for you. Next time you declare love to a lady, do not suggest another gentleman deserves her more. It isn't a good negotiating position. I'm afraid such incompetence would get you dismissed from the diplomatic service."

"I shall rely on you in the future to advise me in all my missions. Let me try again."

He went down on his knees at her feet, his boyish grin making her heart flip. "My lady," he said, seizing her hands and fervently kissing them. "I love you to the point of madness and I will never stop. If any other man tries to take you away I will kill him, or at least apply severe diplomatic sanctions."

"My lord," she replied. "I am happy to see you have recovered from your attack of stupidity. It should be of considerable relief to the Foreign Office." Trembling, she brushed the hair back from his noble forehead. His beautiful eyes bored into her, inciting a rush of desire.

"How can we make sure I don't relapse into idiocy and endanger the future of the country?"

She arched into him shamelessly. "Do you have an idea?"

Beneath her skirts he caressed her legs and started on the task of removing her garters. "It is my considered opinion that we should remove all your clothing."

Author's Note

The silk industry centered on Spitalfields in the East End of London was huge and prosperous, employing thousands of skilled workers in the eighteenth century. The series of laws known as the Spitalfields Acts regulated the wages of the silk workers. Economists, then and now, disagree about the consequences of the acts. For the purposes of my story I decided to interpret them as beneficial; I also invented an extra act between those of 1792 and 1811.

I slotted Damian into Sir John Malcolm's embassy to Persia, intended to protect British interests in India and prevent a Persian alliance with the French. The new Shah Futteh Aly (Fath-Ali in modern usage) was a patron of the arts and a cultivated man. He is said to have read the entire *Encyclopaedia Britannica*, a fact I couldn't fit into this story so I'm sharing it with you now. Alt-Brandenburg and its prince, on the other hand, are entirely invented, as is the Falleron collection of paintings. Exactly what the Duke of Denford was up to in France will be revealed in my next book.

Lady Windermere's Lover is the third novel in The Wild Quartet series. Earlier books are *The Importance of Being Wicked* (Caro Townsend and the Duke of Castleton) and *The Ruin of a Rogue* (Anne Brotherton and Macrus, Viscount Lithgow). In addition, there is a prequel novella, *The Second Seduction of a Lady*. The fourth and final novel will be *The Duke of Dark Desires*, featuring Julian, Duke of Denford, and an unknown lady.

As usual, *Lady Windermere's Lover* required the help and support of many friends, relatives, and colleagues to come to the page. My gratitude goes to Jill Tuennerman, Kathy Greer, Megan Mulry, Caroline Linden, Sarah MacLean, Katharine Ashe, Maya Rodale, Isobel Carr, Rebecca Mallary, Celia de Borchgrave, Susan Hanewald, and Meredith Bernstein. I would like to extend special thanks to my new editor, Chelsey Emmelhainz.

Miranda

At Avon Books, we know your passion for romance—once you finish one of our novels, you find yourself wanting more.

May we tempt you with . . .

- **Excerpts** from our upcoming releases.

- Entertaining **extras**, including authors' personal photo albums and book lists.

- Behind-the-scenes **scoop** on your favorite characters and series.

- **Sweepstakes** for the chance to win free books, romantic getaways, and other fun prizes.

- Writing **tips** from our authors and editors.

- **Blog** with our authors and find out why they love to write romance.

- **Exclusive content** that's not contained within the pages of our novels.

Join us at
www.avonbooks.com

AVON
An Imprint of HarperCollins*Publishers*
www.avonromance.com

Available wherever books are sold or please call 1-800-331-3761 to order.

FTH 1013